Juvenile Justice

Other Books in the Issues on Trial Series:

Juvenile Justice

Jean Leverich, Book Editor

GREENHAVEN PRESS
A part of Gale, Cengage Learning

GALE
CENGAGE Learning™

Detroit • New York • San Francisco • New Haven, Conn • Waterville, Maine • London

GALE
CENGAGE Learning

Christine Nasso, *Publisher*
Elizabeth Des Chenes, *Managing Editor*

© 2009 Greenhaven Press, a part of Gale, Cengage Learning

For more information, contact:
Greenhaven Press
27500 Drake Rd.
Farmington Hills, MI 48331-3535
Or you can visit our Internet site at gale.cengage.com.

For product information and technology assistance, contact us at

Gale Customer Support, 1-800-877-4253
For permission to use material from this text or product, submit all requests online at www.cengage.com/permissions

Further permissions questions can be emailed to permissionrequest@cengage.com

Articles in Greenhaven Press anthologies are often edited for length to meet page requirements. In addition, original titles of these works are changed to clearly present the main thesis and to explicitly indicate the author's opinion. Every effort is made to ensure that Greenhaven Press accurately reflects the original intent of the authors. Every effort has been made to trace the owners of copyrighted material.

Cover photograph by The Library of Congress.

LIBRARY OF CONGRESS CATALOGING-IN-PUBLICATION DATA

Juvenile justice / Jean Leverich, book editor.
    p. cm. -- (Issues on trial)
    Includes bibliographical references and index.
    ISBN-13: 978-0-7377-4178-0 (hardcover)
    1. Juvenile justice, Administration of--United States--Juvenile literature. 2. Due process of law--United States--Juvenile literature. 3. Parent and child (Law)--United States--Juvenile literature. I. Leverich, Jean.
    KF9779.J89 2009
    345.73'08--dc22

                                                        2008038176

Printed in the United States of America
1 2 3 4 5 6 7 12 11 10 09 08

Contents

Chapter 3: Balancing Juveniles' Rights to Individual Privacy with School Safety

Chapter 4: Death Penalty for Juvenile Offenders Is Cruel and Unusual Punishment

Foreword

The U.S. courts have long served as a battleground for the most highly charged and contentious issues of the time. Divisive matters are often brought into the legal system by activists who feel strongly for their cause and demand an official resolution. Indeed, subjects that give rise to intense emotions or involve closely held religious or moral beliefs lay at the heart of the most polemical court rulings in history. One such case was *Brown v. Board of Education* (1954), which ended racial segregation in schools. Prior to *Brown*, the courts had held that blacks could be forced to use separate facilities as long as these facilities were equal to that of whites.

For years many groups had opposed segregation based on religious, moral, and legal grounds. Educators produced heartfelt testimony that segregated schooling greatly disadvantaged black children. They noted that in comparison to whites, blacks received a substandard education in deplorable conditions. Religious leaders such as Martin Luther King Jr. preached that the harsh treatment of blacks was immoral and unjust. Many involved in civil rights law, such as Thurgood Marshall, called for equal protection of all people under the law, as their study of the Constitution had indicated that segregation was illegal and un-American. Whatever their motivation for ending the practice, and despite the threats they received from segregationists, these ardent activists remained unwavering in their cause.

Those fighting against the integration of schools were mainly white southerners who did not believe that whites and blacks should intermingle. Blacks were subordinate to whites, they maintained, and society had to resist any attempt to break down strict color lines. Some white southerners charged that segregated schooling was *not* hindering blacks' education. For example, Virginia attorney general J. Lindsay Almond asserted, "With the help and the sympathy and the love and re-spect of the white people of the South, the colored man has risen under that educational process to a place of eminence and respect throughout the nation. It has served him well." So when the Supreme Court ruled against the segregationists in *Brown*, the South responded with vociferous cries of protest. Even government leaders criticized the decision. The governor of Arkansas, Orval Faubus, stated that he would not "be a party to any attempt to force acceptance of change to which the people are so overwhelmingly opposed." Indeed, resistance to integration was so great that when black students arrived at the formerly all-white Central High School in Arkansas, fed-eral troops had to be dispatched to quell a threatening mob of protesters.

Nevertheless, the *Brown* decision was enforced, and the South integrated its schools. In this instance, the Court, while not settling the issue to everyone's satisfaction, functioned as an instrument of progress by forcing a major social change. Historian David Halberstam observes that the *Brown* ruling "deprived segregationist practices of their moral legitimacy. . . . It was therefore perhaps the single most important moment of the decade, the moment that separated the old order from the new and helped create the tumultuous era just arriving." Considered one of the most important victories for civil rights, *Brown* paved the way for challenges to racial segregation in many areas, including on public buses and in restaurants.

In examining *Brown*, it becomes apparent that the courts play an influential role—and face an arduous challenge—in shaping the debate over emotionally charged social issues. Judges must balance competing interests, keeping in mind the high stakes and intense emotions on both sides. As exempli-fied by *Brown*, judicial decisions often upset the status quo and initiate significant changes in society. Greenhaven Press's Issues on Trial series captures the controversy surrounding in-fluential court rulings and explores the social ramifications of such decisions from varying perspectives. Each anthology highlights one social issue—such as the death penalty, students' rights, or wartime civil liberties. Each volume then focuses on key historical and contemporary court cases that helped mold the issue as we know it today. The books include a compendium of primary sources—court rulings, dissents, and immediate reactions to the rulings—as well as secondary sources from experts in the field, people involved in the cases, legal analysts, and other commentators opining on the implications and legacy of the chosen cases. An annotated table of contents, an in-depth introduction, and prefaces that overview each case all provide context as readers delve into the topic at hand. To help students fully probe the subject, each volume contains book and periodical bibliographies, a comprehensive index, and a list of organizations to contact. With these features, the Issues on Trial series offers a well-rounded perspective on the courts' role in framing society's thorniest, most impassioned debates.

Introduction

Although the juvenile justice system in America is a relatively modern invention, its philosophical underpinnings date back to the ancient Greeks when the philosopher Aristotle posited that the ideal government should have a policing function (to protect its citizens from harm) and a caretaking function (to provide for those who cannot care for themselves). Over the past century, the juvenile justice system in the United States has struggled to strike a balance between punishing troubled youth and caring for them so that they are rehabilitated and become productive citizens.

Prior to the establishment of a separate juvenile court system in 1899, children accused of serious or violent crimes were tried in the same criminal courts as adults, faced the same punishments as adults, and served time in the same jails as adults, where they often suffered severe abuse. According to the Coalition for Juvenile Justice, in the nineteenth century at least ten juveniles under age fourteen were executed by hanging for their offenses.[1] Orphans, truants, and children accused of petty crimes were generally placed in Houses of Refuge, or reformatories, where they were worked hard, disciplined by beatings, and sometimes taught a trade. Although historical evidence suggests that many children were abused in these reformatories, the stated purpose of the reformatory or house of refuge was to educate and rehabilitate children, not punish them.

The landmark case *Ex parte Crouse* (1838) was the first American court case to assert that the state could supersede the parents' wishes in determining the best interests of a wayward or incorrigible child. In *Ex parte Crouse*, the Pennsylvania Supreme Court ruled that a minor child, Mary Ann

---

1. Coalition for Juvenile Justice, *A Celebration or a Wake: The Juvenile Court After 100 Years*. Washington, DC: Coalition for Juvenile Justice, 1998.

Crouse, who was found to be "incorrigible," could be removed from the family home against her father's wishes and placed in a house of refuge. The Supreme Court of Pennsylvania found that, as a minor child, Mary Ann was not entitled to a trial with representation and asserted that the Court had the right to supersede her parents' rights in determining her best interests. The 1838 ruling explicitly states that when parents are unable to properly care for or control a child, the state may intervene and act as a parent. "May not the natural parents, when unequal to the task of education, or unworthy of it, be superseded by the *parens patriae,* or common guardian of the community?"[2] The philosophy of *parens patriae* (Latin for *father of the nation,* meaning that the Court has the right to determine the best interests of a child) served as a guide for many court rulings on minor children throughout the nineteenth century and was instrumental to the founding of the modern juvenile justice system.

The first separate juvenile court was established in Chicago, Illinois, in 1899 as an outgrowth of the child-rescue movement, in which middle class social reformers attempted to rescue impoverished, largely immigrant children from life on the streets. Alarmed by the growing numbers of recent immigrants living in poverty and concerned that impoverished and neglected children were exposed to the criminal element both in their home environments and in the criminal justice system, middle class social reformers such as Jane Addams, founder of Hull House in Chicago, pushed for the founding of a separate court for juveniles that focused on addressing the environmental causes of delinquency.

Soon after the establishment of a juvenile court in Chicago, similar juvenile courts sprang up throughout the country. The juvenile court embraced the idea of *parens patriae,* maintaining that due to their immaturity, children could not be held responsible for criminal behavior in the same way that

2. *Ex parte Crouse,* 4 Wharton, Pa. 9 (1838).

adults were. Additionally, the juvenile court system emphasized child welfare, often advocating for the removal of the child from the corrupting environment and for the rehabilitation of the child with the help of newly professional social workers and juvenile probation officers. Youth were no longer tried as adult offenders. Their cases were heard in a somewhat informal court designed for juveniles, often without the assistance of attorneys. Extenuating evidence outside the legal facts surrounding the crime or delinquent behavior was taken into consideration by the judge. Early reform houses were, in many ways, similar to orphanages. Indeed, many of the youth housed in the reformatories were orphans and homeless children.

The establishment of the juvenile justice system occurred at a time of great social change called the Progressive Era. Between 1900 and 1918, Americans fought for woman's suffrage and the eight-hour work day and campaigned against child labor and corruption in big business. The juvenile court system protected children from interacting with hardened criminals, but at a price. Following the position of *parens patriae* articulated in *Ex parte Crouse*, the juvenile court system did not provide children with legal representation or the due process that a trial would afford them. The proceedings were confidential; usually, a juvenile court judge would confer with social workers, then decide how best to deal with a troubled child. Because juvenile court proceedings were informal and determined by the judge's discretion without a trial, in most jurisdictions, there were no transcripts, no formal presentations of evidence, no cross-examination of witnesses, and no right of appeal. The state assumed the responsibility of parenting the children until they began to exhibit positive changes or became adults. The new juvenile court system intended to remove procedural and legal obstacles so that the court could quickly move to protect a child in danger; however, the informal *ad hoc* nature of the juvenile justice system in the early twentieth century gave judges nearly unlimited power over children and their families, resulted in inconsistent punishments, and deprived children of the constitutional and legal protections found in the criminal court system.

Despite these flaws, for most of the twentieth century, the juvenile court system remained a confidential, informal affair in which judges, working with social workers and other helping professionals, determined the fate of the accused minor and continued to emphasize the need to address environmental factors and provide rehabilitation. While the informality of the juvenile justice system may have been appropriate for cases of petty theft or school truancy, the lack of due process for children accused of wrongdoing inevitably caused situations in which juveniles were placed in detention facilities without access to a lawyer or another advocate.

In the turbulent 1960s, with calls for civil liberties from minorities and for "law and order" from conservatives, fifteen-year-old Gerald Gault was arrested for making obscene phone calls to a neighbor. Gault, a repeat offender, was arrested for delinquency and placed in jail without his parents' knowledge. The judge declared him guilty and sentenced him to a reform school until his twenty-first birthday—nearly six years of confinement. No transcript was made of the confidential hearing, and Gault, like other accused juveniles, had no recourse to appeal the judge's decision in juvenile court. Gault's family took his case to the Supreme Court, arguing that the entire case violated his constitutional rights to due process.

In *In re Gault* (1967), the U.S. Supreme Court ruled in Gault's favor. "Under our Constitution the condition of being a boy does not justify a kangaroo court," the Court wrote in a decision that forced juvenile courts to give minors the complete due process protections afforded adults tried in criminal court. These protections included the right to notice of charges, the right to counsel, the right to confront and cross-examine witnesses, the right of appeal, and the privilege against self-incrimination. The opinion also explicitly rejected the doctrine of *parens patriae* as the founding principle of juvenile justice. The Supreme Court described the meaning of *parens patriae* as "murky" and characterized its "historic credentials" as having "dubious relevance." In his dissent, however, Justice Potter Stewart expressed concern that the court's decision would "convert a juvenile proceeding into a criminal prosecution." Stewart wrote that the historical intent of the juvenile justice system was not to prosecute and punish young offenders, but to "correct a condition" and meet society's "responsibilities to the child."

Although the intent of the Supreme Court's decision in *Gault* was to protect juveniles' civil rights by granting them the same rights afforded adult offenders, one of the consequences of the ruling was that the Court's emphasis shifted from rehabilitation to determining guilt and punishment in a trial. Since *Gault*, a tension has existed between the right to due process, which affords an accused minor the same civil rights as an adult, and the separate juvenile court system that grants judges *parens patriae* and recognizes that children are developmentally, psychologically, and emotionally less mature than adults and are, therefore, less legally culpable for their actions. One of the consequences of *In re Gault* is that today prosecutors can ask that juveniles be tried in an adult criminal court rather than in the juvenile civil court.

A steep rise in juvenile crime that occurred between the late 1980s and mid-1990s led legislators to "get tough on crime," amending the 1974 Juvenile Justice and Delinquency Prevention Act so that states could try minors as adults for some violent crimes and weapons violations. Some states also put into place minimum detention standards. The anticrime sentiment of the period caused changes to be implemented to the juvenile justice system that made it increasingly similar to the adult criminal justice system. The shift Justice Stewart had predicted in 1967, with the implementation of formal trials for youth, reflected an increasingly common view that juvenile offenders were not youth begging rehabilitation, but young criminals. As suggested by the Court's finding in *New Jersey v. T.L.O.* (1985), rehabilitation became less important than public safety in the aggressive campaign against crime of the 1980s and 1990s.

In the late 1990s, a spate of school shootings and other horrendous offenses caused the public to call for violent youth to be tried in adult courts and has even resulted in juveniles on death row. In the case of *Roper v. Simmons* (2005), the Supreme Court held that it is cruel and unusual punishment to execute individuals who were minors at the time of their crime, no matter how violent the act. Citing psychological research, the Court maintained that adolescents were not as mature as adults and that their immaturity should be considered as a mitigating factor.

Throughout the history of juvenile justice, the desire to punish offending youth has conflicted with the goals of rehabilitation; likewise, a tension exists between granting minor offenders the same right to due process as adult offenders and a separate status that acknowledges their immaturity and the obligation of the state to protect and rehabilitate them. This anthology seeks to explore these issues by looking at four of the major Court decision related to juvenile justice and children's rights in America: *Ex parte Crouse* (1838), *In re Gault* (1967), *New Jersey v. T.L.O.* (1985), and *Roper v. Simmons* (2005). By presenting the Supreme Court's decisions, the views of dissenting justices, and commentary on the impact of the cases, *Issues on Trial: Juvenile Justice* provides a comprehensive overview of an important issue with which American society continues to grapple.

CHAPTER 1

Establishing the State's Role as Parent

Case Overview

Ex parte Crouse (1838)

In 1838, a sixteen-year-old girl named Mary Ann Crouse was committed to the Philadelphia House of Refuge by her mother, who claimed Mary Ann was "incorrigible," meaning disobedient and uncontrollable. Mary Ann's mother, however, did not inform the girl's father of the decision. Mary Ann's father took the case to court, arguing that Mary Ann was illegally incarcerated because she had not been given a trial and had been imprisoned without his consent. In the court case *Ex parte Crouse*, the Pennsylvania Supreme Court argued that Mary Ann was not entitled to a trial because she was a minor and had not been imprisoned, but rather rescued from a harmful situation. The Court also ruled that the state has the right to remove children from their parents' homes. In the Court's decision, Justice John Bannister Gibson wrote, "May not the natural parents, when unequal to the task of education, or unworthy of it, be superseded by the *parens patriae*, or common guardian of the community?" He also contended that the parents were unfit and that Mary Ann "ha[d] been snatched from a course which must have ended in confirmed depravity."

Although there was no juvenile justice system in the United States until 1899, for most of American history, children who were accused of petty crimes such as vagrancy, begging, or chronic incorrigibility were routinely placed in Houses of Refuge, which were supposed to train young offenders in a trade and prevent them from growing up to be criminals. Often the children who were placed in these institutions were from poor, ethnic, immigrant families.

For the most part, the precedent of *Ex parte Crouse* went unchallenged, with a few exceptions. In *People v. Turner* (1870), the Illinois Supreme Court reversed the sentencing of fourteen-year-old Daniel O'Connell to the Chicago Reform School after his father petitioned for his release. The Court ruled that children cannot be "confined for 'the good of society'" "without crime, without the conviction of any offense." The Illinois Supreme Court found that O'Connell had not been given due process and was unjustly imprisoned even though he had not been convicted of a crime (O'Connell had been accused of vagrancy). Furthermore, the Court determined that a child could not be removed from a home unless the parents demonstrated "gross misconduct or almost total unfitness."

Because of the O'Connell case, only children who had committed felonies could be sent to reform schools. Homeless, impoverished, and exploited children, however, continued to draw attention and concern among the social reformers who were part of what was known as the Child Rescue Movement. Influenced by the principle of *parens patriae* and the desire to lift children from poverty and a life of crime but cognizant of the *People v. Turner* ruling, influential social reformers such as Jane Addams of the Hull House community and Caroline Brown of the Chicago Woman's Club lobbied for the establishment of a separate juvenile court system to protect and rehabilitate at-risk children.

The first juvenile court was founded on July 1, 1899, in Chicago, Illinois, and every state quickly established their own. The juvenile court system was separate from the criminal courts and was to address cases involving juveniles to age sixteen or seventeen, depending on the state. The juvenile justice system differed from criminal courts in several key ways, namely an emphasis on rehabilitation, a focus on "the best interests of the child," and a large degree of judicial latitude. The juvenile justice system was designed to be much more informal than the criminal system. Juvenile courts adjudicated, rather than convicted, young offenders. The cases were sealed, hearings were closed to the public, records were confidential, and lawyers were unnecessary because the proceedings were considered civil rather than criminal matters. Because the focus was on rehabilitation, as in *Ex parte Crouse*, judges continued to have great discretion in determining consequences for youthful offenders.

> "To this end may not the natural parents, when unequal to the task of education, or unworthy of it, be superseded by the parens patriae, or common guardian of the community?"

The State Supreme Court's Decision: The Government Must Protect Children

John Bannister Gibson

John Bannister Gibson (1780–1853) served as the chief justice of the Pennsylvania Supreme Court from 1827 until 1851. His remarkable range of knowledge and diligent study made him an authority on common law, and his many forceful, well-worded decisions, based on principles rather than precedents, showed great ability to adapt the law to a particular society and did much to mold Pennsylvania law.

In Ex parte Crouse *(1839), Gibson argues that parental control may be natural, but not inalienable, and that in situations in which children are neglected or deemed uncontrollable by the parent, the state does not need the parents' permission or the child's consent to remove the child to a state institution. This case turns upon the right of the state to remove a child from the parents' home against the parents' will and to place the child in a House of Refuge, or state-run reformatory school for delinquent children.*

John Bannister Gibson, *per curiam* opinion, *Ex parte Crouse*, Supreme Court of Pennsylvania, 1839.

The provisions of the acts of 23d of March, 1826, and 10th of April 1835, which authorizes the committal of infants to the House of Refuge, under certain circumstances, and their detention there, without a previous trial by jury, are not unconstitutional.

This was a *habeas corpus* [Latin phrase, meaning "you should have the body," is the name of a writ or legal action through which defendants seek relief from unlawful imprisonment] directed by the keeper and managers of the "House of Refuge," in the county of Philadelphia, requiring them to produce before the court one Mary Ann Crouse, an infant [minor child], detained in that institution. The petition for the *habeas corpus* was in the name of her father.

By the return to the writ it appeared, that the girl had been committed to the custody of the managers by virtue of a warrant under the hand and seal of Morton McMichael, Esq., a justice of the peace in the county of Philadelphia, which recited that complaint and due proof had been made before him by Mary Crouse, the mother of the said Mary Ann Crouse, "that the said infant by reason of vicious conduct, has rendered her control beyond the power of the said complainant, and made it manifestly requisite that from regard to the moral and future welfare of the said infant she should be placed under the guardianship of the managers of the House of Refuge;" and the said alderman certified that in his opinion the said infant was "proper subject for the said House of Refuge." Appended to the warrant of commitment were the names and places of residence of the witnesses examined, and the substance of the testimony given by them respectively, upon which the adjudication of the magistrate was founded.

House of Refuge

The House of Refuge was established in pursuance of an Act of Assembly passed on the 23d day of March 1826. The sixth section of that act declared that the managers should, "at their discretion, receive into the said House of Refuge, such children who shall be taken up or committed as vagrants, or upon any criminal charge, or duly convicted of criminal offences, as may be in the judgment of the Court of Oyer and Terminer, or of the Court of Quarter Sessions of the peace of the county, or of the Mayor's Court of the city of Philadelphia, or of any alderman or justice of the peace, or of the managers of the almshouse and house of employment, be deemed proper objects." By a supplement to the act passed on the 10th day of April 1835, it was declared, that in lieu of the provisions of the act of 1826, it should be lawful for the managers of the House of Refuge "at their discretion to receive into their care and guardianship, infants, males under the age of twenty-one years, and females under the age of eighteen years committed to their custody in either of the following modes, viz [namely]: First: Infants committed by an alderman or justice of the peace on the complaint and due proof made to him by the parent, guardian or next friend of such infant, that by reason of incorrigible or vicious conduct such infant has rendered his or her control beyond the power of such parent, guardian or next friend, and made it manifestly requisite that from regard to the morals and future welfare of such infant, he or she should be placed under the guardianship of the managers of the House of Refuge. Second: Infants committed by the authority aforesaid, where complaint and due proof have been made that such infant is a proper subject for the guardianship of the managers of the House of Refuge, in consequence of vagrancy, or of incorrigible or vicious conduct, and that from the moral depravity or otherwise of the parent or next friend in whose custody such infant may be, such parent or next friend is incapable or unwilling to exercise the proper care and discipline over such incorrigible or vicious infant. Third: Infants committed by the courts of the Commonwealth in the mode provided by the act to which this is a supplement."

Mr. W.L. Hirst, for the petitioner, now contended, that those provisions, so far as they authorized the committal and detention of an infant without a trial by jury, were unconstitutional. . . .

Parens Patriae: State as Parent

The House of Refuge is not a prison, but a school. Where reformation, and not punishment, is the end, it may indeed be used as a prison for juvenile convicts who would else be committed to a common goal; and in respect to these, the constitutionality of the act which incorporated it, stands clear of controversy. It is only in respect of the application of its discipline to subjects admitted on the order of the court, a magistrate or the managers of the Almshouse, that a doubt is entertained. The object of the charity is reformation, by training its inmates to industry; by imbuing their minds with principles of morality and religion; by furnishing them from the corrupting influence of improper associates. To this end may not the natural parents, when unequal to the task of education, or unworthy of it, be superseded by the *parens patriae*, or common guardian of the community? It is to be remembered that the public has a paramount interest in the virtue and knowledge of its members, and that of strict right, the business of education belongs to it. That parents are ordinarily entrusted with it is because it can seldom be put into better hands; but where they are incompetent or corrupt, what is there to prevent the public from withdrawing their faculties, held, as they obviously are, at is sufferance? The right of parental control is a natural, but not an unalienable one. It is not excepted by the declaration of rights out of the subjects of ordinary legislation; and it consequently remains subject to the ordinary legislation; and it consequently remains subject to the ordinary legislative power which, if wantonly or inconveniently used, would soon be constitutionally restricted, but the competency of which, as the government is constituted, cannot be doubted.

27

As to abridgement of indefeasible rights by confinement of the person, it is no more than what is borne, to a greater or less extent, in every school; and we know of no natural right to exemption from restraints which conduce to an infant's welfare. Nor is there a doubt of the propriety of their application in the particular instance. The infant has been snatched from a course which must have ended in confirmed depravity; and, not only is the restraint of her person lawful, but it would be an act of extreme cruelty to release her from it.

Remanded

"The available investigations and records of nineteenth century juvenile institutions offer compelling evidence that the state was not a benevolent parent. In short, there was significant disparity between the promise and practice of parens patriae.*"*

Ex parte Crouse Paved the Way for Juvenile Institutions That Were Less than Ideal

Alexander W. Pisciotta

Alexander Pisciotta is a professor of criminal justice at Kutztown University in Kutztown, Pennsylvania. A well-known authority on both juvenile and adult reformatory movements, Pisciotta received the New York State Archives Outstanding Researcher Award in 1995 and the 1997 Outstanding Book Award given by the Academy of Criminal Justice Sciences for his book Benevolent Repression: Social Control and the American Reformatory-Prison Movement.

Ex parte Crouse (1938) asserted the right of the state to intervene in juvenile matters based on the assumption that the best interests of the children were being protected. In the following essay, Pisciotta argues that although the notion of parens patriae—*or, the agreement as parent—made explicit in the* Ex parte Crouse *decision provided a compelling rationale for plac-*

Alexander W. Pisciotta, "Saving the Children: The Promise and Practice of Parens Patriae, 1838-98," *Crime & Delinquency,* 1982. Reprinted by permission of Sage Publications, Inc., conveyed through Copyright Clearance Center, Inc.

ing neglected and delinquent minors into reformatories in the nineteenth century, in practice, the reformatories and similar institutions often exploited minors and seldom acted in their best interests.

The landmark decision incorporating *parens patriae* [the concept of the government as parent] into the American legal structure was ruled upon by the supreme court justices of the state of Pennsylvania in 1838. In this case, the Pennsylvania court was presented with an appeal on a writ of *habeas corpus* submitted by the father of one of the inmates immured in the Philadelphia House of Refuge—Mary Ann Crouse. Mr. Crouse maintained that his daughter (who had been committed by his wife, without his knowledge, as "incorrigible") was illegally detained because she had not been granted the benefit of a trial on account of her age. Unfortunately for Mary Ann and her father, the justices of the Pennsylvania court rejected this interpretation of the law and rendered a unanimous decision which concluded that the Bill of Rights (in this case the sixth and ninth sections) did not apply to minors. The justices based their opinion on the doctrine of *parens patriae*, which, heretofore, had been an English jurisprudential innovation. "May not the natural parents, when unequal to the task of education, or unworthy of it," asked the judges, "be superseded by the *parens patriae*, or common guardian of the community?"

The justices' *per curiam* ["by the court"] opinion clearly indicates that they based their ruling on the assumption that the Philadelphia House of Refuge had a beneficial influence on its charges: "The House of Refuge is not a prison, but a school. Where reformation and not punishment is the end." The justices also clearly specified their reasons for assuming that the Philadelphia institution was a "school" and not a prison: "The object of charity is reformation, by training . . . inmates to industry; by imbuing their minds with the principles of morality and religion; by furnishing them with means to earn a living; and, above all, by separating them from the corrupting influence of improper associates. . . ."

There was, however, a significant flaw in the logic of the courts: Their knowledge about the internal operations and "benevolent effect" of reformatories was derived almost solely from information imparted by the managers of these institutions. The justices ruling in the case of Mary Ann Crouse assumed that the Philadelphia House of Refuge had a beneficial effect on the children because the prominent members of the board of managers assured the court that their charges were receiving moral, religious, and educational instruction at the same time that they were learning a trade. Judges in other states blindly followed the precedent established by the Pennsylvania court and repeated its error by not closely investigating the internal affairs of these institutions in order to make certain that they were, indeed, "great charities." The result, as might be expected, was that the opinions rendered by the courts in juvenile cases throughout the century were "distressingly similar. . . ."

An examination of the records of a number of juvenile institutions, as well as investigative reports, strongly suggests that there was a significant disparity between the theory and practice of these reformatories. In short, justices across the country, throughout the nineteenth century, invoked *parens patriae* on premises which were, at best, questionable.

The State as Disciplinarian

One of the conditions under which the courts reserved the right to invoke *parens patriae* and separate children from their natural parents occurred when the parents physically abused their offspring. Judges justified this intervention by promising to place the children under the care of reformatory school administrators who were humane and compassionate; and the managers of the "benevolent institutions" reinforced this belief by describing their methods of discipline in terms that were almost identical to those employed by the keepers of the Western House of Refuge in 1851: "The discipline of the institution is intended to be mild, conciliatory and parental but firm." There was, however, often a considerable difference between the rhetoric of the keepers and the reality confronting the inmates; even for an age in which stern corporal punishment was expected of parents, the techniques of subjection applied in many reformatories could not, by any reasonable standard, be described as "parental" in nature.

An investigation into the internal affairs of the Providence Reform School in 1868, for example, revealed that inmates were punished with rattans and a "cat" with six twelve-inch leather thongs attached to a wooden handle—for recalcitrant children, the wooden handle was used as a whipping surface. Eban J. Bean was one of a number of former employees who described Superintendent James Talcott's method of discipline:

> *Bean*: He was stripped naked in the room, his fingers put on the wall as high as he could reach, and he was licked with what I should call a cat o'nine tails. . . . He was licked til the blood ran down his back.
>
> *Alderman*: How long did the punishment last?
>
> *Bean*: I should say about five or ten minutes. He boxed the boy first, he boxed his face, and slapped his face. He bloodied the floor considerably. He first talked, and then the boy stripped for him. . . .

Female inmates were treated with almost as much severity. The testimony revealed that it was a common practice to have their "dresses taken down, so as to expose the upper part of their back and shoulders, and punishment by the strap." In defense of this mode of discipline, the superintendent pointed out that a female officer was "usually present" to supervise the whipping. The girls were also subjected to the punishment of being tied and "ducked" under water in a large tub. . . .

An investigation of the State Reform School at Westborough, Massachusetts, in 1877 revealed an even more elaborate system of punishments. Flogging with the "cat" was, once again, the primary method of maintaining order, and each of the officers was permitted to administer corporal punishments at his own discretion. . . .

The keepers of the Westborough Reform School also placed their more obstreperous children in a "sweatbox," which was ten inches deep and fourteen inches wide with three one-inch slits in the front for air holes; one boy testified that he was locked in the "sweatbox" for seven days from half past five in the morning until a quarter past six at night with his hands strapped behind him. The straightjacket was also commonly used; and, for those children who would not submit to any of these forms of punishment, the keepers applied a steady stream of ice cold water from a hose until the recalcitrant child repented. . . .

The Value of Hard Labor

Throughout most of the nineteenth century, reformatory managers used a system of contract labor in order to fulfill the mandate of the *Crouse* decision of "training its inmates to industry" and "furnishing them with a means to earn a living." Although there were a number of variations, the programs of labor were essentially similar. Private businessmen supplied machinery, material, and overseers; the inmates supplied their labor; and the managers of the institution were paid on a per diem or piece-price basis. The inmates received either a menial sum or, as was more generally the case, no remuneration at all. The items produced in the New York House of Refuge in 1857 were almost identical to the goods produced in other institutions. The boys worked under contract for five to seven hours each day making shoes, clothes, wire, sofa springs, and cane chairs, while the girls were responsible for the institution's domestic chores. "Every child from the oldest to the youngest has a daily task wisely adapted to its age and ability," explained the chaplain of the New York House of Refuge. "A trade in most instances is thus secured." The managers of the Cincinnati House of Refuge expressed the optimism of managers across the country when they proclaimed that "the contracting system is decidedly the most advantageous in all respects."

In practice, however, the system of contract labor did not fulfill the expectations of judges who believed that they were sentencing minors to a term of vocational education. An investigation of the system of contract labor in fourteen institutions in New York State in 1870 by the noted penologist, Enoch C. Wines, is most enlightening. The unequivocal conclusion of Wines's committee was that "[t]he contract system is bad and should be abolished," a finding certainly not consistent with the exhortatory evaluations of the managers. . . .

The primary beneficiary of the contract labor system was not the inmates; rather, it was the contractor, George Whitehouse. After hearing the contractor's former bookkeeper, George Coffin, testify that shoes produced in the open market for $.50 could be made by the boys for $.15, Wines's committee investigated the financial status of Mr. Whitehouse. Their findings were not at all consistent with the presumed rehabilitative effects of contract labor. In 1869 the contractor realized a profit of $183,875 from the labor of the 575 boys in the institution. "We put it to all fair-minded men, we put it to the managers themselves," asked the commissioners in disbelief, "whether the contractor on Randall's Island pays a fair price for the labor he obtains there? . . . In the thirteen years during which he has held the shoe contract on Randall's Island, the contractor has built up a large fortune for himself." The effects of working for Mr. Whitehouse, and of being in the refuge were, perhaps, most aptly stated by bookkeeper Coffin. "I have known boys sent there for some trivial offence [sic] who were not bad boys at bottom when they first went there, but who became, in a short time, as thoroughly hardened as in any institution." In contrast with the assurances of the managers that their institution was a "school," Coffin concluded that "it is generally understood up there that the boys are not reformed."

Saving Fallen Youth

Nineteenth century judges and reformers who cited the doctrine of *parens patriae* also did so on the grounds that by placing wayward children in reformatories they were saving them from a godless existence by "imbuing their minds with the principles of morality and religion." Almost without exception, religious instruction consisted of nonsectarian chapel services on Sunday mornings followed by Sunday school classes in the afternoon, as well as daily prayer. The managers of reformatories, once again, did not hesitate to reassure the courts that they were fulfilling the principles of *Ex parte Crouse*. "The Chaplain's Department," concluded the keepers of the State Reform School at Westborough, "is one of vast importance to the highest welfare of the boys, involving worth of the spiritual as well as the temporal well-being of those under its charge." The managers of the New York House of Refuge supported their claims of salvation in the same year by noting that although 66 percent of the children had never learned any verses of Scripture at the time of entering the refuge, 53,166 verses had been committed to memory and recited by the end of the year.

In reality, however, control over the religious instruction of children in reformatories was a symbolic source of dispute between the Protestant managers, who maintained that they were saving the children of foreign-born Catholics from lives of depravity and crime by exposing them to nonsectarian services, and Catholic clergymen and parents, who felt that their sons and daughters were being stolen from them and molded into heretics. . . .

Reintegration

The ultimate test of the success of juvenile institutions in transforming neglected, dependent, and delinquent minors into God-fearing, law-abiding, and hard-working citizens, in accordance with the principles of *parens patriae*, was, in the view of the keepers, reflected in the successful reintegration of the youths into the community through apprenticeships. The system instituted at the New York House of Refuge in 1825, once again, served as a model throughout the nineteenth century. Once the inmates had resided in the New York institution for a sufficient amount of time, and had participated in the regimen of reform with a significant degree of compliance, they appeared before the institution's "indenture committee," which was composed of several members of the board of managers. At the discretion of the board, the children—who were always committed for indeterminate terms which could not extend beyond the age of majority—could be returned to their parents or discharged to a master who was required to sign a contract wherein he agreed to provide the apprentice with food, clothes, shelter, religious instruction, and a nominal payment when the apprentice reached the age of majority. Boys were generally apprenticed to farmers in the country, and girls were exclusively placed as domestics. In essence, the apprentice system transferred the responsibility of *parens patriae* from the state to the master. . . .

The terms of indenture contract were generally not fulfilled. A random sample of 210 case histories selected between 1857 and 1862 from the records of the New York House of Refuge reveals that 72 percent of the inmates either ran away, voluntarily returned to the refuge because they were not pleased with their placement, were returned to the refuge by their master, or committed an offense and were incarcerated in another institution. . . .

Thomas Collier was forced to run away because he was "badly clothed and stated that he ran away because he [his master] abused him, and had tied and whipped him." A number of female apprentices faced a different type of problem. When Mary Gash returned to the superintendent and informed him that she was pregnant by Mr. Rue, her master, the superintendent, perhaps naively, "advised her to return to Mr. Rue and inform Mrs. Rue of her condition . . . and ask for care and protection. . . ."

The State Is Not the Best Parent

The available investigations and records of nineteenth century juvenile institutions offer compelling evidence that the state was not a benevolent parent. In short, there was significant disparity between the promise and practice of *parens patriae*. Discipline was seldom "parental" in nature, inmate workers were exploited under the contract labor system, religious instruction was often disguised proselytization, and the indenture system generally failed to provide inmates with a home in the country. The frequency of escapes, assaults, incendiary incidents, and homosexual relations suggests that the children were not, as the Pennsylvania court presumed in 1838, "separated from the corrupting influence of improper associates. . . ."

If there is any practical lesson to be learned from evaluating the historical record of *parens patriae*, it is, perhaps, that contemporary child savers would be well advised to assess objectively, rather than assume, the "benevolent" effects of their rehabilitative efforts. It is certainly ironic, and perhaps even tragic, that the humanitarian imagery projected by supporters of the juvenile justice system has, for decades, buried the "evidence" that the child "receives the worst of both worlds."

"Unfortunately, traditional delinquency treatment strategies, employed in both prevention and intervention programs, have been shaped largely by common-sense assumptions about the needs of youth, generally boys."

The Notion of *Parens Patriae* Promotes Gender Bias in the Juvenile Justice System

Randall G. Shelden

Randall G. Shelden is a professor of criminal justice at the University of Nevada, Las Vegas. He is the author or coauthor of five books including Delinquency and Juvenile Justice in American Society *(2006).*

In the following article, Randall G. Shelden argues that the child-saving movement of the nineteenth century was predicated upon middle-class assumptions about femininity and the proper role for girls and women in society. He suggests that just as nineteenth-century reformers failed to meet the needs of the working-class girls who entered reformatories and houses of refuge, all too often the contemporary juvenile justice system inadequately addresses the concerns of girls who enter the system due to abuse or neglect. The concept of parens patriae, *or the state as parent, was established in juvenile law by the 1839 case* Ex parte Crouse. *Shelden contends that* parens patriae *brings with it any gender bias already present in society.*

Randall G. Shelden, PhD, "Confronting the Ghost of Mary Ann Crouse: Gender Bias in the Juvenile Justice System," *Juvenile and Family Court Journal,* Winter 1998. Copyright © 1998 NCJFCJ All rights reserved. Reproduced by permission.

M any early activities of the child savers revolved around monitoring young girls', particularly immigrant girls', behavior. . . .

Girls' were the losers in this reform effort. Studies of early family court activity reveal that almost all girls who appeared in these courts were charged with immorality or waywardness. The sanctions for such misbehavior were extremely severe. For example, the Chicago family court sent half the girl delinquents but only a fifth of the boy delinquents to reformatories between 1899 and 1909. In Milwaukee, twice as many girls as boys were committed to training schools. In Memphis, females were twice as likely as males to be committed to training schools. In Honolulu during 1929–1930, over half the girls referred to juvenile court were charged with "immorality," which meant there was evidence of sexual intercourse; 30 percent were charged with "waywardness. . . ."

There was a slight modification of the *parens patriae* [state as parent] doctrine during this period [the early twentieth century]. The "training" of girls was shaped by the image of the ideal woman that had evolved during the early part of the nineteenth century. According to this ideal (which was informed by what some have called the "separate-spheres" notion), a woman belonged in the private sphere, performing such tasks as rearing children, keeping house, caring for a husband, and serving as the moral guardian of the home. In this capacity, she was to exhibit qualities like obedience, modesty, and dependence. Her husband's domain was the public sphere: the workplace, politics, and the law. He was also, by virtue of his public power, the final arbiter of public morality and culture. This white middle-class "cult of domesticity" was, of course, very distant from the lives of many working- and lower-class women who by necessity were in the labor force. . . . A statement by the Ladies Committee of the New York House of Refuge summed up the attributes early court advocates sought to instill:

> The Ladies wish to call attention to the great change which takes place in every girl who has spent one year in the Refuge; she enters a rude, careless, untrained child, caring nothing for cleanliness and order; when she leaves the House, she can sew, mend, darn, wash, iron, arrange a table neatly and cook a healthy meal.

The institutions established for girls set about to isolate them from all contact with males while training them in feminine skills and housing them in bucolic rural settings. The intention was to hold the girls until marriageable age, and to occupy them in domestic pursuits during their sometimes lengthy incarceration. The child savers had little hesitation about such extreme intervention in girls' lives. They believed "delinquency" to be the result of a variety of social, psychological and biological factors, and they were optimistic about the juvenile court's ability to remove girls from influences that were producing delinquent behavior. For this reason, the juvenile court was to function in a way totally unlike other courts. The juvenile court judge, for example, was to serve as a benevolent yet stern father. The proceedings were to be informal, without the traditional judicial trappings: initially no lawyers were required; constitutional safeguards were not in place; no provisions existed for jury trials; and so on. Consistent with the *parens patriae* doctrine, the courts were freed from many of the usual constraints because it was thought they were acting in the best interests of the child. . . .

Focusing on the Needs of Girls

Hearings held in conjunction with the 1992 reauthorization of the Juvenile Justice and Delinquency Prevention Act addressed for the first time the "provision of services to girls within the juvenile justice system." Witnesses discussed both the double standard of juvenile justice and the paucity of services for girls. . . .

Perhaps as a result of this landmark hearing, the 1992 reauthorization included specific provisions requiring plans from each state receiving federal funds to include "an analysis of gender-specific services for the prevention and treatment of juvenile delinquency, including the types of such services available and the need for such services for females and a plan for providing needed gender-specific services for the prevention and treatment of juvenile delinquency. . . ."

Alternatives to Incarceration

Girls on the economic and political margins, particularly those who find their way into the juvenile justice system, share many problems with their male counterparts. They are likely to be poor, from disrupted and violent families, and having trouble in school. In addition, though, girls also confront problems unique to their sex: notably sexual abuse, sexual assault, dating violence, depression, unplanned pregnancy, and adolescent motherhood. Both their experience of the problems they share with boys, and the additional special problems that they face, then, are conditioned by their gender, as well as their class and race. Specifically, since families are the source of many of the serious problems that girls face, solutions must take into account that some girls may not be able to stay safely at home.

Programming for girls clearly must be shaped by girls' unique situations, and must address the special problems girls have in a gendered society. Unfortunately, traditional delinquency treatment strategies, employed in both prevention and intervention programs, have been shaped largely by common-sense assumptions about the needs of youth, generally boys, need. Sometimes these programs will meet the needs of girls and sometimes they will not address girls' problems at all.

There is a tremendous shortage of information on programs that have been proven effective in work with girls. Indeed, many studies that have evaluated particular approaches do not deal with special gender issues, and frequently programs do not even serve girls. In addition, programs that have been carefully evaluated are often set in training schools (clearly not the ideal place to try any particular strategy). Finally, careful evaluation of most programs tends to show that even the most determined efforts to intervene and help often show very poor results. Of course, the last two points may well be related; programs set in closed, institutional settings are clearly at a disadvantage and, as a consequence, tend to be less effective. . . .

After two decades of "de-institutionalization efforts," girls remain, in the words of [Sue Davidson,] "all but invisible in programs for youth and in the literature available to those who work with youth." Further, funding for programs for young women in general (and for delinquents, in particular) has been a low priority in our society. For instance, a 1975 report by the Law Enforcement Assistance Administration revealed that only 5% of federally funded juvenile delinquency projects were specifically directed at girls, and that only 6% of all local monies for juvenile justice were spent on girls. A 1989 review of seventy-five private foundations revealed that funding "targeted specifically for girls and women hovered around 3.4%."

Girls Fall Between the Cracks

An exhaustive study of virtually all program evaluation studies done since 1950 [by Mark Lipsey in 1992] located reports on some 443 delinquency programs; of these 34.8% were exclusively male and an additional 42.4% served "mostly males." This study found that only about 2% of the surveyed programs explicitly served only girls, and only 6% of the programs served "some males," meaning that most of the programs' participants were girls.

Finally, a 1993 study by the San Francisco Chapter of the National Organization for Women found that less than 10% (8.7%) of the programs funded by the major city organization funding children and youth programs "specifically addressed the needs of girls." Not surprisingly, then, a 1995 study of youth participation in San Francisco after school or summer sports programs found that only 26% of the participants were girls.

What are the specific needs of young women in general, and in particular, of those who come into contact with the juvenile justice system, either as victims or offenders? Davidson argues that:

> The most denigrate need of many young women is to find the economic means of survival. White females today are still being socialized to believe that their security lies in marriage and motherhood, surveys of teenage mothers indicate that approximately 90% receive no financial aid from the fathers of their children.

Likewise, a study of homeless youth in Waikiki, about half of whom were girls, revealed that their most urgent needs are housing, jobs, and medical services. Finally, a survey conducted in a very poor community in Hawaii (Waianae) revealed that pregnant and parenting teens saw medical care for their children, financial assistance, and child care as their major needs. Social workers in the same community, by contrast, saw parenting classes as the girls' most important need, followed by child care, educational and vocational training, and family planning. These findings suggest that while youth understand that economic survival is their most critical need, such is not always the case among those working with them.

The Minnesota Women's Fund noted that the most frequent risk factors for girls and boys differ, and that for girls the list includes emotional stress, physical and sexual abuse, negative body image, disordered eating, suicide, and pregnancy. For boys the list included alcohol, polydrug use, accidental injury, and delinquency. While clearly not all girls at risk will end up in the juvenile justice system, this gendered examination of youth problems sets a standard for examination of delinquency prevention and intervention programs.

Providing Economic and Emotional Support

Among other needs that girls' programs should address include dealing with the physical and sexual violence in their lives (from parents, boyfriends, pimps, and others), confronting the risk of AIDS, coping with pregnancy and motherhood, drug and alcohol dependency, facing family problems, vocational and career counseling, managing stress, and developing a sense of efficacy and empowerment. Many of these needs are universal and should be part of programs for all youth. However, most of these are particularly important for young women.

[C.] Alder points out that serving girls effectively will require different and innovative strategies since "young men tend to be more noticeable and noticed than young women." When girls go out, they tend to move in smaller groups, there are greater proscriptions against girls "hanging out," and they may be justly fearful of being on the streets at night. Finally, the domestic expectations (e.g., taking care of children, cooking, cleaning, etc.) for girls far exceed those for boys, and these may keep them confined to their homes. Alder notes that this may be a particular issue for immigrant girls.

There is some encouraging news as organizations serving girls (like the YWCA, Girls Incorporated, etc.) begin to realize their responsibility for girls in the juvenile justice system. Recent reviews of promising programs for girls indicate the emergence of programs which specifically target the housing and employment needs of youth, while also providing them with the specific skills they will need to survive on their own. These programs often include a built-in caseworker/service broker, as well as counseling components. Clearly, many girls will require specialized counseling to recover from the ravages of sexual and physical victimization, but the research cautions that approaches that rely simply on providing counseling services are likely to fail.

Programs must also be scrutinized to assure that they are culturally specific as well as gender specific. As increasing numbers of minority girls are drawn into the juvenile justice system (and bootstrapped into correctional settings), while their white counterparts are deinstitutionalized, there is a need for programs to be rooted in specific cultures. Minority girls have different experiences of their gender, as well as different experiences with the dominant institutions in the society, programs to divert and deinstitutionalize must be sensitive to these issues.

Rewarding Innovative Programs

Innovative programs must receive the same sort of stable funding generally accorded their more traditional/institutional counterparts (which are generally far less innovative and flexible). A careful reading of the descriptions of novel programs reveals that many relied on federal funds or private foundation grants; the same reading reveals how pitifully few survive for any length of time. To survive and thrive, they must be able to count on stable funding. . . .

Finally, though, programs must also be continually scrutinized to guarantee that they serve as genuine alternatives to girls' incarceration, rather than simply functioning to extend the social control of girls. There is a tendency for programs serving girls to become more "security" oriented in response to girls' propensity to run away. Indeed, a component of successful programming for girls must be advocacy and continuous monitoring of the closed institutions. A careful reading of the rocky history of nearly two decades of efforts to decarcerate youth forces us to appreciate how difficult these efforts are and how easily their gains can be eroded. Finally, much more work needs to be done to support the fundamental needs of girls on the margin. We must do a better job of recognizing that they need less "programming" and more support to live on their own, since many cannot or will not be able go back home again.

> *"The juvenile court system of justice has consistently reflected the values held by society, particularly the traditional notions of parental control of children and that children do not enjoy the same status as adults."*

The Juvenile Court System Protects Children's Rights

Raymond E. Chao

Raymond E. Chao is an assistant state's attorney in Cook County, Illinois, where he is assigned to the child protection division. Both in private practice and as a staff attorney with the Children's Rights Project of the Legal Assistance Foundation of Metropolitan Chicago, he represented parents, children, and foster parents. He is also a part-time instructor at the Loyola University Chicago School of Law.

Ex parte Crouse *(1839) established the notion of* parens patriae, *wherein the state acted as parent for neglected and delinquent juveniles. Noting that the court has shifted away from a focus on rehabilitation in delinquency cases, Raymond E. Chao argues that although society's ideas about when to draw the "bright line" between childhood and adulthood and what constitutes appropriate punishment have changed over the last two centuries, the philosophy of* parens patriae *continues to evolve. He suggests that the juvenile court's role should always be to protect children's rights, even as the court itself adapts to reflect changing notions of what constitutes a child.*

Raymond E. Chao, "From Crouse to Roper: Juveniles Continue to Deserve Separate Court," *Children's Legal Rights Journal,* vol. 25, Summer 2005, pp. 33–39. Reproduced by permission.

The notion of a separate judicial system for children has often been criticized by courts and commentators. Yet, the spirit of American juvenile courts remains largely unchanged and surprisingly resilient since the first system was established in Illinois in 1899. The birth of the juvenile court system occurred at the end of the nineteenth century when many American cities, like Chicago, were experiencing tremendous growth as well as facing increased social concerns associated with industrialization, immigration, migration, and an ever-increasing social divide based on wealth. This article will . . . consider the historical context in which the Juvenile Court system was created[,] . . . explain the doctrine of *parens patriae* [the government as parent,] and . . . argue that juvenile courts are not only necessary to protect the best interests of children, but also to maintain society's traditional notion that children are inherently different from adults.

Originally, the Illinois legislature grouped delinquent, neglected, abused, abandoned, and poor children together with no discernable category for children who needed protection from abuse or neglect. Notably, the primary concern was that children be brought before the court, not as adults, but as a distinct, separate class from adults. Significantly, children, unlike adults, had a right not to liberty, but to custody. Consequently, all juvenile court proceedings were characterized as civil rather than criminal. The nation's first juvenile court act established the ages for delinquent children at under seventeen years old for males, and under eighteen years old for females. This marked a departure from existing common criminal law, which generally applied to persons as young as seven years old and treated children no differently from adults. The philosophy of the original juvenile court was that a child who broke the law was to be treated by the state, not as a criminal, but as a child in need of care, education, and protection. Other states quickly adopted similar acts establishing juvenile courts. Notably, from its inception, juveniles charged with seom "confirmed depravity." The court's opinion began, "The ouse of Refuge is not a prison, but a school." Moreover, be-use the goal is reformation, and not punishment, the "right parental control is a natural, but not an unalienable one" d may be "superseded by the *parens patriae*." Remarkably, e *Crouse* case predated the first juvenile court act by sixty ars, but clearly provided the foundation for the creation of a parate judicial system for minors.

Today, the case involving the minor Crouse could not be sily defined within the modern juvenile justice scheme. On e one hand, *Crouse* has been analyzed as a case involving a linquent minor. On the other hand, *Crouse* is an example of ild protection. In many ways, the court did not need to cat-orize Mary Ann's case as either a delinquency case or a de-ndency case since the doctrine of *parens patriae* would pro-de a proper basis for either category. The state was sponsible for protecting children from abuse as well as pro-cting children from a life of crime. Thus, delinquency was e result of the parents' failure to maintain their child's wel-re or provide adequate parental guidance and the child was unwilling victim of influences beyond his control.

he Relationship Between Juvenile Justice d Juvenile Protection

cause juvenile justice and juvenile protection were born om the same womb, changes in one often impact the her. . . .

In 1944, the Court decided *Prince v. Massachusetts*, and cognized three distinct interests: (1) the parent's right to ise a child, including the right to teach the child the tenets d practices of their faith; (2) the child's right to observe ese teachings; and (3) the state's authority to regulate these eedoms. The Court acknowledged the delicate task required hen accommodating the freedoms of parents and their chil-en and the state's authority. Ultimately, the Court held that

rious crimes in Illinois were always subject to both j
and criminal court proceedings. By 1907, however, the
legislature gave the juvenile court discretion to proce
criminal court and dismiss the juvenile court's petitic
mechanism allowing the transfer of a juvenile delin
case to adult criminal court arose as a method througl
the juvenile court could dispose of the most serious
offenders not amenable to treatment. Thus, despite
ation of a separate juvenile court system, some deli
have always been subject to adult criminal cou
punishment. . . .

The Origins of *Parens Patriae*

The state, as *parens patriae*, was obliged to intervene ;
young offenders toward productive and crime-free !
deed, the U.S. Supreme Court consistently upholds t
ciple. Similarly, the emphasis on individualized treatr
rehabilitation for offenders has been recognized histc
the principle canon of the juvenile court. Thus, the
objective was to protect and rehabilitate all children
delinquent children as well as children abused or neg
their parents. Essentially, the original goal of the
court was to ensure that society protected children fr
and society was protected from certain children.

By design, the juvenile courts operated differentl
adversarial legal proceedings that characterized
criminal courts. Juvenile court judges worked with (
fessionals including social workers, probation off
mental health professionals and were given broad dis
making decisions that were in the "best interests" of

The case of Mary Ann Crouse has often been ci
first time a court relied on the concept of *parens*
justify a statutory commitment. In that case, the
Court of Pennsylvania denied her father's request f
after she was committed to an institution in order 1

"The family itself is not beyond regulation" and the rights of parenthood are not beyond limitation and upheld the doctrine of *parens patriae*. . . .

In the end, the court's reliance on *parens patriae* continues to this day. However, in delinquency cases, there has been a noticeable shift away from rehabilitation. Critics of the juvenile court argue that a separate legal system is no longer necessary because the juvenile court, having been formalized by the U.S. Supreme Court, closely parallels the adult criminal system and the abolition of the juvenile courts would save judicial resources and money. Arguably, merging the two systems would also benefit society by ensuring delinquents are adequately punished while affording minors the full gamut of constitutional guarantees provided by the adult criminal system.

This suggestion, however, ignores the basic utility of the juvenile court, a system based on a bright line rule that designates a particular age as the boundary between childhood and adulthood regardless of actual maturity. Prior to the end of the nineteenth century, children were never afforded separate legal status and were simply regarded as miniature adults. Under common law, there were no separate juvenile courts. Minors were subject to the same laws as adults and punished in a similar fashion. Eventually, this view shifted and children were increasingly seen as vulnerable, innocent, passive, and dependent. Moreover, there was a general understanding that children lack the capacity to make sound decisions. . . .

Primary responsibility for the welfare of children is given to their parents. The law presumes that parents possess the maturity, experience, and capacity for judgment required to act in the best interests of their children. As the Supreme Court of Pennsylvania noted in 1905, "the right of parental control is a natural, but not an unalienable one." However, using the theory of *parens patriae*, the court in *Crouse* upheld a state's authority to commit a child to an institution over the objection of a parent. Most courts followed suit. The case of Mary Ann Crouse began when her mother complained that she was "vicious" and uncontrollable. The minor was committed to the House of Refuge to safeguard her well-being and future welfare. Subsequently, courts followed the *Crouse* case and held that procedural safeguards were not necessary when the state was acting as *parens patriae*. . . .

Natural Law and the Bright Line Between Childhood and Adulthood

More recently, in March 2005, the U.S. Supreme Court held in *Roper v. Simmons* that the execution of minors for crimes committed when the offender was less than eighteen years of age is unconstitutional. The Court identified three general differences between juveniles and adults: (1) a lack of maturity and an underdeveloped sense of responsibility, which often results in impetuous and ill-considered actions; (2) vulnerability or susceptibility to negative influences; and (3) a lack of fixed personality traits. Thus, "from a moral standpoint it would be misguided to equate the failings of a minor with those of an adult." The Court found these broad differences to be significant and well understood. In a dissenting opinion, Justice [Sandra Day] O'Connor conceded "it is beyond cavil [objection] that juveniles as a class are generally less mature, less responsible, and less fully formed than adults, and that these differences bear on juveniles' comparative moral culpability." Clearly, the qualities that distinguish juveniles from adults do not disappear when the individual turns eighteen. But, the Court noted, a line must be drawn somewhere. Without this bright line, under common law, there would be no impediment to the execution of a seven-year-old child today.

These two cases, *Crouse* and *Roper*, suggest a tradition and acceptance by the courts and society that children are not the same as adults. Thus, there is a continuing need for a separate court system. Since at least 1839 when *Crouse* was decided, courts have been given a strong social mandate with respect to children: "save kids." All judges possess their own respective definitions of justice. No judge is free from personal and philosophical views on society expressed through its values, mores, and culture. Ultimately, the various laws and court opinions are merely a reflection of the values that society holds at any given time. Thus, there is no "universal" natural law; only law that is specific to time and culture. The juvenile court system of justice has consistently reflected the values held by society, particularly the traditional notions of parental control of children and that children do not enjoy the same status as adults. As noted by the Supreme Court of Illinois in 1870, "the parent has the right to the care, custody and assistance of his child. The duty to maintain and protect it is a principle of natural law." Moreover, as noted in *Crouse*, there is "no natural right to exemption from restraints which conduce to an infant's welfare."

The most important element of natural law is its capacity to evolve with time as the morals of a culture change. . . . The U.S. Supreme Court demonstrated in *Roper* that the treatment of juveniles in court continues to evolve with societal views; and the Court must view juveniles as a distinct category within society with specific needs and concerns. Moreover, the traditional notions that children are different from adults continue to justify a separate juvenile court system. The juvenile court system was established with the philosophy that children brought before the court, for whatever reason, are in need of care, education, and protection. Thus, the goodwill of the juvenile court is consistent with natural law that emphasizes human good and morality. Under natural law, moral truths are to be derived from truths about human nature. The juvenile court system recognizes the inherent differences between children and adults: differences that have been, and continue to be, recognized and honored by society.

CHAPTER 2

Establishing the Right to Due Process for Juveniles

Case Overview

In re Gault (1967)

From the beginning of the twentieth century, the juvenile justice system had operated under the principle of *parens patriae*, the paternalistic attitude that the state has the right to decide what is in the "best interests" of youthful offenders. The philosophy of *parens patriae*, along with the flexibility and informality of the juvenile justice system, often resulted in a failure of due process for young defendants subjected to overly harsh and seemingly arbitrary sentences. At the height of the Civil Rights Movement, in *In re Gault* (1967) the Supreme Court determined that children were entitled to the same due process rights given to adults.

On June 8, 1964, fifteen-year-old Gerald Gault was taken into custody in his hometown of Gila County, Arizona, for allegedly making obscene phone calls. Gault's parents, who were at work, were not notified that he was being held in detention, nor were they served the petition for a preliminary hearing in juvenile court. Gerald Gault was not provided with an attorney or with the opportunity to confront or cross-examine his accuser. Gault was convicted almost entirely on the basis of his admission that he had taken part in the phone call and the fact that he was already on probation for his involvement in a petty theft. The court declared Gault a juvenile delinquent and committed him to the State Industrial School for a period of up to six years. Had Gault been an adult, he would have received a maximum punishment of a $50 fine or up to two months in jail. Arizona did not permit appeals for juvenile cases.

Gault's parents filed a petition for *habeas corpus* in the Arizona Supreme Court, requesting that their son be released on grounds that he had been illegally detained. When their petition was denied, they then appealed to the U.S. Supreme Court to determine whether the procedures used to commit Gerald Gault were constitutionally legitimate under the due process clause of the Fourteenth Amendment.

The Supreme Court found that the Arizona Juvenile Court failed to comply with the Constitution and also declared that the proceedings for juveniles must comply with the requirements of the Fourteenth Amendment. These requirements included adequate notice of charges, notification of both the parents and the child of the juvenile's right to counsel, opportunity for confrontation and cross-examination at the hearings, and adequate safeguards against self-incrimination. The Court found that the procedures used in Gault's case met none of these requirements.

In the majority Court opinion, Justice Abe Fortas attacked the whole notion of *parens patriae* as paternalistic:

> The right of the state, as *parens patriae,* to deny to the child procedural rights available to his elders was elaborated by the assertion that a child, unlike an adult, had a right "not to liberty but to custody." . . . On this basis, proceedings involving juveniles were described as "civil" not "criminal" and therefore not subject to the requirements which restrict the state when it seeks to deprive a person of his liberty. . . . The constitutional and theoretical basis for this peculiar system is—to say the least—debatable. . . . Juvenile Court history has again demonstrated that unbridled discretion, however benevolently motivated, is frequently a poor substitute for principle and procedure.

The sole dissenter, Justice Potter Stewart, expressed concern that the rules governing juvenile and adult criminal courts would be indistinguishable, so that the youth and immaturity of an offender was no longer considered and that juveniles might be given the same penalties as adult offenders.

> "It would indeed be surprising if the privilege against self-incrimination were available to hardened criminals but not to children."

The Court's Decision: The Due Process Clause Applies to Minors Tried in Juvenile Court

Abe Fortas

Abe Fortas (1910–1982) was a Supreme Court Justice from 1965 to 1969. A graduate of Yale Law School, Fortas defended victims of McCarthyism and litigated cases such as Gideon v. Wainwright, *which established the right of indigent defendants to counsel in state criminal cases. He was a close friend and advisor to President Lyndon B. Johnson, who appointed him to the Supreme Court. There, he continued to support the expansion of civil rights and joined with other liberal justices in most civil liberties cases including* In re Gault *(1967). In 1969, Fortas resigned his Supreme Court position after* Life *magazine disclosed that he had accepted—and then returned—a fee of $20,000 from a charitable foundation controlled by the family of an indicted stock manipulator.*

In his majority opinion in In re Gault, *Fortas argues that the juvenile court in Arizona failed to comply with the Constitution. He contends that although juvenile proceedings are civil rather than criminal in nature, the court still had to comply with the requirements of the Fourteenth Amendment—namely, adequate*

Abe Fortas, majority opinion, *In re Gault*, U.S. Supreme Court, 1967.

notice of charges, notification of both the parents and the child of said child's right to counsel, opportunity for confrontation and cross-examination at the hearings, and adequate safeguards against self-incrimination. Fortas found that the procedures used in the case against Gerald Gault met none of these requirements. In re Gault involved the question of whether juveniles, though charged in a separate, less formal justice system, were explicitly entitled to the same constitutional rights afforded adults in criminal court. A landmark case, In re Gault made explicit procedural constitutional protections for youthful offenders.

Appellants allege that the Arizona Juvenile Code is unconstitutional or alternatively that the proceedings before the Juvenile Court were constitutionally defective because of failure to provide adequate notice of the hearings. No notice was given to Gerald's parents when he was taken into custody on Monday, June 8, 1964. On that night, when Mrs. Gault went to the Detention Home, she was orally informed that there would be a hearing the next afternoon and was told the reason why Gerald was in custody. The only written notice Gerald's parents received at any time was a note on plain paper from Officer Flagg delivered on Thursday or Friday, June 11 or 12, to the effect that the judge had set Monday, June 15, "for further Hearings on Gerald's delinquency. . . ."

Adequate Notice Was Not Provided

The Supreme Court of Arizona rejected appellants' claim that due process was denied because of inadequate notice. It stated that "Mrs. Gault knew the exact nature of the charge against Gerald from the day he was taken to the detention home." The court also pointed out that the Gaults appeared at the two hearings "without objection." The court held that because "the policy of the juvenile law is to hide youthful errors from the full gaze of the public and bury them in the graveyard of the forgotten past," advance notice of the specific charges or basis for taking the juvenile into custody and for the hearing is not necessary. It held that the appropriate rule is that "the infant and his parent or guardian will receive a petition only reciting a conclusion of delinquency. But no later than the initial hearing by the judge, they must be advised of the facts involved in the case. If the charges are denied, they must be given a reasonable period of time to prepare."

We cannot agree with the court's conclusion that adequate notice was given in this case. Notice, to comply with due process requirements, must be given sufficiently in advance of scheduled court proceedings so that reasonable opportunity to prepare will be afforded, and it must "set forth the alleged misconduct with particularity." It is obvious, as we have discussed above, that no purpose of shielding the child from the public stigma of knowledge of his having been taken into custody and scheduled for hearing is served by the procedure approved by the court below. The "initial hearing" in the present case was a hearing on the merits. Notice at that time is not timely, and even if there were a conceivable purpose served by the deferral proposed by the court below, it would have to yield to the requirements that the child and his parents or guardian be notified, in writing, of the specific charge or factual allegations to be considered at the hearing, and that such written notice be given at the earliest practicable time, and in any event sufficiently in advance of the hearing to permit preparation. Due process of law requires notice of the sort we have described—that is, notice which would be deemed constitutionally adequate in a civil or criminal proceeding. It does not allow a hearing to be held in which a youth's freedom and his parents' right to his custody are at stake without giving them timely notice, in advance of the hearing, of the specific issues that they must meet. Nor, in the circumstances of this case, can it reasonably be said that the requirement of notice was waived.

Juveniles Must Be Given Right to Counsel

Appellants charge that the Juvenile Court proceedings were fatally defective because the court did not advise Gerald or his parents of their right to counsel, and proceeded with the hearing, the adjudication of delinquency and the order of commitment in the absence of counsel for the child and his parents or an express waiver of the right thereto. The Supreme Court of Arizona pointed out that "[t]here is disagreement [among the various jurisdictions] as to whether the court must advise the infant that he has a right to counsel." It noted its own decision in *Arizona State Dept. of Public Welfare v. Barlow* (1956), to the effect "that the parents of an infant in a juvenile proceeding cannot be denied representation by counsel of their choosing." It referred to a provision of the Juvenile Code which it characterized as requiring "that the probation officer shall look after the interests of neglected, delinquent and dependent children, including representing their interests in court." The court argued that "The parent and the probation officer may be relied upon to protect the infant's interests." Accordingly it rejected the proposition that "due process requires that an infant have a right to counsel." It said that juvenile courts have the discretion, but not the duty, to allow such representation; it referred specifically to the situation in which the Juvenile Court discerns conflict between the child and his parents as an instance in which this discretion might be exercised. We do not agree. Probation officers, in the Arizona scheme, are also arresting officers. They initiate proceedings and file petitions which they verify, as here, alleging the delinquency of the child; and they testify, as here, against the child. And here the probation officer was also superintendent of the Detention Home. The probation officer cannot act as counsel for the child. His role in the adjudicatory hearing, by statute and in fact, is as arresting officer and witness against the child. Nor can the judge represent the child. There is no material difference in this respect between adult and juvenile proceedings of the sort here involved. In adult proceedings, this contention has been foreclosed by decisions of this Court. A proceeding where the issue is whether the child will be found to be "delinquent" and subjected to the loss of his liberty for years is comparable in seriousness to a felony prosecution. The juvenile needs the assistance of counsel to cope with problems of law, to make skilled inquiry into the facts, to insist upon regularity of the proceedings, and to ascertain whether he has a defense and to prepare and submit it. The child "requires the guiding hand of counsel at every step in the proceedings against him." Just as in *Kent v. United States* (1966), we indicated our agreement with the United States Court of Appeals for the District of Columbia Circuit that the assistance of counsel is essential for purposes of waiver proceedings, so we hold now that it is equally essential for the determination of delinquency, carrying with it the awesome prospect of incarceration in a state institution until the juvenile reaches the age of 21. . . .

We conclude that the Due Process Clause of the Fourteenth Amendment requires that in respect of proceedings to determine delinquency which may result in commitment to an institution in which the juvenile's freedom is curtailed, the child and his parents must be notified of the child's right to be represented by counsel retained by them, or if they are unable to afford counsel, that counsel will be appointed to represent the child.

At the *habeas corpus* proceeding, Mrs. Gault testified that she knew that she could have appeared with counsel at the juvenile hearing. This knowledge is not a waiver of the right to counsel which she and her juvenile son had, as we have defined it. They had a right expressly to be advised that they might retain counsel and to be confronted with the need for specific consideration of whether they did or did not choose to waive the right. If they were unable to afford to employ counsel, they were entitled in view of the seriousness of the charge and the potential commitment, to appointed counsel, unless they chose waiver. Mrs. Gault's knowledge that she could employ counsel was not an "intentional relinquishment or abandonment" of a fully known right.

Rights to Confrontation and Cross–Examination

Appellants urge that the writ of *habeas corpus* should have been granted because of the denial of the rights of confrontation and cross-examination in the Juvenile Court hearings, and because the privilege against self-incrimination was not observed. The Juvenile Court Judge testified at the *habeas corpus* hearing that he had proceeded on the basis of Gerald's admissions at the two hearings. Appellants attack this on the ground that the admissions were obtained in disregard of the privilege against self-incrimination. If the confession is disregarded, appellants argue that the delinquency conclusion, since it was fundamentally based on a finding that Gerald had made lewd remarks during the phone call to Mrs. Cook, is fatally defective for failure to accord the rights of confrontation and cross-examination which the Due Process Clause of the Fourteenth Amendment of the Federal Constitution guarantees in state proceedings generally.

Our first question, then, is whether Gerald's admission was improperly obtained and relied on as the basis of decision, in conflict with the Federal Constitution. For this purpose, it is necessary briefly to recall the relevant facts.

Mrs. Cook, the complainant, and the recipient of the alleged telephone call, was not called as a witness. Gerald's mother asked the Juvenile Court Judge why Mrs. Cook was not present and the judge replied that "she didn't have to be present." So far as appears, Mrs. Cook was spoken to only once, by Officer Flagg, and this was by telephone. The judge did not speak with her on any occasion. Gerald had been questioned by the probation officer after having been taken into custody. The exact circumstances of this questioning do not appear but any admissions Gerald may have made at this time do not appear in the record. Gerald was also questioned by the Juvenile Court Judge at each of the two hearings. The judge testified in the *habeas corpus* proceeding that Gerald admitted making "some of the lewd statements . . . [but not] any of the more serious lewd statements." There was conflict and uncertainty among the witnesses at the *habeas corpus* proceeding—the Juvenile Court Judge, Mr. and Mrs. Gault, and the probation officer—as to what Gerald did or did not admit.

We shall assume that Gerald made admissions of the sort described by the Juvenile Court Judge, as quoted above. Neither Gerald nor his parents were advised that he did not have to testify or make a statement, or that an incriminating statement might result in his commitment as a "delinquent."

Protection Against Self-Incrimination

The Arizona Supreme Court rejected appellants' contention that Gerald had a right to be advised that he need not incriminate himself. It said: "We think the necessary flexibility for individualized treatment will be enhanced by a rule which does not require the judge to advise the infant of a privilege against self-incrimination."

In reviewing this conclusion of Arizona's Supreme Court, we emphasize again that we are here concerned only with a proceeding to determine whether a minor is a "delinquent" and which may result in commitment to a state institution. Specifically, the question is whether, in such a proceeding, an admission by the juvenile may be used against him in the absence of clear and unequivocal evidence that the admission was made with knowledge that he was not obliged to speak and would not be penalized for remaining silent. In light of *Miranda v. Arizona* (1966), we must also consider whether, if the privilege against self-incrimination is available, it can effectively be waived unless counsel is present or the right to counsel has been waived. . . .

This Court has emphasized that admissions and confessions of juveniles require special caution. . . .

The privilege against self-incrimination is, of course, related to the question of the safeguards necessary to assure that admissions or confessions are reasonably trustworthy, that they are not the mere fruits of fear or coercion, but are reliable expressions of the truth. The roots of the privilege are, however, far deeper. They tap the basic stream of religious and political principle because the privilege reflects the limits of the individual's attornment to the state and—in a philosophical sense—insists upon the equality of the individual and the state. In other words, the privilege has a broader and deeper thrust than the rule which prevents the use of confessions which are the product of coercion because coercion is thought to carry with it the danger of unreliability. One of its purposes is to prevent the state, whether by force or by psychological domination, from overcoming the mind and will of the person under investigation and depriving him of the freedom to decide whether to assist the state in securing his conviction.

It would indeed be surprising if the privilege against self-incrimination were available to hardened criminals but not to children. The language of the Fifth Amendment, applicable to the States by operation of the Fourteenth Amendment, is unequivocal and without exception. And the scope of the privilege is comprehensive. . . .

With respect to juveniles, both common observation and expert opinion emphasize that the "distrust of confessions made in certain situations" to which [legal scholar John Henry] Wigmore [Dean of Northwestern University Law School from 1901–1929] referred is imperative in the case of children from an early age through adolescence. In New York, for example, the recently enacted Family Court Act provides that the juvenile and his parents must be advised at the start of the hearing of his right to remain silent. The New York statute also provides that the police must attempt to communicate with the juvenile's parents before questioning him, and that absent "special circumstances" a confession may not be obtained from a child prior to notifying his parents or relatives and releasing the child either to them or to the Family Court. . . .

Juveniles and Parents Must Be Informed of Rights

The authoritative "Standards for Juvenile and Family Courts" concludes that, "Whether or not transfer to the criminal court is a possibility, certain procedures should always be followed. Before being interviewed [by the police], the child and his parents should be informed of his right to have legal counsel present and to refuse to answer questions or be fingerprinted if he should so decide."

Against the application to juveniles of the right to silence, it is argued that juvenile proceedings are "civil" and not "criminal," and therefore the privilege should not apply. It is true that the statement of the privilege in the Fifth Amendment, which is applicable to the States by reason of the Fourteenth Amendment, is that no person "shall be compelled in any criminal case to be a witness against himself." However, it is also clear that the availability of the privilege does not turn upon the type of proceeding in which its protection is invoked, but upon the nature of the statement or admission and the exposure which it invites. The privilege may, for example, be claimed in a civil or administrative proceeding, if the statement is or may be inculpatory.

It would be entirely unrealistic to carve out of the Fifth Amendment all statements by juveniles on the ground that these cannot lead to "criminal" involvement. In the first place, juvenile proceedings to determine "delinquency," which may lead to commitment to a state institution, must be regarded as "criminal" for purposes of the privilege against self-incrimination. To hold otherwise would be to disregard substance because of the feeble enticement of the "civil" label-of-convenience which has been attached to juvenile proceedings. Indeed, in over half of the States, there is not even assurance that the juvenile will be kept in separate institutions, apart from adult "criminals." In those States juveniles may be placed in or transferred to adult penal institutions after having been found "delinquent" by a juvenile court. For this purpose, at least, commitment is a deprivation of liberty. It is incarceration against one's will, whether it is called "criminal" or "civil." And our Constitution guarantees that no person shall be "compelled" to be a witness against himself when he is threatened with deprivation of his liberty—a command which this Court has broadly applied and generously implemented in accordance with the teaching of the history of the privilege and its great office in mankind's battle for freedom.

Youthful Offenders Must Be Granted the Same Rights as Adults

In addition, apart from the equivalence for this purpose of exposure to commitment as a juvenile delinquent and exposure to imprisonment as an adult offender, the fact of the matter is that there is little or no assurance in Arizona, as in most if not all of the States, that a juvenile apprehended and interrogated by the police or even by the Juvenile Court itself will remain outside of the reach of adult courts as a consequence of the offense for which he has been taken into custody. In Arizona, as in other States, provision is made for Juvenile Courts to relinquish or waive jurisdiction to the ordinary criminal courts. In the present case, when Gerald Gault was interrogated concerning violation of a section of the Arizona Criminal Code, it could not be certain that the Juvenile Court Judge would decide to "suspend" criminal prosecution in court for adults by proceeding to an adjudication in Juvenile Court.

It is also urged, as the Supreme Court of Arizona here asserted, that the juvenile and presumably his parents should not be advised of the juvenile's right to silence because confession is good for the child as the commencement of the assumed therapy of the juvenile court process, and he should be encouraged to assume an attitude of trust and confidence toward the officials of the juvenile process. This proposition has been subjected to widespread challenge on the basis of current reappraisals of the rhetoric and realities of the handling of juvenile offenders.

In fact, evidence is accumulating that confessions by juveniles do not aid in "individualized treatment," as the court below put it, and that compelling the child to answer questions, without warning or advice as to his right to remain silent, does not serve this or any other good purpose.... It seems probable that where children are induced to confess by "paternal" urgings on the part of officials and the confession is then followed by disciplinary action, the child's reaction is likely to be hostile and adverse—the child may well feel that he has been led or tricked into confession and that despite his confession, he is being punished.

Further, authoritative opinion has cast formidable doubt upon the reliability and trustworthiness of "confessions" by children....

The Privilege Against Self-Incrimination Must Be Protected

We conclude that the constitutional privilege against self-incrimination is applicable in the case of juveniles as it is with respect to adults. We appreciate that special problems may arise with respect to waiver of the privilege by or on behalf of children, and that there may well be some differences in technique—but not in principle—depending upon the age of the child and the presence and competence of parents. The participation of counsel will, of course, assist the police, Juvenile Courts and appellate tribunals in administering the privilege. If counsel was not present for some permissible reason when an admission was obtained, the greatest care must be taken to assure that the admission was voluntary, in the sense not only that it was not coerced or suggested, but also that it was not the product of ignorance of rights or of adolescent fantasy, fright or despair.

The "confession" of Gerald Gault was first obtained by Officer Flagg, out of the presence of Gerald's parents, without counsel and without advising him of his right to silence, as far as appears. The judgment of the Juvenile Court was stated by the judge to be based on Gerald's admissions in court. Neither "admission" was reduced to writing and, to say the least, the process by which the "admissions" were obtained and received must be characterized as lacking the certainty and order which are required of proceedings of such formidable consequences. Apart from the "admissions," there was nothing upon which a judgment or finding might be based. There was no sworn testimony. Mrs. Cook, the complainant, was not present. The Arizona Supreme Court held that "sworn testimony must be required of all witnesses including police officers, probation officers and others who are part of or officially related to the juvenile court structure." We hold that this is not enough. No reason is suggested or appears for a different rule in respect of sworn testimony in juvenile courts than in adult tribunals. Absent a valid confession adequate to support the determination of the Juvenile Court, confrontation and sworn testimony by witnesses available for cross-examination were essential for a finding of "delinquency" and an order committing Gerald to a state institution for a maximum of six years.

The recommendations in the Children's Bureau's "Standards for Juvenile and Family Courts" are in general accord with our conclusions. They state that testimony should be under oath and that only competent, material and relevant evidence under rules applicable to civil cases should be admitted in evidence. The New York Family Court Act contains a similar provision.

As we said in *Kent v. United States*, with respect to waiver proceedings, "there is no place in our system of law for reaching a result of such tremendous consequences without ceremony. . . ." We now hold that, absent a valid confession, a determination of delinquency and an order of commitment to a state institution cannot be sustained in the absence of sworn testimony subjected to the opportunity for cross-examination in accordance with our law and constitutional requirements.

Due Process Must Be Maintained

Appellants urge that the Arizona statute is unconstitutional under the Due Process Clause because, as construed by its Supreme Court, "there is no right of appeal from a juvenile court order. . . ." The court held that there is no right to a transcript because there is no right to appeal and because the proceedings are confidential and any record must be destroyed after a prescribed period of time. Whether a transcript or other recording is made, it held, is a matter for the discretion of the juvenile court.

This Court has not held that a State is required by the Federal Constitution "to provide appellate courts or a right to appellate review at all." In view of the fact that we must reverse the Supreme Court of Arizona's affirmance of the dismissal of the writ of *habeas corpus* for other reasons, we need not rule on this question in the present case or upon the failure to provide a transcript or recording of the hearings—or, indeed, the failure of the Juvenile Judge to state the grounds for his conclusion. [See] *Kent v. United States*, supra, at 561, where we said, in the context of a decision of the juvenile court waiving jurisdiction to the adult court, which by local law, was permissible: ". . . it is incumbent upon the Juvenile Court to accompany its waiver order with a statement of the reasons or considerations therefor." As the present case illustrates, the consequences of failure to provide an appeal, to record the proceedings, or to make findings or state the grounds for the juvenile court's conclusion may be to throw a burden upon the machinery for *habeas corpus*, to saddle the reviewing process with the burden of attempting to reconstruct a record, and to impose upon the Juvenile Judge the unseemly duty of testifying under cross-examination as to the events that transpired in the hearings before him.

For the reasons stated, the judgment of the Supreme Court of Arizona is reversed and the cause remanded for further proceedings not inconsistent with this opinion.

It is so ordered.

> "Whether treating with a delinquent
> child, a neglected child, defective child,
> or a dependent child, a juvenile
> proceeding's whole purpose and mis-
> sion is the very opposite of the mission
> and purpose of a prosecution in a
> criminal court. The object of the one is
> correction of a condition. The object of
> the other is conviction and punishment
> for a criminal act."

Dissenting Opinion: Juvenile Proceedings Are Not Criminal Trials and Should Not Impose the Same Restrictions

Potter Stewart

Potter Stewart (1915–1985) was appointed to the Supreme Court by President Dwight Eisenhower in 1958, and he served as a Supreme Court justice until 1981. Although Stewart's background was ideologically conservative, he often played the role of centrist on the Supreme Court, voting with liberal justices on First Amendment issues and with conservative justices on matters of equal protection, as in In re Gault. *Although Stewart cast opinions in many important court cases, including* Roe v. Wade *(1973), he is best remembered for his statement in the obscenity case* Jacobellis v. Ohio *(1964) in which he attested that although he could not articulate a precise definition of pornography, "I know it when I see it."*

Potter Stewart, dissenting opinion, *In re Gault*, U.S. Supreme Court, 1967.

Potter Stewart argues that the Court's majority opinion in In re Gault *is unsound as a matter of constitutional law because juvenile and family courts have different judicial purposes than criminal courts. He also argues that it is unwise as a matter of judicial policy, citing fears that an unintended consequence will be courts trying and punishing children as adults.* In re Gault *established that the constitutional protections of the due process clause apply to youthful offenders.*

The Court today uses an obscure Arizona case as a vehicle to impose upon thousands of juvenile courts throughout the Nation restrictions that the Constitution made applicable to adversary criminal trials. I believe the Court's decision is wholly unsound as a matter of constitutional law, and sadly unwise as a matter of judicial policy.

Juvenile proceedings are not criminal trials. They are not civil trials. They are simply not adversary proceedings. Whether treating with a delinquent child, a neglected child, a defective child, or a dependent child, a juvenile proceeding's whole purpose and mission is the very opposite of the mission and purpose of a prosecution in a criminal court. The object of the one is correction of a condition. The object of the other is conviction and punishment for a criminal act.

In the last 70 years many dedicated men and women have devoted their professional lives to the enlightened task of bringing us out of the dark world of Charles Dickens in meeting our responsibilities to the child in our society. The result has been the creation in this century of a system of juvenile and family courts in each of the 50 States. There can be no denying that in many areas the performance of these agencies has fallen disappointingly short of the hopes and dreams of the courageous pioneers who first conceived them. For a variety of reasons, the reality has sometimes not even approached the ideal, and much remains to be accomplished in the administration of public juvenile and family agencies—in personnel, in planning, in financing, perhaps in the formulation of wholly new approaches.

Juvenile Proceedings Are Not Criminal Proceedings

I possess neither the specialized experience nor the expert knowledge to predict with any certainty where may lie the brightest hope for progress in dealing with the serious problems of juvenile delinquency. But I am certain that the answer does not lie in the Court's opinion in this case, which serves to convert a juvenile proceeding into a criminal prosecution.

The inflexible restrictions that the Constitution so wisely made applicable to adversary criminal trials have no inevitable place in the proceedings of those public social agencies known as juvenile or family courts. And to impose the Court's long catalog of requirements upon juvenile proceedings in every area of the country is to invite a long step backwards into the nineteenth century. In that era there were no juvenile proceedings, and a child was tried in a conventional criminal court with all the trappings of a conventional criminal trial. So it was that a 12-year-old boy named James Guild was tried in New Jersey for killing Catharine Beakes. A jury found him guilty of murder, and he was sentenced to death by hanging. The sentence was executed. It was all very constitutional.

A State in all its dealings must, of course, accord every person due process of law. And due process may require that some of the same restrictions which the Constitution has placed upon criminal trials must be imposed upon juvenile proceedings. For example, I suppose that all would agree that a brutally coerced confession could not constitutionally be considered in a juvenile court hearing. But it surely does not follow that the testimonial privilege against self-incrimination is applicable in all juvenile proceedings. Similarly, due process clearly requires timely notice of the purpose and scope of any proceedings affecting the relationship of parent and child. But it certainly does not follow that notice of a juvenile hearing must be framed with all the technical niceties of a criminal indictment.

In any event, there is no reason to deal with issues such as these in the present case. The Supreme Court of Arizona found that the parents of Gerald Gault "knew of their right to counsel, to subpoena and cross-examine witnesses, of the right to confront the witnesses against Gerald and the possible consequences of a finding of delinquency." It further found that "Mrs. Gault knew the exact nature of the charge against Gerald from the day he was taken to the detention home." And, as MR. JUSTICE WHITE correctly points out, no issue of compulsory self-incrimination is presented by this case.

I would dismiss the appeal.

"Studies show that transfer [to adult court] fails to deter violent juvenile offenders. In fact, various studies have indicated that transfer actually increases recidivism among those offenders."

In re Gault Led to Transferring of Juveniles to Adult Criminal Courts

Enrico Pagnanelli

A 2007 graduate of Georgetown University Law Center, Enrico Pagnanelli was articles and notes editor for the American Criminal Law Review. *He is currently an associate at Duane Morris LLP in Philadelphia, where he specializes in corporate and intellectual property law.*

Enrico Pagnanelli discusses how increasing public fears about youth violence and youth crime has contributed to juveniles being tried as adults in the adult criminal court system. Pagnanelli contends that transferring juveniles to adult courts does not protect the public; instead, it increases recidivism and socializes troubled youngsters to the community of hardened criminals. The juvenile court system, with its emphasis on rehabilitation, he argues, is much more effective at reintegrating offenders into society.

Enrico Pagnanelli, "Children as Adults: The Transfer of Juveniles to Adult Courts and the Potential Impact of *Roper v. Simmons*," *The American Criminal Law Review*, Winter 2007. Reproduced by permission.

[According to Kareem L. Jordan, in *Violent Youth in Adult Court* (2006),] during the 1950s, legislators began to question "whether the juvenile court could successfully rehabilitate youth." Namely, many believed that the institutionalization of juveniles was ineffective and that juveniles lacked procedural safeguards in the adjudication process. Several Supreme Court cases originating in the 1960s addressed these concerns, expanding due process rights for juveniles, but not without substantially impacting the increasing mechanisms and volume of transfer [to adult courts]. These cases integrated procedural due process rights from the criminal court system into juvenile proceedings, guaranteeing the growing trend of transfer, and even leading to a reaction by many states to create laws circumventing these new procedural rights to expedite the transfer process.

"From its inception . . . the juvenile court could relinquish its jurisdiction and subject some young offenders to prosecution in adult criminal courts[," write Mary R. Podkopacz and Barry C. Feld in *Judicial Waiver Policy and Practice* (1995).] But in *Kent v. United States* (1966) the Supreme Court held that where juvenile court jurisdiction is waived as a result of judicial waiver, a hearing with the essentials of due process must be provided. The case involved a sixteen-year old boy convicted as an adult in criminal court of burglary, robbery, and rape. In deciding whether or not the boy had been properly denied exclusive jurisdiction by the juvenile court of the District of Columbia, the Supreme Court created a due process-like framework for courts to consider when waiving a juvenile's jurisdiction and allowing transfer.

While many states reexamined their waiver statutes to abide by the criteria laid out in *Kent*, a large number of states took steps to overcome this procedural boundary and created "automatic transfer" or "legislative waiver" statutes. In fact, in some jurisdictions, district attorneys were given the power to make transfer decisions without providing juveniles any of the procedural safeguards specified in *Kent*. Others wrote statutes that defined 'juvenile' in such a way as to "exclude persons of a certain age when they were charged with certain crimes."

The Expansion of Due Process Rights for Juveniles

In *In re Gault*, on an appeal from the Supreme Court of Arizona, the United States Supreme Court further extended constitutional due process rights to accused juvenile offenders. *Gault* and its progeny provided minors with the following constitutional due process safeguards: "representation by counsel; notice of charges; confrontation and cross-examination of witnesses; protection against self-incrimination; protection from double jeopardy; proof of delinquency charges 'beyond a reasonable doubt'; and protection from judicial transfer to criminal court without hearing, effective counsel, or a statement of reasons." Other decisions also expanded the convergence of procedural due process into juvenile delinquency proceedings.

The intention in *Kent* and *Gault* was clear: to provide juveniles the same procedural rights afforded to adults. The effect—presumably unintended—was the erosion of the rehabilitative ideal of juvenile justice. The judicial and legislative bent became not how to treat children *differently* from adults, but how to treat them the *same*. *Gault* undermined the ideological assumptions of the juvenile system and "engrafted some formal procedures at trial onto the [juvenile court's] individualized treatment schema[, and thereby] . . . fostered a procedural and substantive convergence with criminal courts[," according to Barry C. Feld in *Will the Juvenile Court Survive?*]. A new retributive stance on juvenile delinquency translated into various responses: "purpose clauses" in some states were modified to focus on punishment as a goal; some juvenile proceedings became public; and in some jurisdictions, the age for delinquency adjudication was lowered and "determinate and/or mandatory minimum sentences" were mandated for some offenses.

Consequently, *Kent, Gault,* and their progeny merged the juvenile court system with the criminal court system. The once rehabilitative ideal of the juvenile justice system gave way to aggressive implementation of transfer policies and procedures representing a new retributive focus. For example, in *United States v. Bland* [(1992)], the D.C. Circuit upheld a District of Columbia statute (notably, created a few years after *Kent*) that excluded people aged 16 and up who committed a murder, rape, or other serious offenses from the definition of "juvenile." [As Feld explains,] the D.C. Circuit acknowledged in upholding the statute against due process and equal protection claims that the laws were a response to "substantial difficulties in transferring juvenile offenders charged with serious felonies to the jurisdiction of the adult court under present law. . . ." This judicial endorsement of transfer policy and the concomitant loss of faith in the rehabilitative capabilities of the juvenile system, combined with the influx of procedural safeguards, all reinforced the new retributive focus.

Fears of Violent Crime Drove Policy

There is a clear consensus among scholars that public concern, particularly for violent crime, was a major factor contributing to the growing trend of transferring juveniles to the adult court system during the 1990s. Research has shown that the perception by adults of juvenile crime during this period was highly and systematically distorted in favor of over-construing the degree of serious juvenile offenses. [In *American Youth Violence* (1998),] Franklin Zimring, a leading scholar in juvenile crime, detects that there is a general sentiment that the youth population has an unusually high share of violent offenders, and consequently there has been a focus on preventing the potential violent crimes of this grown up demographic.

While there was an increase in violent juvenile crime during the period from 1985–1994, recent trends show that the "rate of juvenile violent crime arrests has consistently decreased since 1994, falling to a level not seen since at least the 1970s." Despite the decrease and plateau of violent crime, the hysteria from the 1985–1994 increase in juvenile crime created the perception of a crime wave. Violent crime among juveniles was one of the most hotly discussed topics in the 1990s. The majority who pushed for harsher policies believed the rehabilitative efforts of the juvenile system had failed. Media coverage of high-profile crimes, as well as an overall distortion of seriousness of violent juvenile crimes, only contributed to this negative stigma towards the effectiveness of the juvenile justice system. Consequently, most Americans believed that juveniles should be treated with the same severity as adults, and this in turn led to pressure on legislatures to create laws that provide for transfer to the criminal court system, as well as other procedural mechanisms that treated violent juvenile offenders as adults.

Such pressure resulted in the passing of the Juvenile Justice and Delinquency Prevention Act of 2002 (hereinafter, Juvenile Act). The Juvenile Act sought to increase the accountability of violent juvenile offenders and even mentioned that penalties imposed by the juvenile system were unsuccessful. The clear purpose of the law was to address violent juvenile offenders in a more punitive manner resembling the adult court system. [According to Kareem Jordan,] many state legislatures had already responded "punitively to the youth violence epidemic of the mid-1980s to mid-1990s, and all but six states either expanded or implemented laws that sought to increase the number of juvenile offenders waived to adult criminal court." The Juvenile Act merely represents the federal codification of this trend, enshrining a national shift from a rehabilitative focus on juvenile crime to a new retributive focus on the treatment of violent juvenile offenders in American courts and legislatures.

The Transfer of Juvenile Offenders to Adult Court

There are various methods of transferring a juvenile to criminal court, including: (1) judicial waiver; (2) prosecutorial waiver; (3) legislative waiver; and (4) once-an-adult-always-an-adult statutes. What follows is a review of the various forms of waiver, a statistical review of state transfer statutes, and a discussion of the policy shortcomings of transfer.

Judicial waiver involves a case-by-case analysis of each juvenile by a judge. There are three types of judicial waiver: discretionary, presumptive, and mandatory. With discretionary waiver, the juvenile judge considers the factors laid out in *Kent* (age, prior record, previous offenses, etc.) and makes a decision accordingly. [Jordan explains that] with presumptive waiver, the juvenile and defense counsel must show that the case belongs in juvenile court and if they fail to meet this burden of proof then "the judge is directed to transfer the case to the adult system." Mandatory waiver specifies that juvenile offenders who meet certain criteria, including age and current offense, must automatically be transferred to adult court.

Prosecutorial waiver, often called concurrent jurisdiction because both the juvenile and criminal justice system initially have jurisdiction, involves the district attorney individually deciding whether or not to prosecute the case in criminal court. [According to Jordan,] "This method is the least used . . . but nevertheless the most controversial." Kareem Jordan believes that prosecutors are unsuited to make this decision, having the wrong incentives and being much less attuned to the rehabilitative goals of juvenile justice. The use of prosecutorial discretion further exemplars the growing shift towards a retributive focus on juvenile crime. The prosecutor is not necessarily required to weigh the *Kent* factors, and his or her decisions are not subject to appellate review. One source of a prosecutor's unfettered discretion is evident where even if the legislature mandates a prosecutor file charges against a child in criminal court, a prosecutor can ultimately decide whether to bring adult or juvenile charges.

Excluding Youth from Juvenile Court

Legislative waiver, also known as statutory exclusion, excludes from the juvenile court system children of a certain age who are charged with specific offenses.

Once-an-adult-always-an-adult statutes hold that where a juvenile has been previously transferred and convicted in adult criminal court, he or she is transferred for all subsequent offenses, usually irrespective of severity. This method of transfer is particularly alarming because a juvenile who has been previously transferred under a once-an-adult-always-an-adult jurisdiction is permanently stripped of juvenile status in the judicial system.

The crackdown on violent juvenile crimes and the invasion of retributive ideals into the juvenile justice system has created a multitude of judicial processes that have exponentially increased the transfer of juveniles to the criminal court system. What follows is a review of some compelling statistics on the breadth of juvenile transfer. Through the 2004 legislative session, forty-six states have judicial waiver provisions under which juvenile court judges may waive jurisdiction over individual juveniles, allowing criminal court prosecutions to take place. In forty-five states the waiver decision is left entirely to the judge's discretion, in fifteen states there is a rebuttable presumption in favor of waiver, and in fifteen states a mandatory waiver is provided under certain circumstances. Fifteen states authorize the prosecutor to decide whether to file certain kinds of cases in juvenile or criminal court [according to Patrick Griffith of the National Center for Juvenile Justice]. Twenty-nine states have "laws that exclude certain kinds of cases from the jurisdiction of the juvenile court and required they be tried in criminal court." In addition, [Griffith writes,] thirty-four states have some variation of a once-an-adult-always-an-adult statute, twenty states either "authorize or mandate criminal prosecution of juveniles accused of drug offenses," and twenty-two states even "require or allow criminal prosecution of juveniles accused of certain property offenses."

Transfer, Recidivism, and Failure to Protect the Public

Studies show that transfer fails to deter violent juvenile offenders. In fact, various studies have indicated that transfer actually increases recidivism among these offenders. This increased recidivism manifests a failure to deter, a failure to rehabilitate, and most significantly, a failure to protect society.

In his study, Jeffrey Fagan examined the recidivism rates of fifteen- and sixteen-year-olds charged with robbery. He compared the recidivism rate of such youths charged in criminal court under New York's automatic transfer statute to those charged in New Jersey's juvenile court and found a significant increase in the recidivism of juveniles who had been transferred to the adult system. Another study analyzing recidivism rates among 2,738 juvenile offenders in Florida, found that recidivism was more likely and more severe for juveniles transferred to criminal courts. Similarly, a study in Minnesota found higher recidivism over a two-year period among juveniles who had been waived to adult court when compared to those who had stayed within the juvenile system. Arguably, the transfer of violent juvenile offenders only increases their likelihood of re-offending and has thus failed the inherent objective of transfer: protecting the public.

Why Transfer Increases Recidivism

Transfer has a significant negative effect on a juvenile's development and may, therefore, be a direct cause of increased recidivism among transferred violent juvenile offenders relative to their counterparts in the juvenile system. Instead of rehabilitating, the criminal system may encourage recidivism. [In an article in *The Changing Borders of Juvenile Justice*, edited by Jeffrey Fagan and Franklin E. Zimring (2000), Donna Bishop and Charles Frazier note that] juveniles who are incarcerated are more likely to "learn social rules and norms that legitimate domination, exploitation, and retaliation" from the surrounding adult criminals. The criminal system also may cause juveniles to feel exploited and humiliated by the judicial process, and stigmatized by society. A criminal conviction may also encourage recidivism by severely obstructing the convicted juvenile's future educational, employment, and social opportunities.

A juvenile who has been tried in a criminal court often feels unjustly treated, and juveniles with this negative perception of the adjudication process are more likely to adopt a delinquent self-concept which also causes them to re-offend. Extensive interviews with juvenile offenders in the adult criminal system reveal that they view the system as "duplicious and manipulative, malevolent in intent, and indifferent to their needs[," write Bishop and Frazier. Furthermore,] these reactions are wholly "inconsistent with compliance to legal norms," and highlight a very potent negative effect on incarcerated juveniles which logically contributes to increased rates of recidivism post-transfer.

Transfer may have a very minimal deterrent effect on juveniles because their premature psychological development may prevent them from feeling culpability. Most juveniles do not perceive risks or appreciate the consequences of their actions the way adults do. While research is mixed on whether juveniles contain the necessary level of blameworthiness for culpability, the idea that juveniles may lack culpability because of psychological development is helpful in assessing whether transfer is appropriate. This evidence argues against any mandatory sentencing policy that fails at least to consider mitigating factors such as age, crime, and the capacity of blameworthiness for a juvenile offender.

The juvenile court system has many positive characteristics that help rehabilitate young offenders and reduce recidivism. Many young offenders who engage in chronic delinquency often fail to develop the relationships and attachments crucial to the process of socialization. Juveniles in the juvenile system are able to develop positive relationships with individuals involved in their care, such as judges, practitioners, and caseworkers. These relationships, in conjunction with the nurturing of the juvenile system's rehabilitation process stimulate the development of trust, core values, and character in juveniles and aid their effective reintegration into society.

One could argue that because a child has the legal right to many "adult decisions," treating juveniles as adults makes sense. However, this argument is a fatal misconstruction. That juveniles now enjoy some of the legal rights enjoyed by adults has no bearing on a juvenile's capacity to stand trial. The utilitarian goals of our justice system should not be ignored. The experience of childhood is necessary to socialize juveniles. It is essential that a justice system recognize this and cater to the many social and psychological deficits in the lives of juvenile offenders. Because of the negative effects of transfer, including increased post-transfer recidivism, and the juvenile system's focus on nurturing and resocialization, the juvenile court system is the most appropriate forum for juvenile offenders—even violent offenders—and, ultimately, the most effective means of protecting the public.

"In failing to consider what procedural adaptations were demanded by the special context of juvenile court, Gault reduced the analysis of children's due process rights to the simple-minded question of adult rights or no rights."

Although *In re Gault* Protects Due Process, It Does Not Protect the Interests of Children

Emily Buss

Emily Buss is the Mark and Barbara Fried Professor of Law at the University of Chicago Law School. Her research interests include children's and parents' rights and the legal system's allocation of authority and responsibility between parent, child, and state. As Kanter Director of Policy Initiatives at the University of Chicago Law School, she heads a project aimed at improving the legal system's treatment of children who age out of foster care.

Professor Emily Buss argues that juveniles have different due process needs than adults and that not modifying due process procedures to meet the needs of children—as established by In re Gault—*is little better than providing no due process at all. The core values behind due process procedures, she suggests, are accuracy, fairness, and participation. If adolescents do not know or trust their attorneys, she notes, they may not disclose all the in-*

Emily Buss, "The Missed Opportunity in Gault," *The University of Chicago Law Review,* Winter 2003. Republished with permission of The University of Chicago Law Review, conveyed through Copyright Clearance Center, Inc.

formation they need to ensure the most accurate representation of their situation. Most young people are not able to follow the legal process—or even understand the charges of which they are accused—and therefore are not able to participate meaningfully in their own hearing. She argues that due process proceedings must be modified to ensure accuracy, fairness, and the full participation of the minor.

A century ago, states established a separate system of juvenile courts with a radical new mission. The aim of these courts was to help juvenile offenders rather than punish them, in a context stripped of the formalities of adult criminal court. By the middle of the century, however, these courts were widely perceived as failures that offered neither substantive nor procedural benefits to children. In 1967, the Supreme Court declared the procedural failings unconstitutional in the landmark case of *In re Gault.*

While *Gault* should be celebrated for its recognition that children, too, have constitutional rights, it should be mourned for its limited vision of those rights. In assuming that children's due process rights would, at best, match those of adults, the Court foreclosed any thoughtful consideration of the changes required to make the juvenile justice system fair to children . . . [and] helped establish a pattern of analysis which has stunted the development of children's constitutional rights overall.

The Vision and Reality of Juvenile Court

In 1899, Illinois enacted the first Juvenile Court Act, and other states quickly followed suit. These new juvenile courts had interrelated substantive and procedural aims: The substantive aim was to respond to juvenile offending with rehabilitative treatment rather than retributive punishment. The procedural aim was to replace the formalities of criminal court with "care and solicitude," intended to facilitate achievement of the juvenile courts' rehabilitative goals. . . .

Both substantive and procedural aims, however, proved elusive. Recidivism data collected mid-century suggested that the courts were failing to rehabilitate offenders, and the harshness of many dispositions made clear that the courts continued to pursue a punitive approach. Moreover, the formal procedures of adult court were replaced, not with caring solicitude, but with administrative neglect. Judges were left free to adopt whatever approach and impose whatever disposition they pleased, but the crush of their dockets and the lack of legal and social service support translated that freedom into inattention. The end result was a system the Court aptly described [in *Kent v. United States* (1966)] as "the worst of both worlds," a system in which children received "neither the protections accorded to adults nor the solicitous care and regenerative treatment postulated for children." The overall unfairness of this system set the stage for the Supreme Court's intervention on constitutional grounds.

The Court's Mistake in *In re Gault*

The case of Gerald Gault well illustrates both of these procedural and substantive shortcomings. For making a single obscene phone call of an "irritatingly offensive, adolescent, sex variety," fifteen-year-old Gerald was removed from home without notice to his parents, brought before a Juvenile Court without notice of the charges against him, and convicted and sentenced without any professional assistance and without any real hearing on the relevant facts. Based on the thin representations of a complaining witness who didn't even come to court, and without even identifying which law Gerald had broken, the judge ordered Gerald confined to a prison-like state industrial school for up to six years.

In the face of these facts, the Supreme Court concluded that Gerald's treatment in Juvenile Court violated his due process rights. A proceeding that produced such a substantial deprivation of liberty with such scant procedural protections failed, in the Court's estimation, to meet the due process standard of fundamental fairness. The Court went on, more affirmatively, to list a number of procedural protections to which children were entitled. Drawing on the adult list of criminal procedural protections, the Court declared that children in juvenile court were entitled to written notice, counsel, adult-style protection against self-incrimination, and the opportunity to confront and cross-examine sworn witnesses.

That the state's treatment of Gerald Gault was fundamentally unfair was clearly right. Less clear, however, were the changes required to make the juvenile justice system fair for children. By simply limiting its consideration to those procedural protections afforded adults, the Court avoided giving this second question any serious attention. Focused exclusively on adult-derived rights, the Court produced a juvenile justice system whose procedures are poorly designed to meet its goals and out of step with childhood.

In finding Gerald Gault's treatment unconstitutional, the Court neither challenged the substantive goals of the juvenile justice system nor argued for its abolition. To the contrary, the Court acknowledged the system's value and its distinct "substantive benefits." But it dismissed concerns that importing adult procedural protections into the system would undermine these goals. This was, the Court explained, both because these criminal procedural rights, "intelligently and not ruthlessly administered," were compatible with the goals of the juvenile justice system and because these goals were not being achieved without these rights. It is this second argument that seems to have had more force for the Court: Because a world with no procedural rights had failed to produce a fair system for children, affording children adult rights would surely be an improvement.

What the Court failed to consider was whether children's due process rights could be tailored actually to advance, rather than simply not undermine, the laudable substantive and procedural goals of the juvenile justice system. The procedural vision for the juvenile court contemplated a meaningful engagement between decision maker and child, an engagement that the child would experience as a conversation rather than as litigation, and that would communicate the concern and interest the state took in the child. Through this process, it was envisioned that decision maker and child could develop a plan that would assist the child in whatever ways were required to help him avoid repeating his criminal conduct. There is no reason to think that such a process, if actually achieved, would be unfair. Moreover, it seems likely that such a process, if actually achieved, would enhance the court's chances of affording children real assistance with their lives. . . .

Children Have Different Due Process Needs than Adults

In failing to consider what procedural adaptations were demanded by the special context of juvenile court, *Gault* reduced the analysis of children's due process rights to the simple-minded question of adult rights or no rights. And in the many cases considering accused juveniles' due process rights since *Gault*, the Court has adhered to this narrow and nonsensical framing. Because neither adult rights nor no rights are well designed to secure fairness for children, the Court has waffled between the two creating a patchwork better understood as an attempt to split the difference than to develop a coherent set of due process rights for children.

In *Gault*, impressed by the alarming carelessness with which the juvenile court had consigned Gerald to a potentially lengthy period of confinement, the Court awarded children a long list of adult rights including the right to notice and to counsel, the right of confrontation, and the right against self-incrimination. Close on *Gault*'s heels came *In re Winship* [(1970)], in which the Court added the "beyond a reasonable doubt" standard to the adult rights side of the balance without taking serious account of how the distinct aims of the juvenile justice system might affect the appropriateness of that standard. Then came *McKeiver v. Pennsylvania* [(1971)], in which the Court denied juveniles the right to jury trials on the ground that affording them this right would be too destructive to the achievement of the juvenile justice system's goals.

While *McKeiver* was the Court's first "no rights" decision since *Gault* was decided, the Court made no attempt to explain how its grants and denials of adult rights fit together into a coherent account of fairness to children. Instead, it offered a catalog of the rights-granting cases as an apparent counterweight to its no rights approach to juries. There was enough, the Court seemed to suggest, on the adult rights side of the balance to call for a rebalancing toward no rights which could be well accomplished by denying children juries....

The Court Must Accommodate the Needs of Children

[*In Fare v. Michael C.* (1979),] the Court showed itself incapable of accommodating its analysis to the special circumstances of childhood.

In *Fare*, the police took sixteen-year-old Michael C. into custody for interrogation about his suspected involvement in a murder. The officers who questioned him informed him of his *Miranda* rights, including his right to remain silent and to consult with an attorney. In response to direct questions about whether he was willing to talk, the minor asked for his probation officer. The police officer responded that he couldn't reach the probation officer and reminded Michael C. of his right to an attorney. Michael C. declined the attorney and went on to make incriminating statements that he later sought to suppress. Michael C. clearly asked for his probation officer in an attempt to secure the advice and support of a knowledgeable adult in deciding whether it was in his interest to talk to the police. In contrast, he declined a lawyer, whom he did not know and therefore did not trust ("How I know you guys won't pull no police officer in and tell me he's an attorney?"). Michael C. was, in all innocence, seeking to adapt an adult right to make it work for a child.

The Court, however, refused to make the adaptation. Insisting upon fidelity to the adult-framed right against self-incrimination and the central role the attorney plays in protecting that right, the Court concluded that interpreting the child's right against self-incrimination to extend to his request for the assistance of his probation officer "would impose the burdens associated with the rule of *Miranda* on the juvenile justice system and the police without serving the interests that [the adult] rule was designed simultaneously to protect." Again, the Court refused to see that a modified right might serve a child's interest better than the adult rule, or that this modified right might actually enhance, rather than impair, the workings of the juvenile justice system. . . .

The Court should rework its due process analysis to address what is required to make a separate juvenile justice system fundamentally fair for children.

Providing Due Process for Children

The proper due process inquiry for children, then, should focus not on the list of particulars developed for the adult criminal justice system, but rather on the fairness norms said to be embodied in the list. We should ask, as we do for adults, what process must we afford minors in order to remain faithful to these norms? . . .

While procedural due process is the subject of endlessly varied analysis, most of this analysis reflects three interrelated values—accuracy, dignity, and participation—that are broadly viewed as essential to the fairness of procedures. Fair procedures are those designed to produce accurate results and to treat the individuals whose interests are at stake with respect.

These two values are, in turn, well served by securing the meaningful participation of those interested individuals in the decision-making process. . . .

For children, full adult procedures are likely to thwart meaningful participation, at a cost to children's dignity and the accuracy of the results obtained. . . .

Procedures in juvenile court must take account of children's special developmental status and the unique goals of the juvenile justice system. After considering the significance of these two factors to our due process analysis, I will suggest how we might alter procedures in juvenile court to bring them in line with due process principles.

For children, every aspect of the formalized procedure designed to serve adults' due process interests threatens to undermine children's parallel interests. Children are much less prepared to understand, let alone participate in, such proceeding. Rather than demonstrating respect and neutrality, the formality of the process and the professional distance of the judge are likely to alienate children from the decision-making process. Moreover, the substance of the dispute in question is also likely to elude minors. Studies suggest that children, even teenagers, have considerable difficulty understanding rights as abstractions. That is, they perceive their rights as privileges afforded by adults, commonly the very adults whose authority is, in fact, qualified by those rights. Because of children's lesser ability to sustain thoughts over time, the delays inevitably imposed by affording them formal procedures will reduce their ability to track the proceeding, let alone appreciate its purpose. Affording minors lawyers to speak on their behalf may only make things worse. As already noted, minors are likely to misperceive the lawyer-client relationship in a manner that only increases the distance between child and decision maker.

It is saying nothing new to conclude that children have trouble following and participating in criminal trials. . . . A commitment to the due process principles of accuracy, dignity, and participation suggests that the Constitution requires some modification of the adult procedures to make due process rights meaningful for children.

Allowing Minors to Participate in Proceedings

The different substantive goals of the juvenile system must also be taken into account in assessing what process is due. What it means to be "accurate" and what it will take to make participation meaningful change when we shift from a guilt-and-punishment-focused system to one focused on rehabilitation and caring.

The fact that the aims of the juvenile justice system have shifted over time does not undermine this point, even if it changes the particulars. While states have modified the express aims of their juvenile courts to give more emphasis to community safety and offender accountability, assisting the offender remains a prominent goal. The very continued existence of separate juvenile courts makes clear that states have maintained their commitment to affording at least some children special opportunities and protection not afforded to their adult counterparts. All of these modern goals—providing assistance to offenders, holding them accountable for their wrongs, and securing community safety—call for modifications in the procedures afforded minors, if minors' meaningful participation and the consequent benefits to the accuracy and dignity of the proceedings are to be achieved. . . .

The assignment of criminal responsibility also takes on a different meaning in the juvenile justice system, a meaning that, again, depends on the juvenile's engagement for its success. For adults, the value of assigning criminal responsibility is perceived in largely external terms: In holding a wrongdoer accountable, we aim to achieve retribution and deter repetition of the offense. But in the juvenile justice system, the focus is also on internal development: Holding a child accountable is intended to help teach the child the connection between their prior acts, the present response, and their obligations in the future. While the external aims can be achieved without regard to the offender's subjective experience of the proceeding, the system cannot hope to accomplish its teaching function absent the child's comprehending participation in the process.

Ensuring Children's Meaningful Participation

The achievement of the special aims of the juvenile justice system all depends on a juvenile's effective participation. The special developmental status of children suggests that effective participation requires a set of procedures very different from those afforded adults. But just as with adults, these procedures will need to be protected as rights to withstand the compromising pressures of resource limitations and power disparities.

To secure children's meaningful participation, their proceedings must be comfortable, comprehensible, and swift. Children should be allowed to speak directly with witnesses rather than left to watch their lawyer's formal, and likely inscrutable, examinations. Lawyers might still serve an important role as legal advisors, while relinquishing the role of spokesperson to their child clients. Because judges have no special expertise in communicating with children or assessing their needs, they might be replaced by other more qualified decision makers. Social service professionals would have the benefit of subject matter expertise, whereas nonprofessional adults known to the child might be in the best position to secure the comfortable participation of that child. Whoever the decision maker, the child should be afforded a meaningful opportunity to speak with her directly at considerable length on more than one occasion. To ensure that the accused appreciates the connection between self and offense, and offense and response, proceedings should last no longer than a few weeks from the time of the accusation to the time of final disposition.

This alternative set of procedures resembles, in many respects, the "restorative justice" approaches that have become increasingly popular throughout the world. Dissatisfaction with traditional juvenile court proceedings have led many countries, including the United States, to experiment with a form of restorative justice known as "family group conferencing," which brings together victim, offender, their two communities of support, and law enforcement to discuss the offense and its consequences, and to develop a plan for restitution. These proceedings, stripped of conventional due process protections, have proven highly successful in achieving the due process aims of meaningful participation, and, relatedly, respectful treatment. Offenders who play an active role in the decision-making process report a high degree of satisfaction with the process and demonstrate their commitment to the process by fulfilling their conference-imposed obligations in a large percentage of cases. . . .

To secure children's meaningful participation, the juvenile justice system must offer children a process very different from the formal adversarial process afforded adults charged with crimes. While intentionally less sentimental, the procedural vision set out here bears a strong resemblance to the vision of the juvenile court's founders a century ago. The difference here is to suggest that, for children, some version of these procedures is not only preferable to the adult set but similarly constitutionally required. Just as children's due process rights have protected them from the process failures illuminated in *Gault*, so should they protect them from the process failures *Gault* mistakenly produced.

"In the years that followed In re Gault, *studies revealed that a child's right to counsel, as well as the right to effective representation in juvenile court, was, at best, implemented unevenly across the country."*

After *In re Gault*, Juveniles Are Still Underrepresented by Attorneys in Proceedings

N. Lee Cooper, Patricia Puritz, and Wendy Shang

N. Lee Cooper is a former president of the American Bar Association. He is a partner at Maynard, Cooper & Gale. Patricia Puritz is the director of the American Bar Association Juvenile Justice Center, and Wendy Shang is the staff attorney of the American Bar Association Juvenile Justice Center. The American Bar Association is a national organization of legal professionals and a major component of its mission is to advocate for excellence in the legal profession.

The authors discuss the trend of trying juveniles as adults and note that although Gault *provides a child's right to counsel, more often than not, the counsel that a minor receives is woefully inadequate due to the attorneys' large caseloads, lack of support staff, lack of training, and lack of compensation. They argue that attorneys must be more creative and proactive in representing their child clients in the best light.*

N. Lee Cooper, Patricia Puritz, and Wendy Shang, "Fulfilling the Promise of *In re Gault*: Advancing the Role of Lawyers for Children," *Wake Forest Law Review*, Fall 1998. Reproduced by permission.

In the last decade, juvenile justice professionals have wit-nessed a slow erosion in the foundation of the juvenile court. The furor over juvenile crime has incited all levels of government—federal, state, and local—to re-examine and, in some cases, drastically revise their juvenile codes and policies. For example, many states and cities have begun to institute parental responsibility laws that hold parents accountable for their children's actions. Since 1992, almost all states have en-acted laws that make possible, if not encourage, trying more juveniles as adults. These laws typically lower the age at which juveniles may be tried as adults and/or expand the list of crimes which make juveniles eligible for trial in adult court. Many states have also begun to make juvenile records available to a broader audience, while twenty-two states allow some form of public juvenile hearings. Some states have gone so far as to re-draft or amend their juvenile codes to emphasize pu-nitive rather than rehabilitative ideals. As a result of these changes, the juvenile court has begun to lose many of its unique characteristics that were designed to protect and reha-bilitate children.

The desire to "get tough" on children who commit crimes is fueled by the belief that children are becoming more vio-lent. The media's coverage of juvenile crime has helped in-flame this belief. . . .

Furthermore, the desire to "get tough" on children who commit crimes has rarely been accompanied by recognition of the fact that once children become embroiled in the juvenile court, many often face systemic barriers that impede access to the assistance of competent counsel—a Constitutional right that is often limited or denied completely. The critical role that defense counsel must fulfill in delinquency proceedings cannot be overstated: he or she is the buffer against unfair-ness, and helps to articulate the voice and spirit of the child. Even though it has been more than thirty years since the Su-preme Court guaranteed a child's right to counsel in *In re*

Gault [(1967)], studies show that its promise has not been fully realized for all children. With the continuing threat of punitive sanctions and systemic hostility toward children, the need for competent defense counsel could not be more urgent. . . .

The Supreme Court's decision in *In re Gault* represented a turning point in the concept of the juvenile court. Whereas the early days of the juvenile court prized informality and paternalism to the point of being "antilegal," the result in *In re Gault* led Justice Fortas to write, "Juvenile Court history has once again demonstrated that unbridled discretion, however benevolently motivated, is frequently a poor substitute for principle and procedure." While lawyers had appeared to have little purpose in the *parens patriae* juvenile court, *In re Gault* demonstrated that children required the representation of an attorney to protect their interests and advocate on their behalf. . . .

Right to Counsel Unevenly Implemented for Juveniles

In establishing a constitutional right to counsel for children in the case of *In re Gault*, the Supreme Court rejected arguments that the probation officer or the juvenile court itself could adequately represent a child. Given the "awesome prospect" of incarceration up to the age of majority, the Court found that an accused delinquent is entitled to an attorney "to make skilled inquiry into the facts, to insist upon regularity of the proceedings, and to ascertain whether he has a defense and to prepare and submit it. . . ."

In the years that followed *In re Gault*, studies revealed that a child's right to counsel, as well as the right to effective representation in juvenile court, was, at best, implemented unevenly across the country. Some of the most extensive work on access to counsel has been conducted by Professor Barry Feld at the University of Minnesota. Professor Feld estimates that prior to *In re Gault*, attorneys appeared on behalf of children in 5% of juvenile delinquency cases. Through an analysis of data from six states, gathered from the National Juvenile Court Data Archive, Professor Feld found that many jurisdictions still failed to appoint counsel in a majority of juvenile court cases. . . .

In addition to the basic issue of whether children have *access* to legal representation, researchers have also questioned the quality of representation provided to juveniles. Richard A. Lawrence found that of the attorneys surveyed, 16.7% spent less than one hour, 44.4% spent one to two hours, 27.7% spent three to four hours, and 11.1% spent five or more hours preparing for a juvenile court case. . . .

Spurred by such findings and rising concerns over fundamental fairness in the juvenile courts, Congress re-emphasized the importance of lawyers in juvenile delinquency proceedings when it reauthorized the Juvenile Justice and Delinquency Prevention Act in 1992. The section on Congressional Findings and Declaration of Purpose specifically noted the inadequacies of prosecutorial and public defender offices "to provide individualized justice or effective help," and further added that a purpose of the Act was "to assist State and local governments in improving the administration of justice and services for juveniles who enter the system." Toward that end, Congress instructed the administrator of the Office of Juvenile Justice and Delinquency Prevention to make grants to establish or support the improvement of due process available to children in the juvenile justice system, as well as to improve the quality of legal representation available to children. . . .

The Need to Improve Representation for Children

Together, the American Bar Association Juvenile Justice Center and the Youth Law Center and Juvenile Law Center conducted a national assessment to examine the problems and issues relating to access to counsel and quality of representation for juveniles. The results were published in *A Call for Justice: An Assessment of Access to Counsel and Quality of Representation in Delinquency Proceedings* [(1993)]. *A Call for Justice* determined that while some attorneys were able to vigorously and enthusiastically represent their clients, many dedicated attorneys continued to labor under tremendous systemic burdens. Those burdens, in many cases, severely compromised the attorneys' abilities to provide effective legal services. . . .

High caseloads were identified by defense attorneys as the single most important barrier to effective representation. The average caseload carried by a public defender often exceeded 500 cases per year, more than 300 of which were juvenile cases. . . .

Attorneys representing children were also hampered by a lack of available training and resources which might be considered standard in other settings. Of the public defender offices surveyed, 78% did not have a budget for lawyers to attend training programs, 50% did not have a training program for new attorneys, 48% did not have an ongoing training program, 46% did not have a section in the office training manual for juvenile court lawyers, 35% did not include juvenile delinquency work in the general training program, 32% did not have any training manual, and 32% did not have a training unit. . . .

In some areas, the needs were even more basic, such as the absence of desks, telephones, files, or offices for juvenile defenders. . . .

While substantial deficiencies in access to counsel and the quality of representation exist in juvenile courts across the country, it would be incorrect to conclude that effective representation of young people does not exist. There are excellent defender programs that deliver first-rate legal services to juveniles. In general, such programs have the following characteristics in common:

- the ability to limit/control caseloads;

- support for entering the case early, and the flexibility to represent—or refer—the client in related collateral matters (such as special education);

- comprehensive initial and ongoing training and available resource materials;

- adequate non-lawyer support and resources;

- hands-on supervision of attorneys; and

- a work environment that values and nurtures juvenile court practice. . . .

Entering the case as early as possible, and having adequate time to meet with the client, his or her family, and others, enables counsel to provide much more effective representation at the station-house, detention hearing, and throughout the case. . . .

Defenders have also managed to obtain access to non-lawyer support and resources through the mobilization of volunteer or low-cost labor such as college students and law students. . . . With appropriate training and supervision, students can effectively work in a variety of capacities. College students can serve as mentors, investigators, or tutors, and assist with case preparation and management. Social work students can conduct assessments and social histories. Law students can provide a whole range of assistance, from preparing and researching briefs to assisting with post-dispositional problems.

Law school clinical programs and nonprofit children's law centers play a critical role in building the capacity of the legal system to provide high quality representation and in establishing a future corps of excellence. . . .

Challenges for Children's Attorneys

Beyond the immediate need to provide effective representation to their clients, juvenile defense attorneys face other important challenges in the future. A revamping of the juvenile court and its laws calls for more than a reactive approach. . . .

The combination of increasingly open juvenile courts and heightened public concern over juvenile crime places new demands on juvenile defense attorneys. In terms of public access to the courts, juvenile defense attorneys have traditionally focused on curtailing the public's access to the proceedings. As more states open the doors to the juvenile courts, however, defense attorneys should consider a media strategy to rebut any negative publicity and present the client in the best light, while still maintaining client confidences. . . .

Juvenile defense attorneys must also be more aggressive about participating in public and legislative discussions regarding juvenile crime and improving the media's reporting on juvenile crime. These two interrelated goals are essential to creating a more rational debate on juvenile justice policy. . . .

Defense attorneys can achieve a greater balance in media coverage by reaching out to local print, television and radio reporters, and letting them know that they are willing to comment on general juvenile justice news stories. Journalists often have source lists for different topics and return to those sources which can provide them with diverse points of view. Defense attorneys can also express their views through writing editorials and seeking out participation on juvenile justice task forces or commissions. Helping reporters ask better questions will also improve reporting on juvenile crime. For example, is it more important for a reporter (and his audience) to learn whether a child is the youngest child in the state to be tried as an adult, or is it more important to learn where a child, tried and convicted as an adult, will be held and what rehabilitative services are available? The answer to the first question provides a better lead-in, but the answer to the second question deepens the public's knowledge of juvenile and criminal justice policies.

Likewise, juvenile defense attorneys can also become more involved in the legislative process. Taking the time to write letters or visit legislators in person heightens the presence of juvenile defense attorneys and their concerns. . . .

Attorneys Must Be Proactive Rather than Reactive

In an era where juvenile policy is more often driven by what *sounds* tough rather than what is proven to be effective, juvenile defense attorneys must also begin to marshal some of their resources into research and data collection to challenge programs and policies which are ineffective, unfair, or dangerous for children. Additionally, juvenile defense attorneys must also garner support for defender programs which benefit children and public safety. . . .

Between 1985 and 1994, the number of children judicially waived to adult court increased 71%. . . . The rush to waive children to adult courts has required defense attorneys across the country to become familiar with complex new laws and regulations, to develop new strategies to oppose the waiver of children to adult courts, and to protect their clients once they have been waived. Stemming the tide of children waived into adult courts is one of the greatest challenges facing juvenile defense attorneys today.

To the extent that judges still decide whether certain juveniles will remain in juvenile court or be waived to adult court, juvenile defense attorneys have been, and will continue to be, tested to think not only in terms of *reacting* to the statute and the prosecution, but developing "out of the box" strategies of their own. Some attorneys have ways to convey their client's individuality and strengths through various mediums, including letters written by the child and videotapes documenting various periods of the child's life. Other attorneys have sought to improve their representation of juvenile defendants through the use of expert witnesses on child development and mental health. Some public defender offices have dealt with the issue by changing the organization of attorneys so that a specialized unit can deal with waiver cases exclusively.

In instances where children are transferred to adult court without a hearing and are represented by criminal defense attorneys, juvenile defense attorneys should reach out to these attorneys. Criminal defense attorneys who are accustomed to working with adults may need assistance identifying expert witnesses who specialize in evaluations for adolescents on various issues such as a defendant's mental health needs, medical needs, educational needs, or psychological development, as well as locating programs which meet the specific needs of adolescent offenders. Criminal defense attorneys must also be prepared for the particular challenges of working with a very young client, such as understanding any aspects of the case which may involve juvenile court, social services, or other issues, and identifying issues relating to adolescent development that should be brought before the court.

Competency, for example, is one idea that needs to be further explored by defense attorneys working on waiver hearings or cases where children will he tried in adult court. Dr. Thomas Griaso, professor of psychiatry at the University of Massachusetts, has conducted some of the most extensive research to date on this issue, and suggests that there are serious questions as to whether most children meet the general legal standard of competency, which includes: (1) the ability to understand the nature and possible consequences of charges, the trial process, the participants' roles, and their own rights; (2) the ability to participate with and meaningfully assist counsel in developing and presenting a defense; (3) and the ability to make decisions to exercise or waive important rights. For example, in contrast to adults who view rights as absolute entitlements, many adolescents view rights as "conditional," something that can he bestowed and taken away by authorities. Children also make decisions differently than adults—adolescents are more likely to underestimate risks and are less able to focus on the long-range consequences of their decisions. To the extent that these deficiencies hamper children's ability to participate meaningfully in their own defense, attorneys must be prepared to raise issues of competence to stand trial, and seek out experts who can recognize incompetence to stand trial as a result of developmental immaturity, mental illness, or retardation. . . .

Children Cannot Wait for Effective Representation

The challenges facing juvenile defense attorneys are daunting but not insurmountable. Juvenile defenders must take time to look beyond *In re Gault*, beyond the day-to-day labors in the courtroom, and develop long-term strategies that will elevate the practice of juvenile defense work and more effectively protect the interests of their clients. It is not work that can be undertaken in a vacuum; juvenile defense attorneys must continue to find new allies and colleagues across the country and in their own states.

Defenders also need to look at practices within their own offices which can be revised to improve defense practices. This may include improving access to expert witnesses, creating mentoring programs, or sharing briefs. In some states, the stakes for children have risen so high that juvenile defenders will need to reorganize their offices in order to provide more initial and ongoing training for attorneys, as well as to provide greater incentives for more effective and more experienced attorneys to work in juvenile court and mentor other attorneys.

Juvenile defense attorneys may also need to seek a range of supportive resources to help reshape the delivery of defense services to juveniles. Following the example of how some death penalty clients are represented, law firms may be persuaded to take on routine waiver cases, employing resources and tactics that might not otherwise be available. Bar associations can be persuaded to examine the needs of juvenile defenders more closely, and help organize educational programs. Law schools and children's law centers can also provide various forms of assistance and support.

In the context of juvenile defense, strength in numbers cannot be underestimated. An important organizational tool is the strength derived from the voice of an organization whose numbers and expertise demand that the views of attorneys representing children are heard in the legislatures, the media, and the courtroom. A focus in the evolution of juvenile defense work should be the formation of a national body to develop, represent, and advocate for the concerns of the attorneys who work on behalf of children in trouble.

Thirty years after the landmark *In re Gault* decision, children in the United States cannot afford to wait any longer for the promises of *In re Gault* to be fulfilled. The consequences of having no lawyer, or one that lacks the necessary training and support, have become too great. Juvenile defense attorneys must insist upon receiving the respect and backing that they and their clients deserve.

CHAPTER 3

Balancing Juveniles' Rights to Individual Privacy with School Safety

Case Overview

New Jersey v. T.L.O. (1985)

In 1984, a teacher caught T.L.O. and her friend, high school freshmen at Piscataway High School in Piscataway, New Jersey, smoking cigarettes in the bathroom and brought the girls to the principal's office, where they met with the vice principal. Although the friend admitted she had been smoking in the bathroom, T.L.O. denied that she had been smoking and stated that she had never smoked in her life.

The vice principal demanded that T.L.O. hand over her purse. He searched the purse and found a pack of cigarettes, rolling papers, a bag of marijuana, a pipe, empty plastic bags, a large quantity of money in small bills, what appeared to be a list of students who owed T.L.O. money, and two letters from students that implied T.L.O. was a drug dealer. The vice principal informed T.L.O.'s mother and the police. At the police station, T.L.O. confessed to selling marijuana in the high school.

The State of New Jersey brought delinquency charges against T.L.O. T.L.O. countered with a motion to suppress evidence found in her purse as a violation of her Fourth Amendment constitutional rights against unreasonable and unwarranted searches and seizures. Upon appeal, the New Jersey Supreme Court found that T.L.O.'s constitutional rights against unreasonable searches had been violated.

In *New Jersey v. T.L.O.* (1985), the Supreme Court overturned the New Jersey Supreme Court's decision and held that the search was reasonable under the Fourth Amendment. *New Jersey v. T.L.O.* is a significant case because the Supreme Court's decision indicated that students in a public school do not have equivalent rights to those of adults. Although police need to demonstrate "probable cause" that citizens whom they search have violated or are violating a law, school officials need to have only "reasonable suspicion" of a violation to justify a search of students in school.

In a 6–3 decision, the Supreme Court held that search and seizure by school officials without a warrant was constitutional as long as school authorities deemed the search reasonable. The Court reaffirmed that a balance exists between a student's expectation of privacy and the school's interest in maintaining order and discipline. Accordingly, school officials do not need a warrant to search the belongings of students, but they do require a "reasonable suspicion." The U.S. Supreme Court held that the vice principal's search of T.L.O.'s purse was reasonable because it was relevant to whether T.L.O. was being truthful when she disavowed smoking in the bathroom despite being caught by a teacher. It was therefore reasonable and not just a "hunch" to assume that she would have cigarettes in her purse. The reasonable search for cigarettes led to the plain view of some of the drug paraphernalia, which justified a further search of the purse. In overturning the New Jersey Supreme Court ruling, the U.S. Supreme Court also stated that states have a duty to provide a safe school environment to protect schools' educational mission.

Justice John Paul Stevens dissented, maintaining that although smoking in the bathroom was against the rules, it was not illegal and that he feared the Court's ruling rendered the Fourth Amendment "virtually meaningless in the school context."

A long-lasting implication of *New Jersey v. T.L.O.* is that the Supreme Court gave public school officials a great deal of latitude in determining "reasonable cause" for search and seizure to ensure safety and order in the public schools. Because school officials' responsibility to provide a safe school environment is vital to schools' educational mission, young people in school settings have less right to an expectation of privacy than they do outside school settings.

> "The warrant requirement, in particular, is unsuited to the school environment: requiring a teacher to obtain a warrant before searching a child suspected of an infraction of school rules (or of the criminal law) would unduly interfere with the maintenance of the swift and informal disciplinary procedures needed in the schools."

The Court's Decision: When Searching Students on School Grounds, School Officials Do Not Violate Juveniles' Right to Privacy

Byron R. White

Byron R. White (1917–2002) was perhaps the only Supreme Court justice to play professional football. He played for the Pittsburgh Pirates (now Steelers) before studying at Oxford University on a Rhodes Scholarship. Appointed to the Supreme Court in 1962 by John F. Kennedy, White wrote 994 opinions before retiring in 1993. As a justice, White often took a narrow, fact-specific view of cases before the Court and generally refused to make broad pronouncements on constitutional doctrine. He wrote dissenting opinions in the landmark case Miranda v. Arizona *(1966), arguing that aggressive police practices enhance the individual rights of law-abiding citizens. He also dissented in* Roe v. Wade *(1973), maintaining that the Court's majority opinion in* Roe *was "an exercise in raw judicial power" and*

Byron R. White, majority opinion, *New Jersey v. T.L.O.*, U.S. Supreme Court, 1985.

criticizing the decision for "interposing a constitutional barrier to state efforts to protect human life." Although White consistently supported civil rights, desegregation, and affirmative action, he was often critical of the doctrine of "substantive due process," which involves the judiciary reading substantive content into the term "liberty" in the due process clauses of the Fifth and Fourteenth Amendments.

In the majority opinion of New Jersey v. T.L.O., *White argues that T.L.O., a ninth-grader at a public high school, did not have her Fourth Amendment rights violated when a high school administrator searched her purse and that the illegal drugs found in her purse were admissible as evidence in juvenile proceedings.*

This case considers whether it is lawful for school officials to search the private belongings of students on the grounds of reasonable suspicion.

In determining whether the search at issue in this case violated the Fourth Amendment, we are faced initially with the question whether that Amendment's prohibition on unreasonable searches and seizures applies to searches conducted by public school officials. We hold that it does.

It is now beyond dispute that "the Federal Constitution, by virtue of the Fourteenth Amendment, prohibits unreasonable searches and seizures by state officers" [*Elkins v. United States* (1960)]. Equally indisputable is the proposition that the Fourteenth Amendment protects the rights of students against encroachment by public school officials:

> "The Fourteenth Amendment, as now applied to the States, protects the citizen against the State itself and all of its creatures—Boards of Education not excepted. These have, of course, important, delicate, and highly discretionary functions, but none that they may not perform within the limits of the Bill of Rights. That they are educating the young for

citizenship is reason for scrupulous protection of Constitutional freedoms of the individual, if we are not to strangle the free mind at its source and teach youth to discount important principles of our government as mere platitudes" [*West Virginia State Bd. of Ed. v. Barnette* (1943)].

These two propositions—that the Fourth Amendment applies to the States through the Fourteenth Amendment, and that the actions of public school officials are subject to the limits placed on state action by the Fourteenth Amendment—might appear sufficient to answer the suggestion that the Fourth Amendment does not proscribe unreasonable searches by school officials. On reargument, however, the State of New Jersey has argued that the history of the Fourth Amendment indicates that the Amendment was intended to regulate only searches and seizures carried out by law enforcement officers; accordingly, although public school officials are concededly state agents for purposes of the Fourteenth Amendment, the Fourth Amendment creates no rights enforceable against them.

Fourth Amendment Rights

It may well be true that the evil toward which the Fourth Amendment was primarily directed was the resurrection of the pre-Revolutionary practice of using general warrants or "writs of assistance" to authorize searches for contraband by officers of the Crown. But this Court has never limited the Amendment's prohibition on unreasonable searches and seizures to operations conducted by the police. Rather, the Court has long spoken of the Fourth Amendment's strictures as restraints imposed upon "governmental action"—that is, "upon the activities of sovereign authority" [*Burdeau v. McDowell* (1921)]. Accordingly, we have held the Fourth Amendment applicable to the activities of civil as well as criminal authorities: building inspectors, Occupational Safety and Health Act inspectors, and even firemen entering privately owned premises to battle a fire, are all subject to the restraints imposed by the Fourth Amendment. As we observed in *Camara v. Municipal Court* [(1967)], "[t]he basic purpose of this Amendment, as recognized in countless decisions of this Court, is to safeguard the privacy and security of individuals against arbitrary invasions by governmental officials." Because the individual's interest in privacy and personal security "suffers whether the government's motivation is to investigate violations of criminal laws or breaches of other statutory or regulatory standards" [*Marshall v. Barlow's, Inc.* (1978)], it would be "anomalous to say that the individual and his private property are fully protected by the Fourth Amendment only when the individual is suspected of criminal behavior" [*Camara v. Municipal Court*].

Notwithstanding the general applicability of the Fourth Amendment to the activities of civil authorities, a few courts have concluded that school officials are exempt from the dictates of the Fourth Amendment by virtue of the special nature of their authority over schoolchildren. Teachers and school administrators, it is said, act in *loco parentis* ["in place of the parent"] in their dealings with students: their authority is that of the parent, not the State, and is therefore not subject to the limits of the Fourth Amendment.

Such reasoning is in tension with contemporary reality and the teachings of this Court. We have held school officials subject to the commands of the First Amendment, and the Due Process Clause of the Fourteenth Amendment. If school authorities are state actors for purposes of the constitutional guarantees of freedom of expression and due process, it is difficult to understand why they should be deemed to be exercising parental rather than public authority when conducting searches of their students. More generally, the Court has recognized that "the concept of parental delegation" as a source of school authority is not entirely "consonant with compulsory education laws" [*Ingraham v. Wright* (1977)]. Today's public school officials do not merely exercise authority voluntarily conferred on them by individual parents; rather, they act in furtherance of publicly mandated educational and disciplinary policies. In carrying out searches and other disciplinary functions pursuant to such policies, school officials act as representatives of the State, not merely as surrogates for the parents, and they cannot claim the parents' immunity from the strictures of the Fourth Amendment.

Standards of Reasonableness

To hold that the Fourth Amendment applies to searches conducted by school authorities is only to begin the inquiry into the standards governing such searches. Although the underlying command of the Fourth Amendment is always that searches and seizures be reasonable, what is reasonable depends on the context within which a search takes place. The determination of the standard of reasonableness governing any specific class of searches requires "balancing the need to search against the invasion which the search entails" [*Camara v. Municipal Court*]. On one side of the balance are arrayed the individual's legitimate expectations of privacy and personal security; on the other, the government's need for effective methods to deal with breaches of public order.

We have recognized that even a limited search of the person is a substantial invasion of privacy. We have also recognized that searches of closed items of personal luggage are intrusions on protected privacy interests, for "the Fourth Amendment provides protection to the owner of every container that conceals its contents from plain view" [*United States v. Ross* (1982)]. A search of a child's person or of a closed purse or other bag carried on her person, no less than a similar search carried out on an adult, is undoubtedly a severe violation of subjective expectations of privacy.

Of course, the Fourth Amendment does not protect subjective expectations of privacy that are unreasonable or otherwise "illegitimate." To receive the protection of the Fourth

Amendment, an expectation of privacy must be one that society is "prepared to recognize as legitimate" [*Hudson v. Palmer*]. The State of New Jersey has argued that because of the pervasive supervision to which children in the schools are necessarily subject, a child has virtually no legitimate expectation of privacy in articles of personal property "unnecessarily" carried into a school. This argument has two factual premises: (1) the fundamental incompatibility of expectations of privacy with the maintenance of a sound educational environment; and (2) the minimal interest of the child in bringing any items of personal property into the school. Both premises are severely flawed.

Need for Discipline in Public Schools

Although this Court may take notice of the difficulty of maintaining discipline in the public schools today, the situation is not so dire that students in the schools may claim no legitimate expectations of privacy. We have recently recognized that the need to maintain order in a prison is such that prisoners retain no legitimate expectations of privacy in their cells, but it goes almost without saying that "[t]he prisoner and the schoolchild stand in wholly different circumstances, separated by the harsh facts of criminal conviction and incarceration" [*Ingraham v. Wright*]. We are not yet ready to hold that the schools and the prisons need be equated for purposes of the Fourth Amendment.

Nor does the State's suggestion that children have no legitimate need to bring personal property into the schools seem well anchored in reality. Students at a minimum must bring to school not only the supplies needed for their studies, but also keys, money, and the necessaries of personal hygiene and grooming. In addition, students may carry on their persons or in purses or wallets such nondisruptive yet highly personal items as photographs, letters, and diaries. Finally, students may have perfectly legitimate reasons to carry with them articles of property needed in connection with extracurricular or recreational activities. In short, schoolchildren may find it necessary to carry with them a variety of legitimate, noncontraband items, and there is no reason to conclude that they have necessarily waived all rights to privacy in such items merely by bringing them onto school grounds.

Against the child's interest in privacy must be set the substantial interest of teachers and administrators in maintaining discipline in the classroom and on school grounds. Maintaining order in the classroom has never been easy, but in recent years, school disorder has often taken particularly ugly forms: drug use and violent crime in the schools have become major social problems. Even in schools that have been spared the most severe disciplinary problems, the preservation of order and a proper educational environment requires close supervision of schoolchildren, as well as the enforcement of rules against conduct that would be perfectly permissible if undertaken by an adult. "Events calling for discipline are frequent occurrences and sometimes require immediate, effective action" [*Goss v. Lopez* (1975)]. Accordingly, we have recognized that maintaining security and order in the schools requires a certain degree of flexibility in school disciplinary procedures, and we have respected the value of preserving the informality of the student-teacher relationship.

How, then, should we strike the balance between the schoolchild's legitimate expectations of privacy and the school's equally legitimate need to maintain an environment in which learning can take place? It is evident that the school setting requires some easing of the restrictions to which searches by public authorities are ordinarily subject. The warrant requirement, in particular, is unsuited to the school environment: requiring a teacher to obtain a warrant before searching a child suspected of an infraction of school rules (or of the criminal law) would unduly interfere with the maintenance of the swift and informal disciplinary procedures needed in the schools. Just as we have in other cases dispensed with the warrant requirement when "the burden of obtaining a warrant is likely to frustrate the governmental purpose behind the search" [*Camara v. Municipal Court*], we hold today that school officials need not obtain a warrant before searching a student who is under their authority.

Balancing Privacy with Need for Order

The school setting also requires some modification of the level of suspicion of illicit activity needed to justify a search. Ordinarily, a search—even one that may permissibly be carried out without a warrant—must be based upon "probable cause" to believe that a violation of the law has occurred. However, "probable cause" is not an irreducible requirement of a valid search. The fundamental command of the Fourth Amendment is that searches and seizures be reasonable, and although "both the concept of probable cause and the requirement of a warrant bear on the reasonableness of a search, . . . in certain limited circumstances neither is required" [*Almeida Sanchez v. United States* (1973)]. Thus, we have in a number of cases recognized the legality of searches and seizures based on suspicions that, although "reasonable," do not rise to the level of probable cause. Where a careful balancing of governmental and private interests suggests that the public interest is best served by a Fourth Amendment standard of reasonableness that stops short of probable cause, we have not hesitated to adopt such a standard.

We join the majority of courts that have examined this issue in concluding that the accommodation of the privacy interests of schoolchildren with the substantial need of teachers and administrators for freedom to maintain order in the schools does not require strict adherence to the requirement that searches be based on probable cause to believe that the subject of the search has violated or is violating the law. Rather, the legality of a search of a student should depend simply on the reasonableness, under all the circumstances, of the search. Determining the reasonableness of any search involves a twofold inquiry: first, one must consider "whether the . . . action was justified at its inception," [*Terry v. Ohio* (1968)]; second, one must determine whether the search as actually conducted "was reasonably related in scope to the circumstances which justified the interference in the first place" [ibid.]. Under ordinary circumstances, a search of a student by a teacher or other school official will be "justified at its inception" when there are reasonable grounds for suspecting that the search will turn up evidence that the student has violated or is violating either the law or the rules of the school. Such a search will be permissible in its scope when the measures adopted are reasonably related to the objectives of the search and not excessively intrusive in light of the age and sex of the student and the nature of the infraction.

This standard will, we trust, neither unduly burden the efforts of school authorities to maintain order in their schools nor authorize unrestrained intrusions upon the privacy of schoolchildren. By focusing attention on the question of reasonableness, the standard will spare teachers and school administrators the necessity of schooling themselves in the niceties of probable cause and permit them to regulate their conduct according to the dictates of reason and common sense. At the same time, the reasonableness standard should ensure that the interests of students will be invaded no more than is necessary to achieve the legitimate end of preserving order in the schools.

Questions of Legality

There remains the question of the legality of the search in this case. We recognize that the "reasonable grounds" standard applied by the New Jersey Supreme Court in its consideration of this question is not substantially different from the standard that we have adopted today. Nonetheless, we believe that the

117

New Jersey court's application of that standard to strike down the search of T.L.O.'s purse reflects a somewhat crabbed notion of reasonableness. Our review of the facts surrounding the search leads us to conclude that the search was in no sense unreasonable for Fourth Amendment purposes.

The incident that gave rise to this case actually involved two separate searches, with the first—the search for cigarettes—providing the suspicion that gave rise to the second— the search for marijuana. Although it is the fruits of the second search that are at issue here, the validity of the search for marijuana must depend on the reasonableness of the initial search for cigarettes, as there would have been no reason to suspect that T.L.O. possessed marijuana had the first search not taken place. Accordingly, it is to the search for cigarettes that we first turn our attention.

The New Jersey Supreme Court pointed to two grounds for its holding that the search for cigarettes was unreasonable. First, the court observed that possession of cigarettes was not in itself illegal or a violation of school rules. Because the contents of T.L.O.'s purse would therefore have "no direct bearing on the infraction" of which she was accused (smoking in a lavatory where smoking was prohibited), there was no reason to search her purse. Second, even assuming that a search of T.L.O.'s purse might under some circumstances be reasonable in light of the accusation made against T.L.O., the New Jersey court concluded that Mr. Choplick in this particular case had no reasonable grounds to suspect that T.L.O. had cigarettes in her purse. At best, according to the court, Mr. Choplick had "a good hunch."

Both these conclusions are implausible. T.L.O. had been accused of smoking, and had denied the accusation in the strongest possible terms when she stated that she did not smoke at all. Surely it cannot be said that under these circumstances, T.L.O.'s possession of cigarettes would be irrelevant to the charges against her or to her response to those charges.

T.L.O.'s possession of cigarettes, once it was discovered, would both corroborate the report that she had been smoking and undermine the credibility of her defense to the charge of smoking. To be sure, the discovery of the cigarettes would not prove that T.L.O. had been smoking in the lavatory; nor would it, strictly speaking, necessarily be inconsistent with her claim that she did not smoke at all. But it is universally recognized that evidence, to be relevant to an inquiry, need not conclusively prove the ultimate fact in issue, but only have "any tendency to make the existence of any fact that is of consequence to the determination of the action more probable or less probable than it would be without the evidence." The relevance of T.L.O.'s possession of cigarettes to the question whether she had been smoking and to the credibility of her denial that she smoked supplied the necessary "nexus" between the item searched for and the infraction under investigation. Thus, if Mr. Choplick in fact had a reasonable suspicion that T.L.O. had cigarettes in her purse, the search was justified despite the fact that the cigarettes, if found, would constitute "mere evidence" of a violation.

Defining Reasonable Suspicion

Of course, the New Jersey Supreme Court also held that Mr. Choplick had no reasonable suspicion that the purse would contain cigarettes. This conclusion is puzzling. A teacher had reported that T.L.O. was smoking in the lavatory. Certainly this report gave Mr. Choplick reason to suspect that T.L.O. was carrying cigarettes with her; and if she did have cigarettes, her purse was the obvious place in which to find them. Mr. Choplick's suspicion that there were cigarettes in the purse was not an "inchoate and unparticularized suspicion or 'hunch,'" [Terry v. Ohio]; rather, it was the sort of "commonsense conclusio[n] about human behavior" upon which "practical people"—including government officials—are entitled to rely [United States v. Cortez (1981)]. Of course, even if the teacher's report were true, T.L.O. might not have had a pack of cigarettes with her; she might have borrowed a cigarette from someone else or have been sharing a cigarette with another student. But the requirement of reasonable suspicion is not a requirement of absolute certainty: "sufficient probability, not certainty, is the touchstone of reasonableness under the Fourth Amendment. . ." [*Hill v. California* (1971)]. Because the hypothesis that T.L.O. was carrying cigarettes in her purse was itself not unreasonable, it is irrelevant that other hypotheses were also consistent with the teacher's accusation. Accordingly, it cannot be said that Mr. Choplick acted unreasonably when he examined T.L.O.'s purse to see if it contained cigarettes.

Our conclusion that Mr. Choplick's decision to open T.L.O.'s purse was reasonable brings us to the question of the further search for marijuana once the pack of cigarettes was located. The suspicion upon which the search for marijuana was founded was provided when Mr. Choplick observed a package of rolling papers in the purse as he removed the pack of cigarettes. Although T.L.O. does not dispute the reasonableness of Mr. Choplick's belief that the rolling papers indicated the presence of marijuana, she does contend that the scope of the search Mr. Choplick conducted exceeded permissible bounds when he seized and read certain letters that implicated T.L.O. in drug dealing. This argument, too, is unpersuasive. The discovery of the rolling papers concededly gave rise to a reasonable suspicion that T.L.O. was carrying marijuana as well as cigarettes in her purse. This suspicion justified further exploration of T.L.O.'s purse, which turned up more evidence of drug-related activities: a pipe, a number of plastic bags of the type commonly used to store marijuana, a small quantity of marijuana, and a fairly substantial amount of money. Under these circumstances, it was not unreasonable to extend the search to a separate zippered compartment of the purse; and when a search of that compartment revealed an index card containing a list of "people who owe me money" as well as two letters, the inference that T.L.O. was involved in marijuana trafficking was substantial enough to justify Mr. Choplick in examining the letters to determine whether they contained any further evidence. In short, we cannot conclude that the search for marijuana was unreasonable in any respect.

Because the search resulting in the discovery of the evidence of marijuana dealing by T.L.O. was reasonable, the New Jersey Supreme Court's decision to exclude that evidence from T.L.O.'s juvenile delinquency proceedings on Fourth Amendment grounds was erroneous. Accordingly, the judgment of the Supreme Court of New Jersey is Reversed.

"While school administrators have entirely legitimate reasons for adopting school regulations and guidelines for student behavior, the authorization of searches to enforce them 'displays a shocking sense of all proportion.'"

Court Opinion, Dissenting in Part: Students' Fourth Amendment Expectations to Privacy Must Be Protected Against Unreasonable Search and Seizure

John Paul Stevens

John Paul Stevens (b. 1920) was appointed to the Supreme Court in 1975 by President Gerald Ford. As a justice, Stevens has avoided simple conservative or liberal labels. As the Court moved toward the right during the Reagan and Bush presidencies, however, Stevens appeared more and more liberal relative to the makeup of the Court.

John Paul Stevens, joined by Thurgood Marshall and William Brennan, wrote a minority opinion for New Jersey v. T.L.O., *expressing partial concurrence with and partial dissent from the majority opinion. Stevens concurred with the majority that the Fourth Amendment protection against unreasonable search and seizure applies to searches made by public school officials, but ar-*

John Paul Stevens, concurring in part and dissenting in part opinion, *New Jersey v. T.L.O.*, U.S. Supreme Court, 1985.

gues that in T.L.O., the assistant principal made an unreasonable search because he did not have probable cause to suspect the student had committed a crime. T.L.O. was a ninth-grade student in a public high school suspected of smoking in the school's lavatory, her purse was searched by the assistant vice principal, and, along with cigarettes, marijuana was found.

Assistant Vice Principal Choplick searched T.L.O.'s purse for evidence that she was smoking in the girls' restroom. Because T.L.O.'s suspected misconduct was not illegal and did not pose a serious threat to school discipline, the New Jersey Supreme Court held that Choplick's search of her purse was an unreasonable invasion of her privacy and that the evidence which he seized could not be used against her in criminal proceedings. The New Jersey court's holding was a careful response to the case it was required to decide.

The State of New Jersey sought review in this Court, first arguing that the exclusionary rule is wholly inapplicable to searches conducted by school officials, and then contending that the Fourth Amendment itself provides no protection at all to the student's privacy. The Court has accepted neither of these frontal assaults on the Fourth Amendment. It has, however, seized upon this "no smoking" case to announce "the proper standard" that should govern searches by school officials who are confronted with disciplinary problems far more severe than smoking in the restroom. Although I join Part II of the Court's opinion, I continue to believe that the Court has unnecessarily and inappropriately reached out to decide a constitutional question. More importantly, I fear that the concerns that motivated the Court's activism have produced a holding that will permit school administrators to search students suspected of violating only the most trivial school regulations and guidelines for behavior.

School Administrators Conducted an Illegal Search

The question the Court decides today—whether Mr. Choplick's search of T.L.O.'s purse violated the Fourth Amendment—was not raised by the State's petition for writ of certiorari [request for the Supreme Court to review the decision of a lower court]. That petition only raised one question: "Whether the Fourth Amendment's exclusionary rule applies to searches made by public school officials and teachers in school." The State quite properly declined to submit the former question because "[it] did not wish to present what might appear to be solely a factual dispute to this Court." Since this Court has twice had the threshold question argued, I believe that it should expressly consider the merits of the New Jersey Supreme Court's ruling that the exclusionary rule applies.

The New Jersey Supreme Court's holding on this question is plainly correct. As the state court noted, this case does not involve the use of evidence in a school disciplinary proceeding; the juvenile proceedings brought against T.L.O. involved a charge that would have been a criminal offense if committed by an adult. Accordingly, the exclusionary rule issue decided by that court and later presented to this Court concerned only the use in a criminal proceeding of evidence obtained in a search conducted by a public school administrator.

Having confined the issue to the law enforcement context, the New Jersey court then reasoned that this Court's cases have made it quite clear that the exclusionary rule is equally applicable "whether the public official who illegally obtained the evidence was a municipal inspector, a firefighter, or a school administrator or law enforcement official." It correctly concluded "that if an official search violates constitutional rights, the evidence is not admissible in criminal proceedings."

When a defendant in a criminal proceeding alleges that she was the victim of an illegal search by a school administrator, the application of the exclusionary rule is a simple corollary of the principle that "all evidence obtained by searches and seizures in violation of the Constitution is, by that same authority, inadmissible in a state court" [*Mapp v. Ohio* (1961)]. The practical basis for this principle is, in part, its deterrent effect, and as a general matter it is tolerably clear to me, as it has been to the Court, that the existence of an exclusionary remedy does deter the authorities from violating the Fourth Amendment by sharply reducing their incentive to do so. In the case of evidence obtained in school searches, the "overall educative effect" of the exclusionary rule adds important symbolic force to this utilitarian judgment.

Justice [Louis] Brandeis was both a great student and a great teacher. It was he who wrote:

"Our Government is the potent, the omnipresent teacher. For good or for ill, it teaches the whole people by its example. Crime is contagious. If the Government becomes a lawbreaker, it breeds contempt for law, it invites every man to become a law unto himself; it invites anarchy. . . ."

Schools are places where we inculcate the values essential to the meaningful exercise of rights and responsibilities by a self-governing citizenry. If the Nation's students can be convicted through the use of arbitrary methods destructive of personal liberty, they cannot help but feel that they have been dealt with unfairly. The application of the exclusionary rule in criminal proceedings arising from illegal school searches makes an important statement to young people that "our society attaches serious consequences to a violation of constitutional rights," and that this is a principle of "liberty and justice for all. . . ."

Search Was a Serious Invasion of Privacy

The search of a young woman's purse by a school administrator is a serious invasion of her legitimate expectations of privacy. A purse "is a common repository for one's personal effects and therefore is inevitably associated with the expectation of privacy" [*Arkansas v. Sanders* (1979)]. Although such expectations must sometimes yield to the legitimate requirements of government, in assessing the constitutionality of a warrantless search, our decision must be guided by the language of the Fourth Amendment: "The right of the people to be secure in their persons, houses, papers and effects, against unreasonable searches and seizures, shall not be violated. . . ." [In *Terry v. Ohio* (1968), the Court found that] in order to evaluate the reasonableness of such searches, "it is necessary 'first to focus upon the governmental interest which allegedly justifies official intrusion upon the constitutionally protected interests of the private citizen,' for there is 'no ready test for determining reasonableness other than by balancing the need to search [or seize] against the invasion which the search [or seizure] entails.'"

The "limited search for weapons" in *Terry* was justified by the "immediate interest of the police officer in taking steps to assure himself that the person with whom he is dealing is not armed with a weapon that could unexpectedly and fatally be used against him." When viewed from the institutional perspective, "the substantial need of teachers and administrators for freedom to maintain order in the schools," is no less acute. Violent, unlawful, or seriously disruptive conduct is fundamentally inconsistent with the principal function of teaching institutions, which is to educate young people and prepare them for citizenship. When such conduct occurs amidst a sizable group of impressionable young people, it creates an explosive atmosphere that requires a prompt and effective response.

Thus, warrantless searches of students by school administrators are reasonable when undertaken for those purposes. But the majority's statement of the standard for evaluating the reasonableness of such searches is not suitably adapted to that end. The majority holds that "a search of a student by a teacher or other school official will be 'justified at its inception' when there are reasonable grounds for suspecting that the search will turn up evidence that the student has violated or is violating either the law or the rules of the school." This standard will permit teachers and school administrators to search students when they suspect that the search will reveal evidence of even the most trivial school regulation or precatory guideline for student behavior. The Court's standard for deciding whether a search is justified "at its inception" treats all violations of the rules of the school as though they were fungible. For the Court, a search for curlers and sunglasses in order to enforce the school dress code is apparently just as important as a search for evidence of heroin addiction or violent gang activity.

The majority, however, does not contend that school administrators have a compelling need to search students in order to achieve optimum enforcement of minor school regulations. To the contrary, when minor violations are involved, there is every indication that the informal school disciplinary process, with only minimum requirements of due process, can function effectively without the power to search for enough evidence to prove a criminal case. In arguing that teachers and school administrators need the power to search students based on a lessened standard, the United States as *amicus curiae* relies heavily on empirical evidence of a contemporary crisis of violence and unlawful behavior that is seriously undermining the process of education in American schools. A standard better attuned to this concern would permit teachers and school administrators to search a student when they have reason to believe that the search will uncover evidence that the student is violating the law or engaging in conduct that is seriously disruptive of school order, or the educational process.

A Warrantless Search Must Be Reasonable

This standard is properly directed at "[t]he sole justification for the [warrantless] search." In addition, a standard that varies the extent of the permissible intrusion with the gravity of the suspected offense is also more consistent with common-law experience and this Court's precedent. Criminal law has traditionally recognized a distinction between essentially regulatory offenses and serious violations of the peace, and graduated the response of the criminal justice system depending on the character of the violation. The application of a similar distinction in evaluating the reasonableness of warrantless searches and seizures "is not a novel idea."

In *Welsh* [*v. Wisconsin* (1984),] police officers arrived at the scene of a traffic accident and obtained information indicating that the driver of the automobile involved was guilty of a first offense of driving while intoxicated—a civil violation with a maximum fine of $200. The driver had left the scene of the accident, and the officers followed the suspect to his home where they arrested him without a warrant. Absent exigent [urgent] circumstances, the warrantless invasion of the home was a clear violation of *Payton v. New York* (1980). In holding that the warrantless arrest for the "noncriminal, traffic offense" in *Welsh* was unconstitutional, the Court noted that "application of the exigent-circumstances exception in the context of a home entry should rarely be sanctioned when there is probable cause to believe that only a minor offense . . . has been committed."

The logic of distinguishing between minor and serious offenses in evaluating the reasonableness of school searches is almost too clear for argument. In order to justify the serious intrusion on the persons and privacy of young people that New Jersey asks this Court to approve, the State must identify "some real immediate and serious consequences." While school administrators have entirely legitimate reasons for adopting school regulations and guidelines for student behavior, the authorization of searches to enforce them "displays a shocking lack of all sense of proportion."

The majority offers weak deference to these principles of balance and decency by announcing that school searches will only be reasonable in scope "when the measures adopted are reasonably related to the objectives of the search and not excessively intrusive in light of the age and sex of the student and the nature of the infraction." The majority offers no explanation why a two-part standard is necessary to evaluate the reasonableness of the ordinary school search. Significantly, in the balance of its opinion the Court pretermits any discussion of the nature of T.L.O.'s infraction of the "no smoking" rule.

The "rider" to the Court's standard for evaluating the reasonableness of the initial intrusion apparently is the Court's perception that its standard is overly generous and does not, by itself, achieve a fair balance between the administrator's right to search and the student's reasonable expectations of privacy. The Court's standard for evaluating the "scope" of reasonable school searches is obviously designed to prohibit physically intrusive searches of students by persons of the opposite sex for relatively minor offenses. The Court's effort to establish a standard that is, at once, clear enough to allow searches to be upheld in nearly every case, and flexible enough to prohibit obviously unreasonable intrusions of young adults' privacy only creates uncertainty in the extent of its resolve to prohibit the latter. Moreover, the majority's application of its standard in this case—to permit a male administrator to rummage through the purse of a female high school student in order to obtain evidence that she was smoking in a bathroom—raises grave doubts in my mind whether its effort will be effective. Unlike the Court, I believe the nature of the suspected infraction is a matter of first importance in deciding whether any invasion of privacy is permissible.

A Hunch Is Not Reasonable Suspicion

The Court embraces the standard applied by the New Jersey Supreme Court as equivalent to its own, and then deprecates the state court's application of the standard as reflecting "a somewhat crabbed notion of reasonableness." There is no mystery, however, in the state court's finding that the search in this case was unconstitutional; the decision below was not based on a manipulation of reasonable suspicion, but on the trivial character of the activity that promoted the official search. The New Jersey Supreme Court wrote:

"We are satisfied that when a school official has reasonable grounds to believe that a student possesses evidence of illegal activity or activity that would interfere with school discipline and order, the school official has the right to conduct a reasonable search for such evidence.

"In determining whether the school official has reasonable grounds, courts should consider 'the child's age, history, and school record, the prevalence and seriousness of the problem in the school to which the search was directed, the exigency to make the search without delay, and the probative value and reliability of the information used as a justification for the search.'"

The emphasized language in the state court's opinion focuses on the character of the rule infraction that is to be the object of the search.

In the view of the state court, there is a quite obvious and material difference between a search for evidence relating to violent or disruptive activity, and a search for evidence of a smoking rule violation. This distinction does not imply that a no-smoking rule is a matter of minor importance. Rather, like a rule that prohibits a student from being tardy, its occasional violation in a context that poses no threat of disrupting school order and discipline offers no reason to believe that an immediate search is necessary to avoid unlawful conduct, violence, or a serious impairment of the educational process.

A correct understanding of the New Jersey court's standard explains why that court concluded in T.L.O.'s case that "the assistant principal did not have reasonable grounds to believe that the student was concealing in her purse evidence of criminal activity or evidence of activity that would seriously interfere with school discipline or order." The importance of the nature of the rule infraction to the New Jersey Supreme Court's holding is evident from its brief explanation of the principal basis for its decision:

> "A student has an expectation of privacy in the contents of her purse. Mere possession of cigarettes did not violate school rule or policy, since the school allowed smoking in designated areas. The contents of the handbag had no direct bearing on the infraction.

> "The assistant principal's desire, legal in itself, to gather evidence to impeach the student's credibility at a hearing on the disciplinary infraction does not validate the search."

Like the New Jersey Supreme Court, I would view this case differently if the assistant vice principal had reason to believe T.L.O.'s purse contained evidence of criminal activity, or of an activity that would seriously disrupt school discipline. There was, however, absolutely no basis for any such assumption—not even a "hunch...."

The schoolroom is the first opportunity most citizens have to experience the power of government. Through it passes every citizen and public official, from schoolteachers to policemen and prison guards. The values they learn there, they take with them in life. One of our most cherished ideals is the one contained in the Fourth Amendment: that the government may not intrude on the personal privacy of its citizens without a warrant or compelling circumstance. The Court's decision today is a curious moral for the Nation's youth. Although the search of T.L.O.'s purse does not trouble today's majority, I submit that we are not dealing with "matters relatively trivial to the welfare of the Nation. There are village tyrants as well as village Hampdens, but none who acts under color of law is beyond reach of the Constitution" [*West Virginia State Board of Education v. Barnette* (1943)].

I respectfully dissent.

"The odds of a child being killed at school by gunfire during the 1998–1999 school year were about one in two million. Contrary to media hyperbole about violence in public schools, most school-related injuries are nonviolent in nature, and the majority of crimes that occur in schools are thefts."

The Expansion of Police Power in Schools Diminishes the Rights of Students

Randall R. Beger

Randall R. Beger is a professor of sociology and the coordinator of the criminal justice program at the University of Wisconsin at Eau Claire. He has published many articles on juvenile justice and the legal rights of minors.

Randall R. Beger argues that the increased presence of law enforcement officials on school campuses is out of proportion with actual rates of school violence. In fact, he maintains, this trend has resulted in overly harsh punishments for relatively harmless student behavior. Beger contends that recent court decisions have eroded civil liberties by exempting school environments from Fourth Amendment search-and-seizure protections and asserts that students should be given the most legal protection possible due to their subservient position in schools.

Randall R. Beger, "Expansion of Police Power in Public Schools and the Vanishing Rights of Students," *Social Justice*, vol. 29, no. 1&2, March 2002, pp. 119–130. Reproduced by permission.

Growing public anxiety over acts of violence in schools has prompted educators and state lawmakers to adopt drastic measures to improve the safety of students. In the wake of recent high-profile campus shootings, schools have become almost prison-like in terms of security and in diminishing the rights of students. Ironically, a repressive approach to school safety may do more harm than good by creating an atmosphere of mistrust and alienation that causes students to misbehave.

This article examines law enforcement expansion in schools and the vanishing Fourth Amendment rights of public school children. The climate of fear generated by recent school shootings has spurred school administrators to increase security through physical means (locks, surveillance cameras, metal detectors) and to hire more police and security guards. State lawmakers have eagerly jumped on the school safety bandwagon by making it easier to punish schoolchildren as adults for a wide range of offenses that traditionally have been handled informally by teachers. Instead of safeguarding the rights of students against arbitrary police power, our nation's courts are granting police and school officials *more* authority to conduct searches of students. Tragically, little if any Fourth Amendment protection now exists to shield students from the raw exercise of *police power* in public schools.

The New School Security Culture and the Realities of School Violence

In response to the latest string of sensationalized school shootings, schools everywhere have made safety a top priority. A recent U.S. Department of Education survey of public schools found that 96% required guests to sign in before entering the school building, 80% had a closed campus policy that forbids students to leave campus for lunch, and 53% controlled access to their school buildings. A National School Board Association survey of over 700 school districts throughout the United

States found that 39% of urban school districts use metal detectors, 75% use locker searches, and 65% use security personnel. Schools have introduced stricter dress codes, put up barbed-wire security fences, banned book bags and pagers, and have added "lock down drills" and "SWAT team" rehearsals to their safety programs. Officials in Dallas, Texas, unveiled a $41 million state-of-the-art "security conscious" school that has 37 surveillance cameras, six metal detectors, and a security command center for monitoring the building and grounds. At Tewksbury Memorial High School in Massachusetts, 20 video cameras bring the school into the local police department via remote access technology. According to one source [*Current Events*], "the video cameras record almost everything students say and do at school—eating in the cafeteria, cramming in the library, chatting in the halls." The new security culture in public schools has stirred debate over whether schools have turned into "learning prisons" where the students unwittingly become "guinea pigs" to test the latest security devices.

Since the mid-1990s, a growing number of schools have adopted zero tolerance policies under which students receive predetermined penalties for any offense, no matter how minor. Students have been expelled or suspended from school for sharing aspirin, Midol, and Certs tablets, and for bringing nail clippers and scissors to class. There is no credible evidence that zero tolerance measures improve classroom management or the behavior of students. Such measures are not only ineffectual, but also appear to have a negative impact on children of color. Research indicates that black children are more likely than are whites to be expelled or suspended from school under zero tolerance.

Although most Americans believe that public schools are violent and dangerous places, numerous surveys on school safety contradict this notion. For example, according to U.S. Department of Education statistics, only 10% of public schools experienced one or more serious violent crimes during the

1996–1997 school year. Over the same period, almost half the nation's public schools (43%) reported no incidents of serious crime. Data from the Uniform Crime Reports show a decline of approximately 56% in juvenile homicide arrests between 1993 and 1998. In *Justice Blind? Ideals and Realities of American Criminal Justice*, Matthew Robinson explains why the conventional wisdom that schools are dangerous places is irrational:

> There are more than 51 million students and approximately 3 million teachers in American schools. In 1996, there were approximately 380,000 violent victimizations at school against these roughly 54 million people. This means the rate of violent victimization at U.S. schools is about 704 per 100,000 people. Stated differently, about 0.7% of people can expect to become victims of serious violent crimes at schools.

The odds of a child being killed at school by gunfire during the 1998–1999 school year were about one in two million. Contrary to media hyperbole about violence in public schools, most school-related injuries are nonviolent in nature, and the majority of crimes that occur in schools are thefts.

The Police Buildup in Public Schools

Despite the relative rarity of school violence, officials everywhere are feeling pressure to improve the safety of students and staff. An increasingly popular "quick fix" strategy is to hire police and security guards. According to a U.S. Department of Education study, about 19% of public schools had the full-time presence of a police officer or other law enforcement representative during the 1996–1997 school year.

School police officers take many forms. Some are regular uniformed police officers working on a part-time basis for a school district. Others are hired and trained by school security departments. In New York City alone, some 3,200 uniformed school security officers work in the Division of School Safety of the City Board of Education, "a contingent larger than the Boston Police Department" [according to researcher John Devine.] Many school districts use more than one form of police, such as campus police with support from local police or private security guards.

School Resource Officers (SROs) are the fastest-growing segment of law enforcement officials stationed in public schools. These armed and uniformed law enforcement officials perform multiple tasks, such as patrolling school grounds, assisting with investigations of students who break school rules, and arresting students who commit crimes. SROs also perform nontraditional law enforcement functions that include chaperoning dances, counseling students, and conducting seminars on substance abuse prevention. In 1997, there were 9,446 School Resource Officers in local police departments assigned to public schools in the United States. Their numbers have increased rapidly in recent years due to increased funding at the federal level to hire more officers. In the last two years alone, the Office of Community Oriented Policing Services (COPS) has awarded more than $350 million in grants to the COPS in Schools program to hire over 3,200 School Resource Officers at an annual cost of $54,687 each. Under a federal budget plan supported by President George W. Bush, COPS funding to hire school police will more than double.

Increased Police Power

The large influx of police officers in public schools has shifted the responsibility for maintaining order and discipline in the classroom away from teachers and into the hands of law enforcement officials. In *Maximum Security: The Culture of Violence in Inner-City Schools,* John Devine describes how school security police in New York public schools have "taken on an independent existence, with [their] own organization and procedures, language, rules, equipment, dressing rooms, uniforms, vans, and lines of authority." A school principal admitted to

Devine: "I have no control over security guards, they don't report to me." Recently, the New York City Board of Education, at the urging of former Mayor Rudolph Giuliani, voted to transfer responsibility for school safety to the city police. School boards in other states, including California, Florida, and Nevada, have come out in favor of placing student safety under the control of city police.

The trend in support of moving school discipline in the direction of law enforcement has also been given a push by state lawmakers. In Arizona, for example, a new state law requires that school officials report any crimes or security threats involving students to the local police. Under a new Michigan statute, teachers must involve the police in any search of students' lockers, cars, and personal belongings. The law explicitly states that evidence obtained from a search by a police officer cannot be excluded in a court or school disciplinary hearing. States have also enacted legislation that requires school officials to share information about students with police, including personal information gathered by school therapists and counselors.

Concurrently, state lawmakers have dramatically increased the penalties for crimes committed on school property. In Mississippi, the penalty for having a gun on school property is a fine of up to $5,000 and up to three years in prison. Louisiana law prescribes that any student or nonstudent carrying a firearm on school grounds "shall be imprisoned at hard labor for not more than five years." Most states have also increased the penalties for selling or using drugs on school campuses. Laws in Illinois, New Hampshire, and Michigan call for severe penalties, including imprisonment, for the possession or distribution of drugs in or near schools and have lowered the current age for prosecution of juveniles as adults. Under recent "zero tolerance" initiatives, trivial forms of student misconduct that were once handled informally by teachers and school administrators are now more likely to result in police arrest and referral to juvenile or adult court. Five students in Mississippi were suspended recently and criminally charged for tossing peanuts at each other on a school bus; a peanut hit the bus driver by mistake.

Increasingly, the search efforts of police officials stationed in public schools mirror the actions of prison guards. For example, to create a drug-free environment, schools are allowing police officers to conduct random preemptive searches of students' lockers and personal property using specially trained sniff dogs. Over 1,000 schools in 14 states use drug-sniffing dogs supplied by a Texas company called Interquest Detection Canines. The profit motive is a powerful incentive to expand canine searches to schools that have no demonstrable drug problems. One school board has even formed a partnership with the U.S. Customs Department to send dogs into classrooms for drug-detection training exercises. In writing about canine searches in Boston public schools, journalist Marcia Vigue describes the following scene:

> Secrecy is the key. Students, teachers, and parents are not warned in advance; some student handbooks do not even explain that [searches] might occur from time to time. . . . During the searches, the dogs respond to German commands like "sook"—which means search—by pushing their snouts against lockers and nudging their noses into bags and coats. Sometimes, after students have been told to leave, the dogs pass through classrooms and other rooms to sniff students' belongings.

The personal indignity of forcing students to submit to a suspicionless canine search is something no adult would tolerate.

Besides police-controlled canine searches, schools are turning to sting operations in which undercover law enforcement officials pretend to be students to conduct actual criminal investigations of students suspected of using or dealing drugs in the school setting. In Los Angeles, for example, undercover officers made over 200 drug buys over a five-month period at local schools. Opponents of school-based sting operations say they not only create a climate of mistrust between students and police, but also put innocent students at risk of wrongful arrest due to faulty tips and overzealous police work. When asked about his role in a recent undercover drug probe at a high school near Atlanta, a young-looking police officer who attended classes and went to parties with students replied: "I knew I had to fit in, make the kids trust me and then turn around and take them to jail."

Police have adopted other aggressive search tactics on school campuses, such as herding students into hallways for unannounced weapons searches, known as "blitz operations." At Shawnee Heights and Seaman High School in Kansas City, signs warn students driving into school parking areas that they have just consented to searches of their vehicles "with or without cause" by school administrators or police officers. Scores of other schools across the country have adopted similar vehicle search policies. Groups of students have even been strip-searched by police officers to locate money missing from a classroom. There seems to be no end in sight to the aggressive search methods police are willing to use on students in the name of safety.

The Fourth Amendment and Schools

The Fourth Amendment of the United States Constitution provides the following:

> The right of the people to be secure in their persons, houses, papers, and effects against unreasonable searches and seizures, shall not be violated, and no Warrants shall issue, but upon probable cause, supported by Oath or affirmation, and particularly describing the place to be searched, and the persons or things to be seized.

In the past, courts held that school authorities acted *in loco parentis* ["in place of the parent"] when searching students and as such were not bound by Fourth Amendment restrictions that apply to state officials.

In the 1995 landmark case of *New Jersey v. T.L.O.*, the United States Supreme Court held that the Fourth Amendment did apply to searches conducted by public school officials. The Court specifically considered the search of a student's purse by an assistant vice principal after a teacher had discovered the student, and her friend, smoking in the school washroom in violation of school policy. Upon searching T.L.O.'s purse, the assistant vice principal discovered cigarettes and a package of cigarette rolling papers, which to him suggested involvement with marijuana. A more extensive search revealed a small amount of marijuana, a pipe, empty plastic bags, and letters implicating T.L.O. in selling drugs. Thereafter, the police were notified and the state of New Jersey filed delinquency charges against T.L.O. for possession of marijuana with intent to sell.

On appeal, the U.S. Supreme Court ruled that schoolchildren do not waive their Fourth Amendment rights by bringing purses, books, and items necessary for personal grooming and hygiene to school. However, a certain degree of "flexibility" in school searches was deemed necessary, which made the warrant and probable cause requirements "impractical." Ultimately, the Court held that school officials need only have "reasonable suspicion" for student searches. Reasonable suspicion means that school officials "must have some [articulable] facts or knowledge that provide reasonable grounds" before conducting a search. Under *T.L.O.*, a search is reasonable if, first, the search decision is supported by reasonable suspicion and, second, the scope of the search is not "excessively intrusive" in light of the age and sex of the student and the nature of the infraction.

The *T.L.O.* decision avoided the issue of whether the probable cause or reasonable suspicion standard would apply to police searches in public schools. In the absence of a clear standard to guide police searches on school campuses, appellate courts have fashioned new criteria that give police officers the same search leeway as teachers. The case . . . *People v. Dilworth*, is a good example.

Kenneth Dilworth, a 15-year-old high school student in Joliet, Illinois, was arrested for drug possession by a police detective assigned full-time to a high school for teenagers with behavioral disorders. Detective Francis Ruettiger served as liaison police officer on staff at the school, but was employed by the Joliet police department. Two teachers at the school asked Ruettiger to search a student, Deshawn Weeks, for drugs. The teachers informed Ruettiger that they had overheard Weeks telling other students he had sold some drugs and would bring more drugs with him to school the next day. The detective searched Weeks, but no drugs were found. Ruettiger then escorted the boy to his locker, where the youth and 15-year-old Kenneth Dilworth began talking and giggling. Ruettiger testified he felt "like [he] was being played for a fool." The officer noticed Dilworth had a flashlight and suspected it might contain contraband. He seized it, unscrewed the top, and found cocaine. After discovering cocaine, Ruettiger chased and captured Dilworth, handcuffed him, placed him in a police vehicle, and escorted him to the Joliet police station. Dilworth was subsequently tried and found guilty in adult court for unlawful possession of a controlled substance with intent to deliver on school property. He was sentenced to a four-year term of imprisonment. Dilworth's motion to reconsider the sentence was denied.

The appellate court reversed Dilworth's conviction on the grounds that his motion to suppress evidence discovered in his flashlight should have been granted. In the opinion of the appellate court, Ruettiger's seizure and search of the flashlight were based on only an unparticularized suspicion or "hunch" and did not comport with any standard of reasonableness for searches and seizures of students and their effects by state officials.

However, a divided Illinois Supreme Court in a four-to-three decision reversed the appellate court decision. Claiming that a flashlight in the context of an alternative school could reasonably be construed to be a weapon, the court affirmed Ruettiger's search as reasonable. The majority reasoned that lower expectations of privacy in the school setting, discussed in *T.L.O.*, supported a sharp departure from the probable cause standard for a school liaison officer. Even though detective Ruettiger was employed by the Joliet police department and performed duties at the school more in line with a regular law enforcement officer than a school official, the court maintained the search was proper.

The *Dilworth* decision stands in stark opposition to Fourth Amendment precedents that require the probable cause test to be met when evidence from a search by a law enforcement official forms the basis of a criminal prosecution. For example, in *A.J.M v. State* (1993), the *T.L.O.* standard does not apply to a search by a sheriff's officer who was serving as a school resource officer and was asked to conduct a search by the school principal; in *F.P. v. State* (1988), the *T.L.O.* standard does not apply where a search is carried out at the behest of police.

Justice Nickels, dissenting in *Dilworth*, severely criticized the majority for lowering the search standard for a school police officer when he stated:

> I cannot agree with the majority that a police officer whose self-stated primary duty is to investigate and prevent criminal activity may search a student on school grounds on a lesser [F]ourth Amendment standard than probable cause merely because the police officer is permanently assigned to the school and is listed in the student handbook as a member of the school staff. The majority's departure from a unanimous line of Federal and State decisions places form over substance and opens the door for widespread abuse and erosion of students' [F]ourth Amendment rights to be free from unreasonable searches and seizures by law enforcement officers.

The *Dilworth* decision is representative of a series of recent cases in which trial and appellate courts have lowered the bar for student searches by police officers. Instead of protecting schoolchildren from arbitrary police intrusion, courts have given law enforcement officials the widest latitude to search students. For example, state appellate courts have redefined police search conduct as "minor" or "incidental" to justify application of the reasonable suspicion standard. Appellate courts have also suggested that the lesser reasonable suspicion test should be applied when police search at the request of school officials or are present when school authorities engage in a search. Courts have even upheld dragnet suspicionless searches of school lockers and police-directed canine searches of students' property with no warnings. Due to these decisions, public school children may now be searched on less than probable cause and prosecuted in *adult* court with the evidence from the search.

Students Need Fourth Amendment Protection

In response to widely publicized incidents of schoolyard violence, public schools have adopted rigid and intrusive security measures that diminish the rights of students. In the name of safety, students are being spied on with hidden cameras, searched without suspicion, and subjected to unannounced locker searches by police with drug-sniffing dogs. Concurrently, federal and state lawmakers have significantly increased penalties for crimes committed on school property. Trivial forms of student misconduct that used to be handled informally by teachers and school administrators are now more likely to result in arrest and referral to a juvenile or adult court. Ironically, the current "crackdown" on schoolchildren comes at a time when the level of violence and drug use in public schools has gone down.

Because[, as legal scholar Mai Linh Spencer states,] the school setting demands "constant submission to authority" and is imposing harsher criminal penalties on students who misbehave, the legal rights of schoolchildren ought to be given the highest legal protection afforded by the nation's courts. Regrettably, the opposite is true. Bowing to public fears and legislative pressures, trial and appellate courts have reduced the Fourth Amendment rights of students to an abstraction. The nation's courts no longer seem interested in scrutinizing the specific facts surrounding the search of a student to determine if police had probable cause or even reasonable suspicion. Instead, courts search for a policy justification—e.g., minimizing disruptions to school order or protecting the safety of students and teachers—to uphold the search, even when police use evidence seized under lower and increasingly porous search standards to convict minors in adult criminal court. Given the current atmosphere of widespread fear and distress precipitated by the September 11 tragedy, there is little reason to expect courts will impose any restrictions on searches in schools. Ironically, children are unsafe in public schools today not because of exposure to drugs and violence, but because they have lost their constitutional protections under the Fourth Amendment.

> *"[S]chool officials do not necessarily need reasonable suspicion to conduct, for example, random locker searches. Rather, school officials must balance their legitimate need to search lockers with the privacy rights of students."*

Random School Searches Ensure Safety and Are Constitutional

Mitchell L. Yell and Michael E. Rozalski

Mitchell L. Yell is a professor in programs in special education at the University of South Carolina (USC) whose research interests include special education law. Prior to teaching at USC, Yell was a special education teacher for sixteen years, working with children with learning disabilities, emotional and behavioral disorders, and autism. Michael E. Rozalski is an assistant professor in special education at the State University of New York (SUNY) Geneseo.

In the following article, Mitchell L. Yell and Michael E. Rozalski contend that students' privacy rights must sometimes be waived so that schools can maintain a safe, orderly environment. They review the necessity and legality of random school search policies and conclude that because students have fewer rights than adults, administrators can search their lockers and backpacks if they have reasonable suspicion of illegal activity. They argue that al-

Mitchell L. Yell and Michael E. Rozalski, "Searching for Safe Schools: Legal Issues in the Prevention of School Violence," *Journal of Emotional and Behavioral Disorders*, vol. 8, no. 3, Fall 2000, pp. 187–196. Copyright © 2000 Pro-Ed. Reproduced by permission.

though courts favor the schools' safety over students' privacy interests, students are protected from unreasonable searches.

The two Supreme Court decisions that directly affect how school officials may keep schools safe and orderly while safeguarding the rights of students are *New Jersey v. T.L.O.* (1985) and *Vernonia School District v. Acton* (1995). In fact, [school safety expert Bernard] James referred to the decision in *New Jersey v. T.L.O.* as a virtual blueprint for designing school safety policies. In this case, the Court noted that the interests of teachers and administrators in maintaining discipline in the classroom would be furthered by a less restrictive rule of law that would balance schoolchildren's legitimate expectations of privacy and the school's equally legitimate need to maintain an environment in which learning could take place. We now discuss these very important cases.

New Jersey v. T.L.O.

In 1985, the U.S. Supreme Court in *New Jersey v. T.L.O.* addressed warrantless searches in the schools. A teacher in a New Jersey high school discovered two girls smoking in the school lavatory. The students were taken to the vice-principal's office. The vice-principal took a purse from one of the girls to examine it for cigarettes. In addition to the cigarettes, the purse also contained cigarette-rolling papers. Suspecting that the girl might have marijuana, the vice-principal emptied the contents of the purse. In it he found a pipe, a small amount of marijuana, a large amount of money in small bills, a list of people owing T.L.O. money, and two letters implicating her in marijuana dealing. The girl's parents were called, and the evidence was turned over to police. Charges were brought by the police, and based on the evidence collected by the vice-principal and T.L.O.'s confession, a juvenile court in New Jersey declared T.L.O. delinquent. The parents appealed the decision on the grounds that the search was conducted without a warrant and, therefore, illegal under the Fourth Amendment.

Because the search was conducted illegally, the parents argued, the evidence was inadmissible. The case went to the New Jersey Supreme Court, which reversed the decision of the juvenile court and ordered the evidence obtained during the vice-principal's search suppressed on the grounds that the warrantless search was unconstitutional.

The U.S. Supreme Court eventually heard the case. The Court declared that the Fourth Amendment, prohibiting illegal searches and seizures, applied to students as well as adults. The Court also noted, however, that a student's privacy interests must be weighed against the need of administrators and teachers to maintain order and discipline in schools. Furthermore, the Court noted that maintaining security and order in schools required some easing of the requirements normally imposed on police.

The Court ruled that schools did not need to obtain a search warrant before searching a student; however, the Fourth Amendment's reasonableness standard, a standard lower than that of probable cause, had to be satisfied. *Probable cause* refers to a standard to which police are held; that is, police may only conduct a search if it is more than probable that the search will reveal evidence of illegal activities. Based on this standard, police must usually obtain a warrant prior to conducting the search. The reasonableness standard that school officials must meet holds that a reasonable person would have cause to suspect that evidence of illegal activities be present before conducting the search. If these preconditions are met, school officials may conduct the search. The reasonableness standard is much easier to meet than is the standard of probable cause.

The Court also adopted a two-part test to determine whether a search conducted by school officials was reasonable and, therefore, constitutionally valid. The two parts of this test that must be satisfied are that the search must be (a) justified at inception, and (b) related to violations of school rules or policies. First, the search must be conducted as the result of a legitimate suspicion. This does not mean that school officials must be absolutely certain prior to conducting a search, but rather that there is a common sense probability regarding the necessity of a search. A search cannot be justified on the basis of what was found during the search. Situations that justify a reasonable suspicion include information from student informers, police tips, anonymous tips and phone calls, and unusual student conduct. Second, the scope of the search must be reasonably related to the rule violation that led to the search in the first place. Because the vice-principal's search of T.L.O. met the Supreme Court's test, it reversed the judgment of the New Jersey Supreme Court and ruled that the marijuana was admissible as evidence.

Vernonia School District v. Acton

A school district in Oregon was experiencing a startling increase in drug use, rebelliousness, and disciplinary problems among its students. School officials identified student athletes as the ringleaders in the drug problem. Following unsuccessful attempts at solving the problem through the use of educational programs, a public meeting was held. During the meeting, school officials received unanimous parent support for adopting a drug-testing program for all students participating in sports. The policy required that if a student wanted to participate in interscholastic sports, the student and his or her parents had to sign a consent form submitting to drug testing. If a student and his or her parents did not sign the consent form, the student was not allowed to participate in sports. A seventh-grade student, James Acton, who wanted to play interscholastic football, refused to sign the consent form. When the school did not allow James to play football, his parents sued the school district, alleging that their son's constitutional rights had been violated. The case, *Vernonia School District v. Acton* was heard by the U.S. Supreme Court in 1995. In a six to three decision, the high court ruled in favor of the school district's drug-testing policy. Although the Court's ruling only addressed drug testing of student athletes, the decision has important implications for school districts' search and seizure policies. The Court, citing its decision in *T.L.O.*, stated that the Fourth Amendment to the Constitution required balancing the interests of the student's privacy and the school district's legitimate interest in preserving order and safety. In making this determination, the Court noted that students in school have a decreased expectation of privacy relative to adults in the general population. The Court also considered the relative unobtrusiveness of the drug-testing policy. The primary consideration, therefore, was regarding the special context of public schools, which act as guardians and tutors of the students in their care. Clearly, this decision indicated that in situations involving such preventive measures, courts will favor the needs of the school over the privacy interests of students when the procedures used are reasonable.

Maintaining Safe Schools Is of Utmost Importance

The *T.L.O.* and *Vernonia* decisions affirmed the constitutional rights of students to be free of unreasonable searches and seizures and to possess a reasonable expectation of privacy while at school. In both cases, however, the court granted a great deal of latitude to schools because they have a legitimate duty to educate students in a safe and orderly environment. The high court clearly stated that when the rights of students and those of school officials seem to conflict, the law favors the duties of school officials.

According to the *T.L.O.* decision, the law permits educators to respond to school safety problems as the situation dictates, providing the actions are reasonable. In *Vernonia*, the high court noted that the privacy expectations of students in public schools are less than those of the general public because school authorities act in *loco parentis*. In *loco parentis* is a concept that originated in English common law. According to this concept, when parents place their children in schools, they give a certain amount of their control of their children to school personnel. The principal and teacher, therefore, have the authority to teach, guide, correct, and discipline children to achieve educational objectives.

Factors That School Personnel Must Consider

Nonetheless, these decisions do place some degree of restraint on school personnel. In *T.L.O.* the court held that reasonable grounds must exist to lead school authorities to believe a search is necessary, and the search must be related to the original suspicion. According to [Jeffrey T.] Dise, [Chita S.] Iyer, and [author John H.] Noorman, this standard requires that school officials weigh the credibility of the information prior to making a decision to conduct a search. Court decisions following *T.L.O.* have recognized situations in which searches and seizures in school environments do not give rise to Fourth Amendment concerns (i.e., searches during which even the standard of reasonable suspicion is not required). These situations include searches (a) to which a student voluntarily consents, (b) of material left in view of the school authorities, (c) in an emergency to prevent injury or property damage, (d) by police authorities that are incidental to arrests, and (e) of lost property.

The intrusiveness of the search is also a relevant factor. Considering the nature of the possible offense, the search should not be overly intrusive (e.g., a strip search to locate missing money). When these conditions are met, school officials have a great deal of leeway in conducting searches of students and their property.

In *Vernonia*, the court stated that the interest of the school in taking the action (e.g., random searches, drug tests) must be important enough to justify the procedure. The court saw protecting students from drug use and maintaining a safe and orderly educational environment as "important—indeed compelling".

These decisions are extremely important because they give school officials guidance in using procedures such as targeted and random searches, drug testing, and surveillance. . . .

Targeted Searches of Students' Property

Although the U.S. Supreme Court has not heard a case involving targeted searches of student property, the Court did uphold searches of government offices, desks, and file cabinets based on reasonable suspicion. Lower courts, using this decision as precedent, have upheld school officials' targeted or random searches of student lockers, if the searches are based on reasonable suspicion. Searches by school authorities may also extend to students' cars and locked briefcases, as well as objects in which contraband may be hidden, such as backpacks.

When school officials use tertiary prevention procedures, such as targeted searches of students and their property, they do not have to wait until the illegal behavior affects the school before taking action. School officials are legally permitted to act in response to reasonable suspicion that a student is violating or may have violated school rules or committed an illegal act. That is, they only need reason to believe that the safety or order of the school environment may be threatened by student behavior.

There is, however, another class of procedures that in many situations do not require reasonable suspicion prior to being undertaken. We refer to these as secondary procedures. Secondary procedures include random searches, use of metal detectors, and surveillance. It is legally useful to consider such searches separately from targeted searches and other tertiary procedures because the standard that school officials must meet in using secondary procedures is lower. In the next section, we briefly examine the legality of secondary prevention procedures when used by school officials.

Random, Suspicionless Searches Are Legal

Secondary prevention procedures involve school officials' attempts to seize weapons or contraband materials before they can be used. These procedures typically consist of random searches of students' belongings or property (e.g., lockers, automobiles, desks, backpacks). The use of metal detectors and various means of surveillance also fall into this category. Furthermore, the use of metal detectors to search students, even though there is no suspicion or consent to a search, is permitted. To keep weapons, drugs, and contraband off school property, random searches of students and their property are now common occurrences in public schools, especially at the secondary level Secondary procedures, like tertiary procedures, are governed by the Fourth Amendment to the U.S. Constitution, which prohibits unreasonable searches and seizures. Unlike tertiary procedures, secondary procedures are directed at all students or are conducted randomly and therefore do not require reasonable suspicion.

A decision that has great importance for school districts conducting random searches was *In the Interest of Isaiah B.* (1993). In this decision, the Wisconsin Supreme Court ruled that a student did not have reasonable expectations of privacy in his school locker. The court based its decision largely on the existence of the Milwaukee Public Schools' policy regarding student lockers. According to the school policy,

> School lockers are the property of Milwaukee Public Schools. At no time does the Milwaukee School District relinquish its exclusive control of lockers provided for the convenience of students. School authorities for any reason may conduct pe-

riodic general inspections of lockers at any time, without notice, without student consent, and without a search warrant.

Unless prohibited by state law, [B.] Miller and [W.] Ahrbecker suggested [in "Legal Issues and School Violence"] that schools develop policies regarding locker searches, such as the Milwaukee Public Schools' policy, that notify students and parents that there is no reasonable expectation of privacy in a student locker and that both random and targeted searches of the locker may be conducted without student or parental consent. [Educational law expert Eugene C.] Bjorklun, likewise, concluded that random locker searches may be conducted without individualized suspicion.

Secondary procedures include the use of random searches, surveillance cameras, and metal detectors. These procedures are legally proactive because they serve as a deterrent. School officials attempt to seize contraband and weapons before they are used. Unlike tertiary procedures, the *T.L.O.* standard of reasonable suspicion is not as directly applicable in situations involving random property searches and other secondary procedures. That is, school officials do not necessarily need reasonable suspicion to conduct, for example, random locker checks. Rather, school officials must balance their legitimate need to search lockers with the privacy rights of students. When conducting searches of students and their property, it is important that school district officials adhere to established guidelines and policies that correspond with the case law. Students have diminished expectations of privacy while at school; nevertheless, school officials must notify students and their parents that student property may be subjected to random searches and that surveillance measures will be used and that the purpose of such measures is to ensure that students are educated in a safe and orderly environment.

> *"The teacher's role is as an educator, and the value of a good teacher-student relationship is not going to be enhanced by students viewing the teacher as a safety officer with respect to something as significant as searches."*

Teachers Should Not Conduct Student Searches

Nicole Klaas

Nicole Klaas is a journalist for the Albany, New York, alternative weekly Metroland.

In the following article, Nicole Klaas examines the potential impact of the Student and Teacher Safety Act of September 2006, which requires schools to develop a policy for conducting student searches or risk losing federal funding. While supporters of the legislation claim that the measure would increase school safety and minimize school liability, critics express concern that the bill would not only violate students' constitutional rights, but might undermine the role teachers strive to serve with students.

Adopt a policy for searching students or lose federal funding. That's the ultimatum associated with the Student and Teacher Safety Act, which was passed by the U.S. House of Representatives on Sept. 19, 2006.

The legislation would require school boards to establish a policy allowing full-time teachers and school officials, acting on reasonable suspicion, to search any student they wish in

Nicole Klaas, "Suspicion in the Classroom," *Metroland*, vol. 29, September 28, 2006, pp. 6–7. Copyright Metroland September 28, 2006. Reproduced by permission.

order to ensure that the school remains free from weapons, drugs or other dangerous materials. Districts that fail to enact the guidelines would become ineligible for federal funds through the Safe and Drug Free School program, from which New York state received more than $7 million in the 2006–07 academic year.

Supporters of the Student and Teacher Safety Act argue that the measure would increase safety in schools while alleviating apprehension about liability for teachers and other school officials. Opponents, although they echo the need to improve safety, question the bill's potential to violate students' constitutional rights as well as the appropriateness of expanding the role of educators.

Student and Teacher Safety Act Is Vague

In defining student searches, the Student and Teacher Act fails to describe the scope of permissible searches, said Jesselyn McCurdy, legislative counsel for the American Civil Liberties Union [ACLU], which opposes the legislation because of its broad language. This ambiguity leaves wiggle room for school officials to construe the bill as allowing for random, wide-scale searches of all students, even those for whom there is no suspicion of wrongdoing.

"What we encourage school administrators to do is to have a reasonable suspicion that an individual student or group of students are participating in a violation of school rules or criminal law and base their search on that," McCurdy said, offering an alternative to broad searching policies.

Absent such a clause limiting the scope of searches to those students for whom there is individualized suspicion, the ACLU has stated that the Student and Teacher Safety Act may not stand up to constitutional scrutiny.

Students in public schools are protected by the Fourth Amendment, which guarantees against unreasonable search and seizure, the United States Supreme Court ruled in 1985.

While affirming students' rights against unreasonable searches, the court's decision in *New Jersey v. T.L.O.* acknowledged that certain limits on this right are legitimate because students are minors and in the temporary custody of the state. Student searches, therefore, can be conducted without a warrant and need only be based on "probable cause."

The text of the Student and Teacher Safety Act points to the 1985 decision as justification for the bill's legitimacy. However, that decision is silent on the question of the constitutionality of conducting random searches without suspicion. In another student-search case from 2002, the Supreme Court ruled that random drug testing of students who participate in extracurricular activities was reasonable but again did not clarify whether school-wide searches constitute a violation of the Fourth Amendment.

Suspicionless Searches May Violate Students' Rights

Even though the Supreme Court has not handed down a definitive answer, ACLU representatives argue there's enough evidence to conclude that searches without individualized suspicion infringe upon students' Fourth Amendment rights. They point to court decisions, including language from *New Jersey v. T.L.O.*, which indicate that exceptions to the requirement of individualized suspicion are acceptable only when the privacy interests at stake are minimal and protections are in place to ensure the student's privacy.

Individualized suspicion also is simply good public policy, McCurdy and ACLU director Caroline Fredrickson wrote last week in a letter to the House of Representatives urging opposition to the bill.

Constitutional issues aside, the Student and Teacher Safety Act is getting mixed reviews among education associations. The largest teacher union, the National Education Association, has expressed its support, while other teachers unions, including the American Teachers Federation, have objected to the measure.

Many organizations critical of the legislation point to the increased demand the legislation would put on teachers as the primary source of their concern.

"We do not support putting teachers in that position," said Richard Iannuzzi, president of New York State United Teachers, the state's largest teachers union. "It's a role that really requires a well-trained expert, who understands both the interaction with the students and understands the law and the rights of the students."

Involving teachers in the bill would help keep drugs and violence out of schools while affirming their control of the classroom, said Rep. Geoff Davis (R-Ky.) in a press release from his congressional office.

The Role of Teachers May Be Compromised

"The teacher's role is as an educator, and the value of a good teacher-student relationship is not going to be enhanced by students viewing the teacher as a safety officer with respect to something as significant as searches," said Iannuzzi in response to this argument. "Teachers should clearly be part of making a parent and students feel that a school is a safe place to be, but taking it to what I consider to be the extreme by putting teachers in charge of searches would not be an appropriate step."

Instead, Iannuzzi proposed addressing the root social causes that compromise school safety. The bill is little more than a "diversion" from real issues, Iannuzzi suggested, churned out by mid-election-cycle politicians.

Davis, for example, is in the midst of a fight to retain his seat in Congress. Pollsters show a nearly dead-even competition with his Democratic challenger.

Election-time politics also may have motivated members of the House when they opted for a voice vote on the measure as opposed to the standard roll-call vote, which enables constituents to know how each representative voted.

"I look at it as something that's going to make its mark prior to the election process and is unlikely to follow the flow after that," Iannuzzi said of the chances this bill would also pass the Senate and eventually become law.

The bill now moves to the Senate, which has referred it to committee. The Senate did not have similar legislation on the table prior to passage in the House.

Although it abides by case law from the Supreme Court and the New York State Court of Appeals, New York's Department of Education has no state-mandated policy about student searches. Local districts are free to develop their own policies as long as they satisfy criteria established by the courts.

> "[P]ractitioners [must] seek wise av-
> enues to ensure schools are safe and
> student civil liberties are protected, es-
> pecially after a critical episode. It is
> important to bear in mind that al-
> though T.L.O. provided school officials
> considerable latitude when engaging in
> student searches, whether such latitude
> is justifiable or necessary in every disci-
> plinary incident is a decision that needs
> to be addressed on a local and case-by-
> case basis."

School Violence Has Not Negatively Affected Students' Civil Liberties

Mario S. Torres Jr. and Yihsuan Chen

*Mario S. Torres Jr. is an assistant professor of educational ad-
ministration and human resource development at Texas A&M
University. His research interests include general education law
with an interest in Fourth Amendment and administrative discretion issues. Yihsuan Chen is a doctoral candidate in educational administration at Texas A&M University whose research
interests include school leadership and school policy.*

*Mario S. Torres Jr. and Yishuan Chen examine the impact of the
1999 Columbine shooting on students' civil liberties and how
school leaders use discretion in conducting student searches.*

Mario S. Torres Jr. and Yihsuan Chen, "Assessing Columbine's Impact on Students'
Fourth Amendment Case Outcomes: Implications for Administrative Discretion and Decision Making," *National Association of Secondary School Principals, NASSP Bulletin*,
vol. 9, no. 3, September 2006, pp. 185–206. Reprinted by permission of SAGE Publications, Inc. conveyed through Copyright Clearance Center.

Their findings suggest that the Columbine school shooting had only a minor influence on court outcomes and that courts have not become more tolerant of school officials using excessive discretion.

In 1999, the Columbine High School incident spurred public and private agencies to react to a perceived crisis in schools.... Overnight, school safety evolved into a prominent issue, forcing school systems across the county to take immediate action against school violence. With the media fueling criticism that schools were inept or ill prepared to handle or prevent future incidents, schools were compelled to vamp up security to allay public fear. As a result, administering searches of students became more than a routine preventative option.

The Impact of Columbine

Columbine's impact has been profound—some calling it the "Columbine Effect." In its aftermath, the country was sensitized to school violence through multiple sources. The Clinton administration leveraged Columbine to press for greater federal gun regulation. Interest in home schooling intensified as parental concern over school safety intensified. A "Million Mom March," attracting an estimated 500,000 participants to Washington, D.C., in May 2000, called for stiffer gun control in response to Columbine....

In much the same way, violent episodes like Columbine have prompted schools to institute a variety of searches as part of the daily routine and state legislatures to enact statutes aimed at curbing crime and violence. Yet, in the midst of greater press for safety after Columbine and the U.S. Supreme Court's affirmation that "special needs" circumstances may call for greater administrative latitude, there is little agreement regarding what factors distinguish appropriate from inappropriate administrative discretion.... This study discusses the five search-related variables as they are addressed in the three

Fourth Amendment rulings, and creates a frame from which to examine case outcomes using literature associated with administrative discretion as well as excerpts from High Court rulings reflecting the study's theme that critical events like Columbine may influence how courts treat students' rights. . . . Although this study is largely exploratory, it carries significant implications for how the judicial system and schools act toward student rights after critical episodes like Columbine.

This study examines Columbine's effect on court outcomes involving the lawfulness of student searches. The intent of this study is twofold. The first part examines the degree to which the April 20, 1999, Columbine High School episode affected students' privacy interests through the court system. This section examines case outcomes before and after the event according to four key dimensions: (a) number or scope of students on a campus or district who are suspected of committing an offense (i.e., level of suspicion), (b) the number of separate searches conducted on the student(s), (c) the severity of the suspected offense, and (d) whether a history of drugs or violence in the school district factored into the court's legal reasoning. The secondary purpose of the study uses the findings to draw out implications for students' civil rights and decision making for school leaders in an era stressing greater school safety and control.

Student Searches Before and After Columbine

The scope of Fourth Amendment law in schools has been addressed in large measure in three U.S. Supreme Court cases: *New Jersey v. T.L.O.* (1985), *Vernonia v. Acton* (1995), and *Board of Education v. Earls* (2002). In *T.L.O.* (1985), the Court ruled the Fourth Amendment required schools to extend students a modicum of privacy less than that granted to the private citizen in ordinary situations. The *T.L.O.* decision provided the Fourth Amendment groundwork for two subsequent

High Court rulings: *Vernonia* and *Earls*. Both of these cases considered the constitutionality of drug testing segments of the school population, particularly athletes and students participating in extracurricular activities.

The Fourth Amendment secures citizens the right "to be secure in their persons, houses, papers, and effects, against unreasonable searches and seizures." The Fourteenth Amendment makes this amendment applicable to the states. The Supreme Court in *T.L.O.* ruled that special circumstances of public schools warrant a lesser standard of suspicion than probable cause for justification. The Court fashioned a two-pronged test requiring that searches be justified at their inception and reasonable in scope.

In *Vernonia*, the Supreme Court held that in circumstances when drug use among student athletes threatens safety and order, random drug testing of athletes could be justified. In a three-part analysis, the Court recognized that certain populations of the schools deserve a lesser expectation of privacy (e.g., student athletes) and thus should be subject to greater scrutiny. Second, the Court maintained that the manner in which a search is conducted must be relatively unobtrusive. Third, the Court determined that a severity of the need must be met. Using much of the same rationale in *Vernonia*, the Supreme Court in *Earls* broadened permissible random drug testing to all students participating in extracurricular activities (e.g., band, choir, chess club, and the Future Farmers of America).

As for *T.L.O.*, the touchstone ruling left critical issues unresolved. First, the Court sidestepped the applicability of the exclusionary rule (a rule suppressing unlawfully secured evidence) and what procedures were legally appropriate for handling evidence when presented in court. Second, the High Court offered little insight into the appropriate role of municipal police or school personnel acting in a pseudo police role in student searches. Although the *T.L.O.* Court espoused the more flexible standard of reasonable suspicion for school personnel, the opinion offered little guidance as to the appropriate standard for police or school officials acting in a law enforcement mode. Third, the ruling failed to clearly distinguish circumstances warranting individualized suspicion versus those permitting searches of groups. *Vernonia* and *Earls* would soon confirm that individualized suspicion was not an "irreducible requirement" in every instance. Last, *T.L.O.* failed to fully address student expectations of privacy related to lockers, desks, or other school property. Although courts after *T.L.O.* have recognized privacy interests of students in government-issued storage, there is little agreement across states with regard to what standard should be applied. What these issues imply then is that court rulings largely fall short of comprehensively addressing every practical consideration, and as a result, give school officials a fair degree of discretion. The following subsections give added attention to such variables used in this study.

The Relevance of Fourth Amendment Law to Schools

T.L.O. was the first U.S. Supreme Court case to argue the relevance of Fourth Amendment law to schools. The Court ruled that school officials are held to a standard of reasonableness in requiring that searches are justified at their inception and reasonable in scope. Prior to *T.L.O.*, it was commonly understood that suspicion be narrowed to the individual suspected of violating the law. Whether the same principle applied to schools was not articulated thoroughly in *T.L.O.* because only individualized suspicion was employed in *T.L.O.*'s purse search. The decision did say, however, that individualized suspicion was required but fell short of requiring its need when the "privacy interests implicated by the search [were] minimal" and precautions were in place to protect the individuals from arbitrary discretionary practices. On the whole, the *T.L.O.* ruling offered little to no guidance for searches lacking individualized suspicion.

Two subsequent Fourth Amendment rulings would partially resolve this ambiguity. In *Vernonia*, random drug testing of student athletes was ruled constitutional. In *Earls*, the scope of students that could be randomly drug tested was expanded from only student athletes to all students participating in extracurricular activities. . . .

Giving schools the necessary freedom and flexibility to maintain discipline and order was a primary objective for the *T.L.O.* majority. The Court argued that forcing school officials to obtain probable cause and secure warrants would "unduly interfere with the maintenance of the swift and informal disciplinary procedures in the schools." With regard to multiple searches, *T.L.O.* made no mention of whether reasonable suspicion was required for each subsequent search beyond the original search (e.g., administering a locker search, then a pat down, followed by a strip search). Justice Stevens in *T.L.O.*'s dissent warned that such a vague standard "[would] permit teachers and school administrators to search students when they suspect that the search will reveal evidence of even the most trivial school regulation or precatory guideline for student behavior."

Motives to search students vary widely and range in degree. The Supreme Court in *T.L.O.* held that a search is reasonable in scope "when measures adopted are reasonably related to the objectives of the search and not excessively intrusive in light of the age and sex of the student and the nature of the infraction." According to *T.L.O.*, the intent of "reasonableness" was to give school officials the power and authority to manage and sustain order and discipline through the "dictates of reason and common sense" while at the same time protecting the interests of the student. . . .

The manner by which the judicial system decides the lawfulness of searches by the level of suspicion, number of searches, and severity of the offense can tell much about what judges are accepting of when it comes to how reasonableness is reflected in practice. One might even speculate that given the scope of Columbine's impact on society, judges would be more willing to uphold the legality of searches despite considerable dissimilarities in search justification and scope. Nevertheless, none of the three opinions provides a clear and definitive framework from which to judge and determine appropriate administrative discretion. It is worth emphasizing, however, that inadequate or excessive discretion can be equally troublesome and potentially place schools legally at risk. School officials who negligently fail to act on symptoms of a potential crisis or alternatively police problems overzealously can pose equally troubling consequences. The following section explores the subject of administrative discretion in schools and why this topic deserves added attention after critical episodes like Columbine.

Administrative Discretion

Administrative discretion is complex and multifaceted. In essence, it embodies all policy implementing options or actions not encompassed or governed in formalized law or rules. Although some argue that discretion is indispensable given the complexity of modern agencies and bureaucracies, others view unchecked administrative discretion as potentially threatening to fairness and liberty if rules fail to sufficiently regulate decisions and actions. [In *The Conditions of Discretion*, J. F.] Handler, for instance, argued that although policy such as that which oversees U.S. Social Security may be easily accomplished within rigid regulatory frameworks, other policy such as special education law cannot be strictly governed by tightly controlling rules and demands a fair degree of "judgmental, professional, flexible, and experimental" choice to ensure effectiveness.

165

As for discretion and searches, studies have thoroughly investigated search discretion in the law enforcement area, and much fewer have addressed it from the school perspective. Discretion in schools has been described as largely "particularistic" and reflective of accepted "culture[s] of control." Although the research regarding discretion in student searches is relatively sparse, studies have routinely examined discretion in schools using race and culture as critical lenses to evaluate disciplinary choice and action. For instance, an analysis by [R. J.] Skiba et al. found black students were more likely to be referred to the office for more subjective reasons (e.g., disrespect, excessive noise) than objective violations (e.g., smoking, vandalism) and that discipline for black students was based more on perception than grounded facts. . . .

Current research on discretion demonstrates its puzzling and often misguided nature. Although the research in discretion will likely continue focusing on race, culture, and context, other dimensions such as deciding on the proper forum for affording justice (e.g., the traditional court versus restorative justice models) and selecting more appropriate consequences will deserve greater attention in the future. In the short term, courts will likely continue deferring to the expertise and judgment of school administrators. Whether court outcomes after Columbine seem to endorse greater discretion makes the findings of this study that much more important. In each of the three U.S. Supreme Court cases, a link is drawn between the social environment and the need for school officials to have adequate search powers and discretion. . . .

The Interests of Society

In each of the three Fourth Amendment cases, the U.S. Supreme Court has paid considerable attention to youth culture, giving considerable emphasis to dramatically changing social conditions in schools. At the very minimum, all suggest Fourth Amendment interpretation and application cannot occur in isolation from problems plaguing school youth (i.e., drugs and weapons). . . . In *T.L.O.*, the primary issue was deciding the scope of the Fourth Amendment in schools versus that for common citizens. For ordinary citizens suspected of an offense, a warrant or probable cause is required to administer a search. Ultimately, the *T.L.O.* court ruled that school officials required a less rigid, more practical standard to ensure student safety. The Court concluded that school searches should be "reasonably" justified vis-à-vis mandating school officials to act in a law enforcement capacity by gathering the necessary evidence to build a probable cause case. Aside from the technical legal challenges (e.g., students' expectation of privacy), the majority was clearly troubled by declining societal conditions in schools. In *T.L.O.*, Justice White in the majority opinion addressed the need for greater disciplinary flexibility in view of an escalating drug and violence crisis in schools:

> Maintaining order in the classroom has never been easy, but in recent years, school disorder has often taken particularly ugly forms: drug use and violent crime in the schools have become major social problems. Even in schools that have been spared the most severe disciplinary problems, the preservation of order and a proper educational environment requires close supervision of schoolchildren, as well as the enforcement of rules against conduct that would be perfectly permissible if undertaken by an adult.

This concern prefaced the Court's final determination. In a two-part test, the Court held that searches should be justified at their inception and reasonable in scope. Using "reasonableness" as a standard, the Court held that requiring probable cause would "unduly burden the efforts of school authorities to maintain order in their schools." *T.L.O.* was the first of three cornerstone cases to refer to environmental factors when deciding the extent of the Fourth Amendment in schools. It was significant for many reasons, none more important than it partially resolved issues of administrative power (e.g., *in loco parentis*) and student privacy. Yet, *T.L.O.* was equally noteworthy in its clear suggestion that environmental factors cannot be ignored when deliberating the limits of the Fourth Amendment.

As alluded to earlier, *T.L.O.* provided the framework for two subsequent High Court rulings related to the Fourth Amendment in schools: *Vernonia* and *Earls.* Because the two cases dealt directly with the constitutionality of drug testing in schools, the current youth culture in schools was established as an overriding concern. In *Vernonia,* for instance, Justice Scalia wrote in the majority opinion that the compelling interest of the Immigration and Naturalization Service (INS) in randomly drug screening customs agents is no different than schools interested in eliminating the drug influence. Justice Scalia moreover suggests a societal aim is met through instituting drug testing, particularly among student athletes:

> The effects of a drug-infested school are visited not just upon the users, but upon the entire student body and faculty, as the educational process is disrupted. In the present case, moreover, the necessity for the State to act is magnified by the fact that this evil is being visited not just upon individuals at large, but upon children for whom it has undertaken a special responsibility of care and direction.

Here again, the majority of the Court addressed the potential for a widespread crisis if drug use among a segment of the student population is permitted to continue sans [without] government intervention (i.e., athletes). Although acknowledging the "physical, psychological, and addictive effects of drugs" the Court using no uncertain terms held that the Fourth Amendment "imposed no irreducible requirement of individualized suspicion to justify a search by the government." The message was clear that mass suspicionless searches (i.e., searches lacking individualized suspicious of wrongdoing) fulfilled an important societal purpose.

Whereas *Vernonia* involved drug testing of student athletes, a Supreme Court ruling seven years later would decide the constitutionality of randomly drug testing students participating in extracurricular activities. In *Earls*, Justice Thomas writing for the majority addressed the immediate need for state action in confronting a drug dilemma in schools still evident today. As Justice Thomas contended. "The health and safety risks identified in *Vernonia* apply with equal force to Tecumseh's children. Indeed, the nationwide drug epidemic makes the war against drugs a pressing concern in every school".

As in the two prior rulings, the Court held that school officials be extended the power to counter elements that pose a threat to school safety. The majority hesitated to issue a "constitutional quantum" or a rigid standard to indicate when a lawful necessity for drug testing was met. It opted to allow school districts to make that determination. A statement in the *Earls* ruling captures the considerable emphasis given to the larger societal mission in justifying more intrusive administrative action. Justice Thomas declared that "given the nationwide epidemic of drug use, and the evidence of increased drug use in Tecumseh schools, it [is] entirely reasonable for the school district to enact [such a] drug testing policy."

On the whole, the three rulings confirm that the lawfulness of the search represented only one piece of the final holding. The realization that environmental factors affect legal outcomes raises critical questions about the proper role of courts, appropriate administrative discretion in decisions and actions, and the treatment of students' rights across different settings. Uncertain case law, the court's alertness and sympathetic posture toward problematic student trends, and the emotional nature of Columbine together appear to invite greater administrative discretion in an albeit subtle way....

The Need to Balance Safety and Privacy

Although the findings suggest courts are not influenced by a critical episode like Columbine, civil liberties are far from absolute and could be altered by environmental influences at any time. In such cases, student rights are unsettled and perhaps less respected and honored. Therefore, more attention should be placed on cultivating leadership that ethically balances the safety interests of the school and of the privacy interest of the student. Policy makers should be more mindful of the unintended consequences of critical incidents and be overly cautious when designing policy that may potentially undermine students' privacy rights. Although political pressure may in some way necessitate tougher approaches to student discipline, case law should be carefully reviewed and followed.

This study also reminds practitioners to seek wise avenues to ensure schools are safe and student civil liberties are protected, especially after a critical episode. It is important to bear in mind that although *T.L.O.* provided school officials considerable latitude when engaging in student searches, whether such latitude is justifiable or necessary in every disciplinary incident is a decision that needs to be addressed on a local and case-by-case basis. To prevent inappropriate forms of discretion, local educational agencies and schools should carefully design and word policy so that it explains what circumstances warrant, for instance, searches of classrooms, and specifies what type of search actions are permissible or impermissible (e.g., locker searches versus strip searches of entire classes).

Campus leaders, at minimum, should apprise the faculty of the legal restrictions and also be extra diligent in monitoring the degree to which student race and culture affect search decisions and outcomes. Toward this end, future studies should examine the impact of school and community characteristics on search and seizure discretion and case outcomes. Other studies may also assess the relationship between practitioner knowledge of case law and school leader perceptions of appropriate and inappropriate discretion. By providing stakeholders with a greater awareness of the complex nature of privacy and discretion, the likelihood is greater for socially just policy and practice.

CHAPTER 4

Death Penalty for Juvenile Offenders Is Cruel and Unusual Punishment

Case Overview

Roper v. Simmons (2005)

In 1993, Christopher Simmons, then seventeen years old, broke into Shirley Crook's home, robbed her, tied her up, and tossed her off a bridge in a Missouri state park. Simmons had recruited two younger friends, but one friend, John Tessmer, backed out at the last minute.

At trial, Simmons confessed to the murder. Strong evidence of premeditation existed, as Tessmer testified that Simmons had discussed the plot in advance and then bragged about the murder. Even considering such mitigating factors as his youth, lack of prior criminal history, and troubled background, the jury recommended the death penalty. Citing ineffective counsel, Simmons moved to set aside the conviction and sentence. After the trial court rejected his motion, Simmons appealed.

At each step of the appeal, the courts continued to uphold the death penalty sentence. Almost ten years later, in 2002, the Supreme Court overturned the death penalty for mentally disabled offenders in *Atkins v. Virginia*. After the U.S. Supreme Court ruled that executing the mentally retarded violated the Eighth and Fourteenth Amendment prohibitions on cruel and unusual punishment, because a majority of Americans found it cruel and unusual, the Missouri Supreme Court decided to reconsider Simmons' case.

Using the reasoning from the *Atkins* case, the Missouri court decided, six to three, that the U.S. Supreme Court's 1989 decision in *Stanford v. Kentucky*, which held that executing minors was not unconstitutional, was no longer valid. The opinion in *Stanford v. Kentucky* had relied on a finding that a majority of Americans did not consider the execution of minors to be cruel and unusual. The Missouri court noted that subsequent laws had limited the scope of the death penalty and that a majority of Americans now opposed the execution of juveniles; the court held that such executions were now unconstitutional.

The State of Missouri appealed the decision to the U.S. Supreme Court, which agreed to hear the case. *Roper v. Simmons* (2005) (Donald P. Roper was the superintendent of the correctional facility where Simmons was held), argued that allowing a state court to overturn a Supreme Court decision by looking at "evolving standards of decency" would be dangerous, because state courts could just as easily decide that executions prohibited by the Supreme Court (such as the execution of the mentally disabled in *Atkins v. Virginia*) were now permissible due to a change in the beliefs of the American people.

In a five to four decision, the U.S. Supreme Court upheld the Missouri Supreme Court's ruling, declaring it unconstitutional to impose capital punishment for crimes committed while under the age of eighteen. Writing for the majority opinion, Anthony Kennedy maintained that standards of decency have evolved so that executing minors is "cruel and unusual punishment" prohibited by the Eighth Amendment. The majority cited a consensus against the juvenile death penalty among state legislatures, and its own determination that the death penalty is a disproportionate punishment for minors. Finally the Court pointed to "overwhelming" international opinion against the juvenile death penalty.

> *"The differences between juvenile and adult offenders are too marked and well understood to risk allowing a youthful person to receive the death penalty despite insufficient culpability."*

The Court's Decision: Standards of Decency Insist That the Death Penalty for Juveniles Constitutes Cruel and Unusual Punishment

Anthony M. Kennedy

Anthony M. Kennedy (b. 1936) was appointed to the Supreme Court in 1988 by President Ronald Reagan after the Senate rejected Reagan's first nomination, Robert Bork. A generally conservative justice, Kennedy eschews sweeping conclusions and takes a case-by-case approach to judicial decisions. He has generally voted to restrict the use of the death penalty; in Atkins v. Virginia *and* Roper v. Simmons, *he held that it was unconstitutional to execute the mentally ill and those under eighteen at the time of the crime.*

Roper v. Simmons *involves Christopher Simmons, who, with one acquaintance, broke into the home of Shirley Crook, bound and gagged her, drove her to a state park, and threw her from a bridge, causing her to drown. Simmons was seventeen years old when the crime was committed. Writing the majority opinion, Kennedy argues that under the "evolving standards of decency"*

Anthony Kennedy, majority opinion, *Roper v. Simmons*, U.S. Supreme Court, 2005.

test, it is cruel and unusual punishment to execute a person who was under the age of eighteen at the time of the murder. Citing sociological and scientific research that found that juveniles lack the maturity and judgment of adults, as well as laws prohibiting juveniles from voting, serving on juries, or marrying without parental consent, he notes that a national and international consensus against executing juveniles had developed over the past twenty years. The Court's decision in Roper v. Simmons *overturned its previous ruling in* Stanford v. Kentucky.*

This case requires us to address, for the second time in a decade and a half, whether it is permissible under the Eighth and Fourteenth Amendments to the Constitution of the United States to execute a juvenile offender who was older than fifteen but younger than eighteen when he committed a capital crime. In *Stanford v. Kentucky* (1989), a divided Court rejected the proposition that the Constitution bars capital punishment for juvenile offenders in this age group. We reconsider the question.

At the age of seventeen, when he was still a junior in high school, Christopher Simmons, the respondent here, committed murder. About nine months later, after he had turned eighteen, he was tried and sentenced to death. There is little doubt that Simmons was the instigator of the crime. Before its commission, Simmons said he wanted to murder someone. In chilling, callous terms he talked about his plan, discussing it for the most part with two friends, Charles Benjamin and John Tessmer, then aged fifteen and sixteen respectively. Simmons proposed to commit burglary and murder by breaking and entering, tying up a victim, and throwing the victim off a bridge. Simmons assured his friends they could "get away with it" because they were minors. . . .

Simmons and Benjamin entered the home of the victim, Shirley Crook, after reaching through an open window and unlocking the back door. . . .

Using duct tape to cover her eyes and mouth and bind her hands, the two perpetrators put Mrs. Crook in her minivan and drove to a state park. They reinforced the bindings, covered her head with a towel, and walked her to a railroad trestle spanning the Meramec River. There they tied her hands and feet together with electrical wire, wrapped her whole face in duct tape, and threw her from the bridge, drowning her in the waters below. . . .

The next day, after receiving information of Simmons' involvement, police arrested him at his high school and took him to the police station in Fenton, Missouri. They read him his *Miranda* rights. Simmons waived his right to an attorney and agreed to answer questions. After less than two hours of interrogation, Simmons confessed to the murder and agreed to perform a videotaped reenactment at the crime scene.

The State charged Simmons with burglary, kidnapping, stealing, and murder in the first degree. As Simmons was seventeen at the time of the crime, he was outside the criminal jurisdiction of Missouri's juvenile court system. He was tried as an adult. . . .

Seeking the Death Penalty for a Brutal Murder

The State sought the death penalty. As aggravating factors, the State submitted that the murder was committed for the purpose of receiving money; was committed for the purpose of avoiding, interfering with, or preventing lawful arrest of the defendant; and involved depravity of mind and was outrageously and wantonly vile, horrible, and inhuman. The State called Shirley Crook's husband, daughter, and two sisters, who presented moving evidence of the devastation her death had brought to their lives. . . .

The jury recommended the death penalty after finding the State had proved each of the three aggravating factors submitted to it. Accepting the jury's recommendation, the trial judge imposed the death penalty. . . .

After these proceedings in Simmons' case had run their course, this Court held that the Eighth and Fourteenth Amendments prohibit the execution of a mentally retarded person. Simmons filed a new petition for state postconviction relief, arguing that the reasoning of *Atkins* [*v. Virginia* (2002)] established that the Constitution prohibits the execution of a juvenile who was under eighteen when the crime was committed.

The Missouri Supreme Court agreed. It held that. . .

> a national consensus has developed against the execution of juvenile offenders, as demonstrated by the fact that eighteen states now bar such executions for juveniles, that twelve other states bar executions altogether, that no state has lowered its age of execution below eighteen since *Stanford* [*v. Kentucky* (1989),] five states have legislatively or by case law raised or established the minimum age at eighteen, and that the imposition of the juvenile death penalty has become truly unusual over the last decade.

On this reasoning it set aside Simmons' death sentence and resentenced him to "life imprisonment without eligibility for probation, parole, or release except by act of the Governor."

We granted certiorari, and now affirm.

Evolving Standards of Decency

The Eighth Amendment provides: "Excessive bail shall not be required, nor excessive fines imposed, nor cruel and unusual punishments inflicted." The provision is applicable to the States through the Fourteenth Amendment. As the Court explained in *Atkins*, the Eighth Amendment guarantees individuals the right not to be subjected to excessive sanctions. The right flows from the basic "precept of justice that punishment for crime should be graduated and proportioned to [the] offense." By protecting even those convicted of heinous crimes, the Eighth Amendment reaffirms the duty of the government to respect the dignity of all persons.

The prohibition against "cruel and unusual punishments," like other expansive language in the Constitution, must be interpreted according to its text, by considering history, tradition, and precedent, and with due regard for its purpose and function in the constitutional design. . . .

[In *Atkins v. Virginia* (2002),] we held that standards of decency have evolved since *Penry* [*Penry v. Lynaugh* (1989)] and now demonstrate that the execution of the mentally retarded is cruel and unusual punishment. The Court noted objective indicia of society's standards, as expressed in legislative enactments and state practice with respect to executions of the mentally retarded. When *Atkins* was decided only a minority of States permitted the practice, and even in those States it was rare. On the basis of these indicia the Court determined that executing mentally retarded offenders "has become truly unusual, and it is fair to say that a national consensus has developed against it."

The inquiry into our society's evolving standards of decency did not end there. The *Atkins* Court neither repeated nor relied upon the statement in *Stanford* [*v. Kentucky* (1989)] that the Court's independent judgment has no bearing on the acceptability of a particular punishment under the Eighth Amendment. Instead we returned to the rule, established in decisions predating *Stanford*, that "the Constitution contemplates that in the end our own judgment will be brought to bear on the question of the acceptability of the death penalty under the Eighth Amendment" [quoting *Coker v. Georgia* (1977)]. Mental retardation, the Court said, diminishes personal culpability even if the offender can distinguish right from wrong. The impairments of mentally retarded offenders make it less defensible to impose the death penalty as retribution for past crimes and less likely that the death penalty will have a real deterrent effect. Based on these considerations and on the finding of national consensus against executing the mentally retarded, the Court ruled that the death penalty constitutes an excessive sanction for the entire category of mentally retarded offenders, and that the Eighth Amendment "'places a substantive restriction on the State's power to take the life' of a mentally retarded offender" [quoting *Ford v. Wainwright* (1986)]. . . .

A National Consensus Against the Death Penalty for Juveniles

The evidence of national consensus against the death penalty for juveniles is similar, and in some respects parallel, to the evidence *Atkins* held sufficient to demonstrate a national consensus against the death penalty for the mentally retarded. When *Atkins* was decided, thirty states prohibited the death penalty for the mentally retarded. This number comprised twelve that had abandoned the death penalty altogether, and eighteen that maintained it but excluded the mentally retarded from its reach. By a similar calculation in this case, thirty states prohibit the juvenile death penalty, comprising twelve that have rejected the death penalty altogether and eighteen that maintain it but, by express provision or judicial interpretation, exclude juveniles from its reach. *Atkins* emphasized that even in the twenty states without formal prohibition, the practice of executing the mentally retarded was infrequent. Since *Penry*, only five states had executed offenders known to have an IQ under seventy. In the present case, too, even in the twenty states without a formal prohibition on executing juveniles, the practice is infrequent. Since *Stanford*, six states have executed prisoners for crimes committed as juveniles. In the past ten years, only three have done so: Oklahoma, Texas, and Virginia. In December 2003, the Governor of Kentucky decided to spare the life of Kevin Stanford, and commuted his sentence to one of life imprisonment without parole, with the declaration that "[w]e ought not be executing people who, legally, were children." By this act, the Governor ensured Kentucky would not add itself to the list of states that have executed juveniles within the last ten years even by the execution of the very defendant whose death sentence the Court had upheld in *Stanford v. Kentucky.*

There is, to be sure, at least one difference between the evidence of consensus in *Atkins* and in this case. Impressive in *Atkins* was the rate of abolition of the death penalty for the mentally retarded. Sixteen states that permitted the execution of the mentally retarded at the time of *Penry* had prohibited the practice by the time we heard *Atkins.* By contrast, the rate of change in reducing the incidence of the juvenile death penalty, or in taking specific steps to abolish it, has been slower. Five states that allowed the juvenile death penalty at the time of *Stanford* have abandoned it in the intervening fifteen years—four through legislative enactments and one through judicial decision. . . .

The slower pace of abolition of the juvenile death penalty over the past fifteen years, moreover, may have a simple explanation. When we heard *Penry*, only two death penalty states had already prohibited the execution of the mentally retarded. When we heard *Stanford*, by contrast, twelve death penalty states had already prohibited the execution of any juvenile under eighteen, and fifteen had prohibited the execution of any juvenile under seventeen. If anything, this shows that the impropriety of executing juveniles between sixteen and eighteen years of age gained wide recognition earlier than the impropriety of executing the mentally retarded. In the words of the Missouri Supreme Court: "It would be the ultimate in irony if the very fact that the inappropriateness of the death penalty for juveniles was broadly recognized sooner than it was recognized for the mentally retarded were to become a reason to continue the execution of juveniles now that the execution of the mentally retarded has been barred." . . .

As in *Atkins*, the objective indicia of consensus in this case—the rejection of the juvenile death penalty in the majority of states; the infrequency of its use even where it remains on the books; and the consistency in the trend toward abolition of the practice—provide sufficient evidence that today our society views juveniles, in the words *Atkins* used respecting the mentally retarded, as "categorically less culpable than the average criminal."

The Diminished Capacity of Juveniles

A majority of states have rejected the imposition of the death penalty on juvenile offenders under eighteen, and we now hold this is required by the Eighth Amendment.

Because the death penalty is the most severe punishment, the Eighth Amendment applies to it with special force. Capital punishment must be limited to those offenders who commit "a narrow category of the most serious crimes" and whose extreme culpability makes them "the most deserving of execution." This principle is implemented throughout the capital sentencing process. States must give narrow and precise definition to the aggravating factors that can result in a capital sentence. In any capital case, a defendant has wide latitude to raise as a mitigating factor "any aspect of [his or her] character or record and any of the circumstances of the offense that the defendant proffers as a basis for a sentence less than death." There are a number of crimes that beyond question are severe in absolute terms, yet the death penalty may not be imposed for their commission. The death penalty may not be imposed on certain classes of offenders, such as juveniles under sixteen, the insane, and the mentally retarded, no matter how heinous the crime. These rules vindicate the underlying principle that the death penalty is reserved for a narrow category of crimes and offenders.

Three general differences between juveniles under eighteen and adults demonstrate that juvenile offenders cannot with reliability be classified among the worst offenders. First, as any parent knows and as the scientific and sociological studies respondent and his *amici* cite tend to confirm, "[a] lack of maturity and an underdeveloped sense of responsibility are found in youth more often than in adults and are more understandable among the young. These qualities often result in impetuous and ill-considered actions and decisions." It has been noted that "adolescents are overrepresented statistically in virtually every category of reckless behavior." In recognition of the comparative immaturity and irresponsibility of juveniles, almost every state prohibits those under eighteen years of age from voting, serving on juries, or marrying without parental consent.

The second area of difference is that juveniles are more vulnerable or susceptible to negative influences and outside pressures, including peer pressure. This is explained in part by the prevailing circumstance that juveniles have less control, or less experience with control, over their own environment.

The third broad difference is that the character of a juvenile is not as well formed as that of an adult. The personality traits of juveniles are more transitory, less fixed.

These differences render suspect any conclusion that a juvenile falls among the worst offenders. The susceptibility of juveniles to immature and irresponsible behavior means "their irresponsible conduct is not as morally reprehensible as that of an adult." *Thompson* [*v. Oklahoma* (1988)], *supra*, at 835 (plurality opinion). Their own vulnerability and comparative lack of control over their immediate surroundings mean juveniles have a greater claim than adults to be forgiven for failing to escape negative influences in their whole environment. The reality that juveniles still struggle to define their identity means it is less supportable to conclude that even a heinous crime committed by a juvenile is evidence of irretrievably depraved character. From a moral standpoint it would be misguided to equate the failings of a minor with those of an adult, for a greater possibility exists that a minor's character deficiencies will be reformed. Indeed, "[t]he relevance of youth as a mitigating factor derives from the fact that the signature qualities of youth are transient, as individuals mature, the impetuousness and recklessness that may dominate in younger years can subside." *Johnson* [*v. Texas* (1993)], *supra*, at 368. . . .

Deterrence and Retribution

Once the diminished culpability of juveniles is recognized, it is evident that the penological justifications for the death penalty apply to them with lesser force than to adults. We have held there are two distinct social purposes served by the death penalty "'retribution and deterrence of capital crimes by prospective offenders.'" As for retribution, we remarked in *Atkins* that "[i]f the culpability of the average murderer is insufficient to justify the most extreme sanction available to the state, the lesser culpability of the mentally retarded offender surely does not merit that form of retribution." The same conclusions follow from the lesser culpability of the juvenile offender. Whether viewed as an attempt to express the community's moral outrage or as an attempt to right the balance for the wrong to the victim, the case for retribution is not as strong with a minor as with an adult. Retribution is not proportional if the law's most severe penalty is imposed on one whose culpability or blameworthiness is diminished, to a substantial degree, by reason of youth and immaturity.

As for deterrence, it is unclear whether the death penalty has a significant or even measurable deterrent effect on juveniles, as counsel for the petitioner acknowledged at oral argument. . . . Here, however, the absence of evidence of deterrent effect is of special concern because the same characteristics that render juveniles less culpable than adults suggest as well that juveniles will be less susceptible to deterrence. In particular, as the plurality observed in *Thompson*, "[t]he likelihood that the teenage offender has made the kind of cost-benefit analysis that attaches any weight to the possibility of execution is so remote as to be virtually nonexistent." To the extent the juvenile death penalty might have residual deterrent effect, it is worth noting that the punishment of life imprisonment without the possibility of parole is itself a severe sanction, in particular for a young person.

In concluding that neither retribution nor deterrence provides adequate justification for imposing the death penalty on juvenile offenders, we cannot deny or overlook the brutal crimes too many juvenile offenders have committed. Certainly it can be argued, although we by no means concede the point, that a rare case might arise in which a juvenile offender has sufficient psychological maturity, and at the same time demonstrates sufficient depravity, to merit a sentence of death. . . . Given this Court's own insistence on individualized consideration, petitioner maintains that it is both arbitrary and unnecessary to adopt a categorical rule barring imposition of the death penalty on any offender under eighteen years of age.

We disagree. The differences between juvenile and adult offenders are too marked and well understood to risk allowing a youthful person to receive the death penalty despite insufficient culpability. An unacceptable likelihood exists that the brutality or cold-blooded nature of any particular crime would overpower mitigating arguments based on youth as a matter of course, even where the juvenile offender's objective immaturity, vulnerability, and lack of true depravity should require a sentence less severe than death. In some cases a defendant's youth may even be counted against him.

It is difficult even for expert psychologists to differentiate between the juvenile offender whose crime reflects unfortunate yet transient immaturity, and the rare juvenile offender whose crime reflects irreparable corruption. As we understand it, this difficulty underlies the rule forbidding psychiatrists from diagnosing any patient under eighteen as having antisocial personality disorder, a disorder also referred to as psychopathy or sociopathy, and which is characterized by callousness, cynicism, and contempt for the feelings, rights, and suffering of others. If trained psychiatrists with the advantage of clinical testing and observation refrain, despite diagnostic expertise, from assessing any juvenile under eighteen as having antisocial personality disorder, we conclude that states should refrain from asking jurors to issue a far graver condemnation—that a juvenile offender merits the death penalty. When a juvenile offender commits a heinous crime, the state can exact forfeiture of some of the most basic liberties, but the state cannot extinguish his life and his potential to attain a mature understanding of his own humanity.

Drawing the line at eighteen years of age is subject, of course, to the objections always raised against categorical rules. The qualities that distinguish juveniles from adults do not disappear when an individual turns eighteen. By the same token, some under eighteen have already attained a level of maturity some adults will never reach. For the reasons we have discussed, however, a line must be drawn. The plurality opinion in *Thompson* drew the line at sixteen. In the intervening years the *Thompson* plurality's conclusion that offenders under sixteen may not be executed has not been challenged. The logic of *Thompson* extends to those who are under eighteen. The age of eighteen is the point where society draws the line for many purposes between childhood and adulthood. It is, we conclude, the age at which the line for death eligibility ought to rest. . . .

The Court of World Opinion

Our determination that the death penalty is disproportionate punishment for offenders under eighteen finds confirmation in the stark reality that the United States is the only country in the world that continues to give official sanction to the juvenile death penalty. This reality does not become controlling, for the task of interpreting the Eighth Amendment remains our responsibility. Yet at least from the time of the Court's decision in *Trop* [*v. Dulles* (1958)] the Court has referred to the laws of other countries and to international authorities as instructive for its interpretation of the Eighth Amendment's prohibition of "cruel and unusual punishments." . . .

. . . Article 37 of the United Nations Convention on the Rights of the Child, which every country in the world has ratified save for the United States and Somalia, contains an express prohibition on capital punishment for crimes committed by juveniles under eighteen. No ratifying country has entered a reservation to the provision prohibiting the execution of juvenile offenders Parallel prohibitions are contained in other significant international covenants. . . .

Only seven countries other than the United States have executed juvenile offenders since 1990: Iran, Pakistan, Saudi Arabia, Yemen, Nigeria, the Democratic Republic of Congo, and China. Since then, each of these countries has either abolished capital punishment for juveniles or made public disavowal of the practice. In sum, it is fair to say that the United States now stands alone in a world that has turned its face against the juvenile death penalty.

Though the international covenants prohibiting the juvenile death penalty are of more recent date, it is instructive to note that the United Kingdom abolished the juvenile death penalty before these covenants came into being. The United Kingdom's experience bears particular relevance here in light of the historic ties between our countries and in light of the Eighth Amendment's own origins. The Amendment was modeled on a parallel provision in the English Declaration of Rights of 1689, which provided: "[E]xcessive bail ought not to be required nor excessive fines imposed; nor cruel and unusuall punishments inflicted." . . .

It is proper that we acknowledge the overwhelming weight of international opinion against the juvenile death penalty, resting in large part on the understanding that the instability and emotional imbalance of young people may often be a factor in the crime. The opinion of the world community, while not controlling our outcome, does provide respected and significant confirmation for our own conclusions.

Over time, from one generation to the next, the Constitution has come to earn the high respect and even, as Madison dared to hope, the veneration of the American people. The document sets forth, and rests upon, innovative principles original to the American experience, such as federalism; a proven balance in political mechanisms through separation of powers; specific guarantees for the accused in criminal cases; and broad provisions to secure individual freedom and preserve human dignity. These doctrines and guarantees are central to the American experience and remain essential to our present-day self-definition and national identity. Not the least of the reasons we honor the Constitution, then, is because we know it to be our own. It does not lessen our fidelity to the Constitution or our pride in its origins to acknowledge that the express affirmation of certain fundamental rights by other nations and peoples simply underscores the centrality of those same rights within our own heritage of freedom.

The Eighth and Fourteenth Amendments forbid imposition of the death penalty on offenders who were under the age of eighteen when their crimes were committed. The judgment of the Missouri Supreme Court, setting aside the sentence of death imposed upon Christopher Simmons, is affirmed.

> "The age-based line drawn by the Court
> is indefensibly arbitrary—it quite likely
> will protect a number of offenders who
> are mature enough to deserve the death
> penalty."

Dissenting Opinion: The Death Penalty Should Apply to Juveniles

Sandra Day O'Connor

*Sandra Day O'Connor (b. 1930) was the first woman to be ap-
pointed to the Supreme Court. After graduating with honors
from Stanford Law School, where she served on Law Review, she
found that no law firm wanted to hire her except as a legal sec-
retary, so she accepted a job in public service and then started
her own law firm and became active in the Republican Party.
Before becoming a judge in 1974, O'Connor served briefly in the
U.S. Senate. President Ronald Reagan appointed her to the Supreme Court in 1981 to replace Potter Stewart, who had retired.
O'Connor herself retired in 2006.*

*Sandra Day O'Connor argues that some juveniles are mature
enough to understand the severity of their crimes and are therefore as culpable as adults are. Thus, she concludes, categorically
excluding all juveniles from the death penalty is wrong. The case
of* Roper v. Simmons *involves Christopher Simmons who, at the
age of seventeen, committed murder. He was found guilty and
sentenced to death, but his sentence was reduced to life imprisonment by the Missouri Supreme Court.*

Sandra Day O'Connor, dissenting opinion, *Roper v. Simmons*, U.S. Supreme Court,
2005.

The Court's decision today establishes a categorical rule forbidding the execution of any offender for any crime committed before his eighteenth birthday, no matter how deliberate, wanton, or cruel the offense. Neither the objective evidence of contemporary societal values, nor the Court's moral proportionality analysis, nor the two in tandem suffice to justify this ruling.

Although the Court finds support for its decision in the fact that a majority of the states now disallow capital punishment of 17-year-old offenders, it refrains from asserting that its holding is compelled by a genuine national consensus. Indeed, the evidence before us fails to demonstrate conclusively that any such consensus has emerged in the brief period since we upheld the constitutionality of this practice in *Stanford v. Kentucky* (1989).

Instead, the rule decreed by the Court rests, ultimately, on its independent moral judgment that death is a disproportionately severe punishment for any 17-year-old offender. I do not subscribe to this judgment. Adolescents *as a class* are undoubtedly less mature, and therefore, less culpable for their misconduct, than adults. But the Court has adduced no evidence impeaching the seemingly reasonable conclusion reached by many state legislatures that at least *some* 17-year-old murderers are sufficiently mature to deserve the death penalty in an appropriate case. Nor has it been shown that capital sentencing juries are incapable of accurately assessing a youthful defendant's maturity or of giving due weight to the mitigating characteristics associated with youth. . . .

The Differences Between Adults and Juveniles

Seventeen-year-old murderers must be categorically exempted from capital punishment, the Court says, because they "cannot with reliability be classified among the worst offenders." That conclusion is premised on three perceived differences between "adults," who have already reached their eighteenth birthdays, and "juveniles," who have not. First, juveniles lack maturity and responsibility and are more reckless than adults. Second, juveniles are more vulnerable to outside influences because they have less control over their surroundings. And third, a juvenile's character is not as fully formed as that of an adult. Based on these characteristics, the Court determines that 17-year-old capital murderers are not as blameworthy as adults guilty of similar crimes; that 17-year-olds are less likely than adults to be deterred by the prospect of a death sentence; and that it is difficult to conclude that a 17-year-old who commits even the most heinous of crimes is "irretrievably depraved." The Court suggests that "a rare case might arise in which a juvenile offender has sufficient psychological maturity, and at the same time demonstrates sufficient depravity, to merit a sentence of death." However, the Court argues that a categorical age-based prohibition is justified as a prophylactic rule because "[t]he differences between juvenile and adult offenders are too marked and well understood to risk allowing a youthful person to receive the death penalty despite insufficient culpability". . .

The Court adduces no evidence whatsoever in support of its sweeping conclusion, that it is only in "rare" cases, if ever, that 17-year-old murderers are sufficiently mature and act with sufficient depravity to warrant the death penalty. The fact that juveniles are generally *less* culpable for their misconduct than adults does not necessarily mean that a 17-year-old murderer cannot be *sufficiently* culpable to merit the death penalty. At most, the Court's argument suggests that the average 17-year-old murderer is not as culpable as the average adult murderer. But an especially depraved juvenile offender may nevertheless be just as culpable as many adult offenders considered bad enough to deserve the death penalty. Similarly, the fact that the availability of the death penalty may be *less* likely to deter a juvenile from committing a capital crime does not imply that this threat cannot *effectively* deter some 17-year-olds from such an act. Surely there is an age below which no offender, no matter what his crime, can be deemed to have the cognitive or emotional maturity necessary to warrant the death penalty. But at least at the margins between adolescence and adulthood—and especially for 17-year-olds such as respondent—the relevant differences between "adults" and "juveniles" appear to be a matter of degree, rather than of kind. It follows that a legislature may reasonably conclude that at least *some* 17-year-olds can act with sufficient moral culpability, and can be sufficiently deterred by the threat of execution, that capital punishment may be warranted in an appropriate case.

Simmons' Crime

Indeed, this appears to be just such a case. Christopher Simmons' murder of Shirley Crook was premeditated, wanton, and cruel in the extreme. Well before he committed this crime, Simmons declared that he wanted to kill someone. On several occasions, he discussed with two friends (ages fifteen and sixteen) his plan to burglarize a house and to murder the victim by tying the victim up and pushing him from a bridge. Simmons said they could "'get away with it'" because they were minors. In accord with this plan, Simmons and his 15-year-old accomplice broke into Mrs. Crook's home in the middle of the night, forced her from her bed, bound her, and drove her to a state park. There, they walked her to a railroad trestle spanning a river, "hog-tied" her with electrical cable, bound her face completely with duct tape, and pushed her, still alive, from the trestle. She drowned in the water below. One can scarcely imagine the terror that this woman must have suffered throughout the ordeal leading to her death. Whatever can be said about the comparative moral culpability of 17-year-olds as a general matter, Simmons' actions unquestionably reflect "'a consciousness materially more "depraved" than that of' . . . the average murderer." And Simmons' prediction that he could murder with impunity because he had not yet turned eighteen—though inaccurate—suggests that he *did* take into account the perceived risk of punishment in deciding whether to commit the crime. Based on this evidence, the sentencing jury certainly had reasonable grounds for concluding that, despite Simmons' youth, he "ha[d] sufficient psychological maturity" when he committed this horrific murder, and "at the same time demonstrate[d] sufficient depravity, to merit a sentence of death."

Chronological Age Not an Unfailing Measure

The Court's proportionality argument suffers from a second and closely related defect: It fails to establish that the differences in maturity between 17-year-olds and young "adults" are both universal enough and significant enough to justify a bright-line prophylactic rule against capital punishment of the former. The Court's analysis is premised on differences *in the aggregate* between juveniles and adults, which frequently do not hold true when comparing individuals. Although it may be that many 17-year-old murderers lack sufficient maturity to deserve the death penalty, some juvenile murderers may be quite mature. Chronological age is not an unfailing measure of psychological development, and common experience suggests that many 17-year-olds are more mature than the average young "adult." In short, the class of offenders exempted from capital punishment by today's decision is too broad and too diverse to warrant a categorical prohibition. Indeed, the age-based line drawn by the Court is indefensibly arbitrary— quite likely will protect a number of offenders who are mature enough to deserve the death penalty and may well leave vulnerable many who are not. . . .

Moreover, it defies common sense to suggest that 17-year-olds as a class are somehow equivalent to mentally retarded persons with regard to culpability or susceptibility to deterrence. Seventeen-year-olds may, on average, be less mature than adults, but that lesser maturity simply cannot be equated with the major, lifelong impairments suffered by the mentally retarded.

Individual Sentencing Decisions Are More Appropriate

The proportionality issues raised by the Court clearly implicate Eighth Amendment concerns. But these concerns may properly be addressed not by means of an arbitrary, categorical age-based rule, but rather through individualized sentencing in which juries are required to give appropriate mitigating weight to the defendant's immaturity, his susceptibility to outside pressures, his cognizance of the consequences of his actions, and so forth. In that way the constitutional response can be tailored to the specific problem it is meant to remedy. The Eighth Amendment guards against the execution of those who are "insufficiently culpable," in significant part, by requiring sentencing that "reflect[s] a reasoned *moral* response to the defendant's background, character, and crime." *California v. Brown* (1987). Accordingly, the sentencer in a capital case must be permitted to give full effect to all constitutionally relevant mitigating evidence.

Although the prosecutor's apparent attempt to use respondent's youth as an aggravating circumstance in this case is troubling, that conduct was never challenged with specificity in the lower courts and is not directly at issue here. As the Court itself suggests, such "overreaching" would best be addressed, if at all, through a more narrowly tailored remedy. The Court argues that sentencing juries cannot accurately evaluate a youthful offender's maturity or give appropriate weight to the mitigating characteristics related to youth. But, again, the Court presents no real evidence—and the record appears to contain none—supporting this claim. Perhaps more importantly, the Court fails to explain why this duty should be so different from, or so much more difficult than, that of assessing and giving proper effect to any other qualitative capital sentencing factor. I would not be so quick to conclude that the constitutional safeguards, the sentencing juries, and the trial judges upon which we place so much reliance in all capital cases, are inadequate in this narrow context. . . .

Applicability of the Eighth Amendment

In determining whether the Eighth Amendment permits capital punishment of a particular offense or class of offenders, we must look to whether such punishment is consistent with contemporary standards of decency. We are obligated to weigh both the objective evidence of societal values and our own judgment as to whether death is an excessive sanction in the context at hand. In the instant case, the objective evidence is inconclusive; standing alone, it does not demonstrate that our society has repudiated capital punishment of 17-year-old offenders in all cases. Rather, the actions of the nation's legislatures suggest that, although a clear and durable national consensus against this practice may in time emerge, that day has yet to arrive. By acting so soon after our decision in *Stanford*, the Court both pre-empts the democratic debate through which genuine consensus might develop and simultaneously runs a considerable risk of inviting lower court reassessments of our Eighth Amendment precedents.

To be sure, the objective evidence supporting today's decision is similar to (though marginally weaker than) the evidence before the Court in *Atkins* [*v. Virginia* (2002)]. But, *Atkins* could not have been decided as it was based solely on such evidence. Rather, the compelling proportionality argument against capital punishment of the mentally retarded played a decisive role in the Court's Eighth Amendment ruling. Moreover, the constitutional rule adopted in *Atkins* was tailored to this proportionality argument: It exempted from capital punishment a defined group of offenders whose proven impairments rendered it highly unlikely, and perhaps impossible, that they could act with the degree of culpability necessary to deserve death. And *Atkins* left to the states the development of mechanisms to determine which individual offenders fell within this class.

In the instant case, by contrast, the moral proportionality arguments against the juvenile death penalty fail to support the rule the Court adopts today. There is no question that "the chronological age of a minor is itself a relevant mitigating factor of great weight," and that sentencing juries must be given an opportunity carefully to consider a defendant's age and maturity in deciding whether to assess the death penalty. But the mitigating characteristics associated with youth do not justify an absolute age limit. A legislature can reasonably conclude, as many have, that some 17-year-old murderers are mature enough to deserve the death penalty in an appropriate case. And nothing in the record before us suggests that sentencing juries are so unable accurately to assess a 17-year-old defendant's maturity, or so incapable of giving proper weight to youth as a mitigating factor, that the Eighth Amendment requires the bright-line rule imposed today. In the end, the Court's flawed proportionality argument simply cannot bear the weight the Court would place upon it.

Lack of a Clear National Consensus

Reasonable minds can differ as to the minimum age at which commission of a serious crime should expose the defendant to the death penalty, if at all. Many jurisdictions have abolished capital punishment altogether, while many others have determined that even the most heinous crime, if committed before the age of eighteen, should not be punishable by death. Indeed, were my office that of a legislator, rather than a judge, then I, too, would be inclined to support legislation setting a minimum age of eighteen in this context. But a significant number of states, including Missouri, have decided to make the death penalty potentially available for 17-year-old capital murderers such as respondent. Without a clearer showing that a genuine national consensus forbids the execution of such offenders, this Court should not substitute its own "inevitably subjective judgment" on how best to resolve this difficult moral question for the judgments of the nation's democratically elected legislatures. I respectfully dissent.

"It is our view that courts or legislatures should eliminate waiver of children under eighteen [to criminal court] regardless of the crime or past history. To deal with the problem of how to treat adolescents nearing eighteen, statutes could allow juvenile courts to maintain jurisdiction over the child until age twenty-five."

Juveniles Should Not Be Tried in Adult Criminal Court

Ellen Marrus and Irene Merker Rosenberg

Ellen Marrus is George Butler Research Professor of Law at the University of Houston Law Center and director of the Southwest Juvenile Defender Center. Irene Merker Rosenberg is the Royce R. Till Professor of Law at the University of Houston Law Center.

Ellen Marrus and Irene Merker Rosenberg argue that although Roper v. Simmons *was a capital punishment decision, the differences between adolescents and adults that the Supreme Court considered in reaching its finding should be considered in determining punishment for juveniles who commit serious crimes. They make a case that, given juveniles' capacity for further maturation and their reduced moral culpability, juveniles should not be tried in adult criminal court. They also contend that, based on the conclusions of* Roper v. Simmons, *courts should not allow sixteen- or seventeen-year-olds to be defined as adults.*

Ellen Marrus and Irene Merker Rosenberg, "After *Roper v. Simmons*: Keeping Kids out of Adult Criminal Court," *The San Diego Law Review*, vol. 42, no. 4, Fall 2005, pp. 1151–1183. Reprinted with the permission of the San Diego Law Review.

Roper v. Simmons *involved the case of Christopher Simmons who, at the age of seventeen, committed murder. He was found guilty and assigned the death penalty, a sentence that was subsequently reduced to life in prison.*

The Supreme Court jurisprudence concerning the constitutionality of capital punishment for adolescents is a study in vacillation [going back and forth]. In *Thompson v. Oklahoma* [(1988)], the Court reversed the death penalty imposed on a fifteen-year-old. It was a five-four decision, but only four justices agreed that fifteen-year-olds, across-the-board, were not mature enough to warrant execution. Justice, [Sandra Day] O'Connor's concurrence in the judgment was, however, very narrow. Her concern was that Oklahoma had not made an explicit policy choice that such minors should be executed. She made quite clear that although "adolescents are generally less blameworthy than adults who commit similar crimes—it does not necessarily follow that all fifteen-year-olds are incapable of the moral culpability that would justify the imposition of capital punishment."

A year later, in *Stanford v. Kentucky*, the Supreme Court upheld executions of sixteen- and seventeen-year-olds. The majority noted that the common-law rebuttable presumption of infancy theoretically would have permitted capital punishment to be imposed on those children over the age of seven who demonstrated sufficient *mens rea* [a Latin term meaning intention or state of mind] and moral culpability. Since a majority of states in 1989 authorized capital punishment for sixteen-year-olds, the majority concluded that there was no national consensus that executing such minors was inhumane.

In *Roper v. Simmons* [(2005)], the Supreme Court, again five-four, created an Eighth Amendment categorical bar to execution of persons who commit capital crimes when they are under the age of eighteen. The decision in *Stanford*, rejecting the identical claim, was held to be "no longer controlling on this issue." Justice [Anthony] Kennedy, writing for the majority, relied heavily on *Atkins v. Virginia* [(2002)], which prohibited capital punishment for retarded people. He also made clear that the Court had an obligation to make its "own independent judgment" in determining "whether the death penalty is . . . disproportionate" and thus violates the Eighth Amendment.

Developmental and Psychological Considerations for Juveniles

Although we recognize that capital cases are often *sui generis* [a legal term meaning a specific case that may not have broader application to other cases] and may not be of strong precedential value in other contexts, we think that the developmental and psychological distinctions between adults and adolescents, differences that the *Simmons* Court believed was constitutionally relevant regarding execution, should also be considered in determining the extent of punishment for juveniles who commit serious criminal acts. In particular, we argue that the Court's recognition of the growth capacity of juveniles, and their reduced moral culpability, should weigh heavily in favor of a categorical bar against waiver of children to criminal court. Furthermore, attempts to circumvent such a ruling by defining adults as sixteen or seventeen years of age for purposes of the criminal law should be prohibited.

If these proposals are not accepted, and a child is charged and convicted of a serious crime in criminal court, the kind and extent of punishment imposed should be heavily influenced by the type of evidence relied on by the *Simmons* Court in finding that youths are not death eligible. Either the Court should extend the *Simmons* rationale to prohibit life imprisonment without the possibility of parole, or at the least, create a presumption against such a sentence being imposed on an adolescent. As Justice Kennedy noted, "the punishment of life imprisonment without the possibility of parole is itself a severe sanction, in particular for a young person." Even life imprisonment is rapidly becoming life without possibility of parole. Defendants who use to be paroled in ten or twenty years are now dying in prison of old age.

When children kill, as they always have and probably always will, the state must juggle two distinct and often conflicting concerns: its police power and its *parens patriae* [the state as parent] interest. These concerns are not, however, mutually exclusive. There is a delicate balance that must be maintained. Even during the more savage common-law era, children's diminished responsibility was reflected by the irrebuttable presumption of incapacity for children under seven, and the rebuttable presumption of incapacity for those between seven and fourteen. But we are not wedded to that more primitive assessment of culpability. Evolving standards of decency require that society takes a more refined approach in allocating responsibility and punishment for juveniles. Clearly, the state must incapacitate and punish children who commit serious criminal acts, but, as *Simmons* says, that does not mean that minors can be executed, nor, as we maintain, be consigned to a living death behind bars without any hope of respite. As the Court has said in another context, the legal system must somehow be adjusted "to account for children's vulnerability and their needs for 'concern . . . sympathy and . . . paternal attention.'" . . .

Adolescence, Maturity and Culpability

The *Simmons* majority looked at "scientific and sociological studies" to establish "that juvenile offenders cannot with reliability be classified among the worst offenders." The first trait differentiating juveniles from adults is immaturity and "an underdeveloped sense of responsibility." The Court cited and quoted from an article showing that "adolescents are overrepresented statistically in virtually every category of reckless behavior." The states recognize this fact, and limit ages at which people can marry, serve on juries, vote, drink alcohol, and contract. Juveniles act impulsively, and therefore cannot accurately assess the consequences of their behavior. [As Paul Raeburn writes in "Too Immature For the Death Penalty?,"] Impulsivity means that even "good kids, who know right from wrong sometimes do stupid things." They engage in unprotected sex which often results in out of wedlock pregnancies and disease; they "do drugs;" drink enough to die from alcohol poisoning, even in college; drive recklessly causing their own death and that of others; and are at serious risk of committing suicide. All parents of teenagers have to contend with the problem of impulsivity and have greater or lesser success in helping their children to think before acting. It is true that there are adults who continue to engage in reckless and impulsive behavior, but this conduct is much more common in children and much less prevalent in adults.

The second characteristic the Court focused on in differentiating juveniles from adults was the effect of outside influences on the child's behavior. Indeed, adolescence and peer pressure are inextricably linked—from clothing fads to antisocial behavior. . . .

The American Academy of Child and Adolescent Psychiatry (AACAP) "determined that the brain does not physically stop maturing until a person is about twenty years old." . . . This means that an adolescent's personality and character are not static. The child at sixteen or seventeen is not the adult he or she will be at thirty. Therefore, punishing adolescents the same as adults is akin to punishing them for a developmental lag. Furthermore, even though teenagers may appear to be mature, they are not. [According to Paul Raeburn,] when everything is perfect, they can act like adults. But you add a little bit of stress, and they can break down. . . .

As the law now stands, adolescents cannot be sentenced to death. They are, however, subject to adult sanctions which are often very severe. This happens for one of two reasons. One, the state, across the board, defines adults for all criminal law purposes as sixteen or seventeen and older. Two, the children who would ordinarily be within the jurisdiction of the juvenile courts are waived to criminal court to be tried as adults. Very often the deciding factor for the transfer is the severity of the crime. The lesser culpability of the offender gets lost in the shuffle. We argue that just as the differences between adolescents and adults are relevant to capital punishment, they also must be considered in the decision to transfer and in the legislative determination that adolescents are adults. . . .

The Importance of Juvenile Courts

It is our view that courts or legislatures should eliminate waiver of children under eighteen [to adult court] regardless of the crime or past history. To deal with the problem of how to treat adolescents nearing eighteen, statutes could allow juvenile courts to maintain jurisdiction over the child until age twenty-five. Such an allowance will eliminate arguments that suggest waiver is necessary because older adolescents could not be treated in the limited time the juvenile courts have jurisdiction.

If legislatures eschew [disregard] this approach, a more limited change could be considered, such as a presumption against waiver regardless of age, seriousness of crime, and past criminal behavior. Furthermore, the juvenile courts should be able to consider the kind of evidence that the *Simmons* Court relied on to prohibit the execution of adolescents. . . . To assure that evidence of developmental lag, immaturity, recklessness, and lesser culpability is considered, there must be a list of factors that the district attorney must consider when making the charging decision and some form of review of prosecutorial decisions in this context. . . . We also do not believe that states should define adults as including adolescents under eighteen.

When a child is subject to waiver of any sort, the prominent factors determining whether the child is to be treated as an adult or a juvenile are age, offense, prior adjudications, and, to be frank, the predilections of the juvenile court judge. Except for the latter, those are the same factors that the *Simmons* Court refused to allow a jury to consider in deciding whether an adolescent should be subjected to capital punishment. It is true that the Court reached this conclusion in the context of the death penalty, but conceptually the Court's rationale describing the differences between adults and adolescents and its acceptance of scientific and sociological studies should also apply to decisions regarding whether juveniles should be considered adults for other criminal law purposes. If the child's brain is still growing until either twenty or twenty-five (depending on what study one uses), subjecting a child to adult punishment, especially life without possibility of parole, is irrational. We do not know who that child will be in five years or ten years. Just as teenagers' bodies change as they mature, so do their brains. In effect, waiver constitutes a prediction that the child is not really a child and cannot be helped within the juvenile court system. This prediction, however, is based on factors that may well be different within a few years.

Predicting future criminality is very speculative. The studies show that the measures used to make that determination result in a substantial inclusion of persons who would not, in fact, engage in the predicted criminal behavior. Although the Supreme Court has concluded that "there is nothing inherently unattainable about a prediction of future criminal conduct," it has also acknowledged that "some in the psychiatric community are of the view that clinical predictions as to whether a person would or would not commit violent acts in the future are 'fundamentally of very low reliability,'" and noted studies showing that "psychiatric predictions of future dangerousness were wrong two out of three times." Thus, one cannot know with a high degree of certainty which children will become violent predators.

Caution Is Needed in Determining Punishment for Juveniles

It is true that the state has a right to punish those who violate the criminal law, particularly murderers, even if they would not commit crimes in the future. Retribution has a place in the justification of punishment. Retribution principles do not, however, tell us with any specificity how much punishment is necessary for atonement. . . .

Determining whether a child should be charged in, or waived to, criminal court and subjected to severe punishment such as life without possibility of parole, requires a value choice. Concededly, opting to keep a child within the juvenile court system with its generally lower sentences, risks the possibility of future serious harm to the community. However, studies show that long prison sentences for children result in a greater likelihood of recidivism.

The risks on the other side are very high—the virtual destruction of young people who might benefit society and live productive lives. Since we know that mistakes in predicting future criminality will be made, and that minors have the capacity for growth, which path should we follow? The *Simmons* Court suggests that we err on the side of the child.

People imagine that children who kill are irredeemable—a "bad seed." Both of us have represented children in juvenile court who were charged with serious criminal acts, including murder. Our experiences tell us that even children who commit the most heinous offense, such as joining a group of "friends" to stomp an elderly, defenseless person to death, are ultimately capable of understanding what they had really done. After release from incarceration in a secure facility for juveniles, many of them, although not all, were able to turn their lives around, went to school, and found jobs. This also happens with adults who are killers. When the Supreme Court invalidated the death penalty in 1972, the sentences of many people on death row were commuted to life imprisonment.

Some of them were paroled and most refrained from further illegal conduct. Admittedly, some did bear the mark of [biblical figure] Cain and went on to kill and kill again. The difficulty is that we do not know how to differentiate among the different types of murderers. What we do know, however, is that children and adolescents are growing and maturing and the chances for them "to make it" are much higher than for adults. Knowing that, we must be very cautious when exposing children to adult punishment. They are not adults; they are children. We need to treat them as such.

"Like the decision in Simmons, *the decision in* Atkins *will immediately help only a modest number of inmates. Unlike* Simmons, *however,* Atkins *has dynamic consequences that will reverberate throughout death row."*

The Effect of *Roper v. Simmons* on Death Penalty Cases Is Trivial

David R. Dow

David R. Dow is a professor at the University of Houston Law Center, the founder and director of the Texas Innocence Network, and author of Executed on a Technicality: Lethal Injustice on America's Death Row.

David R. Dow, argues that, while on the surface Atkins v. Virginia *and* Roper v. Simmons *[(2005)] appear similar—prohibiting the execution of mentally retarded people and juveniles on the grounds that they are less culpable for their acts—*Atkins *will have a much greater impact on death row cases than* Simmons. *Because mental retardation is less easily defined than whether or not an offender had turned eighteen at the time of a crime,* Atkins *will encourage more investigation and provide greater opportunity to provide evidence of innocence or mitigating factors.*

David R. Dow, "Cruel, Unusual, and Unconstitutional," *New Politics*, vol. 10, no. 3, Summer 2005, p. 57. Reproduced by permission of the author.

For nearly half a century, the cruel and unusual punishments clause of the Eighth Amendment has been understood as reflecting society's "evolving standards of decency." Stripped to its core, the idea of evolving standards is that something can be permissible—which is to say, constitutional—at a certain historical moment, and unconstitutional later. Once upon a time in America, states could execute people who committed rape, or even robbery. The Supreme Court has held, however, that a state can execute only those who commit homicide. Our standards have evolved. That's one reason that my brother and Justice Scalia are wrong, and that the death penalty is, in fact, unconstitutional.

A second reason is that the Constitution deals not only with results, but also with procedures. Executing someone is a result. How we go about executing them is a procedure. When Justice Harry Blackmun threw up his hands in 1994 and announced that he would no longer tinker with the machinery of death, he was saying that the procedures are inherently flawed. The Constitution permits the death penalty when it's perfect; Justice Blackmun said that he had been mistaken in believing that we are capable of perfection.

The *Simmons* Ruling Is Potentially Damaging

Sometimes the randomness that Justice Blackmun condemned works to our benefit. Three of my clients will not be executed, and none of the credit is mine. They have been saved by the Supreme Court's decision in *Roper v. Simmons*, which held that the states cannot execute murderers who were younger than the age of eighteen at the time they committed a crime. Give or take a score, there are 3,500 people on death row in the United States. The Court's decision in *Simmons* saved perhaps seventy. So *Simmons* affected 2 percent of the nation's death row population. (In Texas, the decision has had a broader impact, nullifying death sentences of around 7 percent of the state's death row population.) As a death penalty opponent, I do not want to sound ungrateful or churlish, but, outside of the people whose cases it immediately affects, the decision in *Simmons* is trivial. It is not especially important doctrinally, and in some respects, it is actually rather damaging.

Two and a half years ago, in *Atkins v. Virginia*, the Supreme Court ruled that the states cannot execute the mentally retarded. Unlike chronological age, which has well-defined boundaries, mental retardation is a comparatively imprecise concept. A murderer was or was not younger than age eighteen at the time of the crime. Whether a murderer is mentally retarded is far less clear and is often controversial. Experts use accepted methods and tests to ascertain mental retardation, but they disagree among themselves on how to interpret those tests. Yet despite the difficulty of saying whether a particular death row inmate is retarded, a conservative estimate is that 5 percent of the nation's death row population satisfies the clinical criteria, and perhaps the number is as large as 10 percent. *Atkins* was an important decision, however, not simply because it affected two to five times as many inmates as *Simmons*, but as well because of the impact it has had on death penalty advocacy.

Like the decision in *Simmons*, the decision in *Atkins* will immediately help only a modest number of inmates. Unlike *Simmons*, however, *Atkins* has dynamic consequences that reverberate throughout death row. The reason is that even though only 5 or 10 percent of death row inmates will prove to be retarded, a much larger number have plausible claims under *Atkins*. Of the dozen death row inmates I currently represent, easily half of them have plausible mental retardation claims. They will, therefore, now receive the benefit of an investigation that they would not otherwise have received.

These investigations are vital because lawyers often find unexpected information, and so the likelihood that something useful will be found is increased. In *Simmons v. South Carolina* [(1994)] (a different Simmons), Justice Scalia complained that death penalty lawyers are like guerillas, always looking for another battlefront to open. I'm not sure why Justice Scalia used the word "guerilla" to describe what death penalty lawyers are supposed to do, but *Atkins* did open the front for us. *Roper v. Simmons* has no such effect.

Juveniles on Death Row Now Lose Right to Counsel

To take just one dramatic example: A death row inmate in Texas was recently set for execution. We believed there was a chance he was mentally retarded, within the meaning of *Atkins*, and therefore, sought out evidence to establish it. We found no proof of his retardation; however, we did locate evidence tending to suggest that the inmate was not in fact guilty at all. Without *Atkins*, the investigation that led us to conclude that he is innocent would never have been undertaken. Unlike *Atkins*, *Simmons* has no such dynamic consequence. There is no mystery as to which 2 percent of the death row population benefits from *Simmons*. There is no incentive for lawyers to do something that they were not already doing. And, in fact, exactly the contrary is true. Under federal law, as well as under the laws of every death penalty state except one, death row inmates are entitled to lawyers to represent them in state and federal habeas corpus proceedings. That is not true for prison inmates not on death row—which means that as soon as the seventy or so juveniles who were on death row when *Simmons* was decided get moved off of death row—they also lose their right to counsel.

Yet of the three juveniles I represent, two of them have exceedingly strong claims of actual innocence, and the third has a nontrivial claim of innocence. Even if I were willing to work on these cases without the prospect of having expenses paid for by a state or federal court, I also have to confront the fact that these cases are no longer urgent. Put somewhat actuarially, my clients still on death row face imminent demise, meaning that my clients not on death row—even assuming I continue to represent them—are constantly pushed to the bottom of my "to do" list.

In the long run, cases that draw lines are trivial because the enterprise of drawing lines has little if any legal or moral content. It doesn't much matter whether the legal age for voting is eighteen or nineteen. In contrast, saying that states cannot prevent women or blacks from voting is a point with profound moral content. I am relieved that, because of *Simmons*, three young men, whom I believe should not be executed, will not be executed. At the same time, I recognize that even if it is true that the death penalty will die from a thousand cuts, the Supreme Court's decision in *Simmons* is barely a pinprick.

And maybe it's actually a styptic pencil [capable of fixing only a small wound or problem]. Every time the Supreme Court says "here's something the states can no longer do," it strengthens the states' entitlement to do everything else. When the Supreme Court announces that the Constitution forbids the execution of the mentally retarded or juveniles, death penalty advocates conclude that the problems have been addressed, and the machinery of death can once again move forward.

"If, as with juveniles and mentally retarded offenders, courts accept that severely mentally ill defendants also have diminished culpability due to the nature of their illness (e.g. impairments in perception and cognition, and frequent inability to control their impulses), justice is not achieved by allowing mentally ill offenders to be sentenced to death—the most extreme penal sanction for crimes."

Roper v. Simmons Opens the Door to Death Penalty Exemptions for the Mentally Ill

Helen Shin

Helen Shin, a third-year law student at Fordham University, is the Notes and Articles editor for the Fordham Law Review.

In this article, Helen Shin considers the reasoning behind the Atkins v. Virginia *and* Roper v. Simmons *rulings as it might apply to the mentally ill. Shin reviews psychiatric and legal opinions on the culpability of the mentally ill, as well as international opinion with regard to execution, to suggest that mentally ill offenders may be the next group to benefit from* Atkins *and* Simmons. *The* Atkins *case prohibits assigning the death penalty to mentally retarded offenders, and* Roper v. Simmons *protects juvenile offenders from capital punishment.*

Helen Shin, "Is the Death of the Death Penalty Near? The Impact of *Atkins* and *Roper* on the Future of Capital Punishment for Mentally Ill Defendants," *Fordham Law Review*, vol. 76, no. 1, October 2007, pp. 465–516. Reproduced by permission.

Although mentally retarded and juvenile offenders are now categorically shielded from receiving the death penalty, there are still many death row prisoners who suffer from severe mental illnesses and/or brain damage, and act under states of delusion or hallucination. Furthermore, many of them come from backgrounds of poverty, child abuse, racism, deprivation, and societal marginalization—factors that may have affected them at the time they committed their crimes. Although such factors can be considered mitigating factors, the absolute protection afforded to juveniles and the mentally retarded against the death penalty has not been afforded to mentally ill criminals as a matter of law. In light of the recent developments regarding capital punishment, it is appropriate to take a fresh look at how such changes may affect mentally ill offenders. . . .

The Legacy of *Atkins* and *Roper*

In *Roper* and *Atkins*, the Supreme Court relied on several factors to conclude that juveniles and mentally retarded persons ought to be categorically exempt from the death penalty. The Court placed the most weight on evidence of a national consensus against executing juveniles and the mentally retarded, stating that standards of decency had evolved significantly since earlier cases when it had denied death penalty exclusion for such classes of offenders. In determining whether a consensus existed against allowing the death penalty for these categories of persons, the Court looked to such things as state legislation, sentencing practices by courts and juries, and popular polls. In addition, it also looked at international and foreign laws and practices, as well as the professional stances of organizations with germane [relevant] expertise, though it noted that such evidence was merely instructive and supportive rather than determinative of the Court's ultimate decision. The Court also performed a proportionality analysis in each case to determine whether the deterrent and retributive goals of the death penalty were being met by allowing mentally retarded and juvenile defendants to be executed.

... This Note applies the analysis the Supreme Court used in *Roper* and *Atkins* to severely mentally ill offenders and examines whether they should be categorically exempt from the death penalty.

Connecticut is the only state that has legislatively proscribed imposing the death penalty on mentally ill defendants who, despite their mental illnesses, were competent to be executed. Connecticut's law states that courts cannot impose a death sentence on a defendant if the jury or court concludes "that at the time of the offense . . . the defendant's mental capacity was significantly impaired or the defendant's ability to conform the defendant's conduct to the requirements of law was significantly impaired but not so impaired in either case as to constitute a defense to prosecution." This single state statute shielding the mentally ill from the death penalty stands in stark contrast to the legislative landscape of the states when *Roper* and *Atkins* were decided. At the time of *Roper* and *Atkins*, there was much greater statutory opposition to the practice of executing juveniles and mentally retarded offenders than there currently is against executing the mentally ill.

There is little evidence that other states are considering following Connecticut's lead in imposing such a categorical ban. However, most states have capital statutes that implicate mental illness as a mitigating factor. Furthermore, twenty-eight of the thirty-eight states that sanction the death penalty allow mental illness to have a mitigating impact by permitting the jury to consider the defendant's capacity "to appreciate the criminality [or wrongfulness] of his conduct or to conform his conduct to the requirements of the law." Several statutes even stipulate that impairments in capacity may be due to mental illness, mental disease, or mental defect. This pattern of inclusion of mental illness provisions in death penalty laws suggests that many states recognize that mental illness can affect a person's culpability and that an offender's mental ill-ness, if present, ought to be considered during sentencing. . . .

The Weight of International Opinion

International communities oppose capital punishment as a general matter, but also specifically for individuals with men-tal disorders. After World War II, the United Nations (U.N.) General Assembly adopted the Universal Declaration of Hu-man Rights, which proclaimed a "right to life." During the 1950s and 1960s, many international human rights treaties were drafted, such as the International Covenant on Civil and Political Rights, which the United States has ratified, and the European Convention on Human Rights, which provided for the right to life and led to many Western European nations stopping their use of the death penalty. By the 1980s, there was a *de facto* abolition of the death penalty in Western Eu-rope. Also, in the 1980s, the U.N. General Assembly adopted the Second Optional Protocol to the International Covenant on Civil and Political Rights, which seeks to abolish the death penalty around the world. Furthermore, in 1990, member na-tions of the Organization of American States signed the Pro-tocol to the American Convention on Human Rights to Abol-ish the Death Penalty.

The European Union and the Council of Europe have conditioned countries' membership on the abolition of the death penalty, and as such, even nations that once had harsh capital punishment systems, such as Turkey, have promised to abandon the death penalty to gain admission to the European Union. In addition, with the exception of Turkey, every Euro-pean country has signed Protocol No. 6 to the Convention for the Protection of Human Rights and Fundamental Freedoms Concerning the Abolition of the Death Penalty, which pro-scribes the death penalty in peacetime. Currently, more than half of the countries in the world have legally or by practice abolished the death penalty. Sixty-nine countries still retain the death penalty, but in 2005, executions occurred in only twenty-two countries, with 94 percent of known executions taking place in just four countries: China, Iran, Saudi Arabia, and the United States.

With regard to mentally ill offenders in particular, the U.N. Commission on Human Rights passed a resolution in 1999 urging countries "not to impose the death penalty on a person suffering from any form of mental disorder." In 2004, it passed another resolution concerning the death penalty, using the same language to call on nations that still maintain the death penalty to stop imposing it on individuals with any form of mental disorder. Certainly, severe mental illness would be considered a form of mental disorder. In 1997, the U.N. Special Rapporteur on Extrajudicial, Summary, or Arbitrary Executions stated in a report that governments that continue to use capital punishment on "the *mentally ill* are particularly called upon to bring their domestic legislation into conformity with international legal standards." In addition, the European Union, whose brief the Supreme Court cited in *Atkins*, has also expressed disapproval of the practice of executing persons with severe mental illness through letters urging states to commute death sentences of mentally ill death row prisoners. . . .

. . . From *Atkins* to *Roper*, reliance on international consensus seems to have grown somewhat because discussion about the views of the world community, which in *Atkins* was limited to a mere footnote in the majority opinion, leapt into the actual text of the *Roper* opinion in a much lengthier discourse. International opinion is still by no means determinative of what the outcome of an issue before the Court ought to be, as explicitly stated in both cases, but nevertheless can be persuasive and at the least can lend support to the Court's resolution on an issue. In particular, if the Supreme Court ever examines whether it is appropriate to allow executions for mentally ill criminals, it may again look to the international community for guidance. If it does, the Court will likely determine that there is ample evidence of international and foreign opposition to executing the mentally ill. . . .

Professional Consensus on the Mentally Ill

Even before the *Atkins* and *Roper* decisions, another mental health organization, the American Psychological Association, also put forward its position on the death penalty and mentally ill offenders, declaring,

> WHEREAS death penalty prosecutions may involve persons with serious mental illness or mental retardation. Procedural problems, such as assessing competency, take on particular importance in cases where the death penalty is applied to such populations,
>
> THEREFORE, BE IT RESOLVED, that the American Psychological Association
>
> Calls upon each jurisdiction in the United States that imposes capital punishment not to carry out the death penalty until the jurisdiction implements policies and procedures that can be shown through psychological and other social science research to ameliorate the deficiencies identified above

In the legal community, the ABA [American Bar Association] passed a resolution at its annual conference on August 8, 2006, recommending that states stop sentencing mentally ill or disabled criminals to death. Without favoring or opposing the death penalty, the ABA urged jurisdictions that permit capital punishment to end their practice of executing or sentencing defendants to death if "at the time of the offense, they had significant limitations in both their intellectual functioning and adaptive behavior resulting from mental retardation, dementia, or a traumatic brain injury." Furthermore, the ABA recommended that defendants who, at the time of their offense, "had a severe mental disorder or disability that significantly impaired their capacity (a) to appreciate the nature, consequences or wrongfulness of their conduct, (b) to exercise rational judgment in relation to conduct, or (c) to conform their conduct to the requirements of the law" should also not be executed or given the death penalty.

The language used by the ABA . . . mirrors the language used by the American Psychiatric Association in its various position statements concerning mental illness and the death penalty. The American Psychiatric Association and the American Psychological Association have both officially endorsed the ABA's resolution. The ABA states that its recommendations are, in part, meant to "prohibit execution of persons with severe mental disabilities whose demonstrated impairments of mental and emotional functioning at the time of the offense would render a death sentence disproportionate to their culpability."

In the aggregate, the opinions and policy positions of respected legal and mental health organizations provide abundant evidence of a professional consensus in opposition to allowing the execution of severely mentally ill offenders.

Deterrence and Retribution

Retribution and deterrence of violent crimes by potential offenders are the two social purposes served by the death penalty. . . .

The goal of retribution requires that an offender be punished in proportion to his or her culpability. In *Roper*, the Court confirmed that once the diminished culpability of a class of offenders is recognized, "the penological justifications for the death penalty apply to them with lesser force." If, as with juveniles and mentally retarded offenders, courts accept that severely mentally ill defendants also have diminished culpability due to the nature of their illness (e.g., impairments in perception and cognition, and frequent inability to control their impulses), justice is not achieved by allowing mentally ill offenders to be sentenced to death—the most extreme penal sanction for crimes. Because capital punishment assumes that a condemned criminal is fully culpable, any diminished culpability results in the punishment of death being disproportionate. Thus, the retributive goal fails. Therefore, the diminished culpability of mentally ill defendants ought to preclude them from the death penalty, since allowing it would not further the goal of retribution.

With respect to deterrence, the theory is that the severity of capital punishment will inhibit prospective criminals from committing violent crimes. The same argument made by the Court in *Atkins* about the weak deterrent effect on mentally retarded defendants can also be made about defendants with severe mental illness. In *Atkins*, the Court stated,

> The same cognitive and behavioral impairments that make [mentally retarded] defendants less morally culpable—for example, the diminished ability to understand and process information, to learn from experience, to engage in logical reasoning, or to control impulses—that also make it less likely that they can process the information of the possibility of execution as a penalty and, as a result, control their conduct based upon that information.

People with severe mental illness manifest many of the same difficulties that mentally retarded people struggle with, such as those the *Atkins* Court listed. The inability of persons with severe mental illness to control their impulses, to engage in logical reasoning, and to control their conduct based on information about the penal consequences of criminal action provides persuasive evidence that the death penalty has little to no deterrent effect on mentally ill offenders. . . . Furthermore, a mentally ill defendant may not refrain from committing a crime because cognitive impairments or delusions may lead to the false belief that he or she is acting according to reality. Moreover, in asserting that the death penalty does not have a strong deterrent effect on severely mentally ill defendants who are often unable to control their actions, Amnesty International points out that "certainly no one believes that the death penalty can deter people from being psychotic." ...

The Death Penalty and the Mentally Ill

The Supreme Court has not yet addressed the issue of whether mentally ill defendants ought to be categorically exempt from being sentenced to death.... Looking at the development of the Supreme Court's death penalty jurisprudence, it is evident that the Court is moving in the direction of narrowing the applicability of the death penalty so as to preclude offenders with diminished culpability. Based on this trend, the Court may again exclude other categories of people if it deems it necessary according to its constitutional interpretations as well as evolving standards of decency. Applying the Supreme Court's analysis of youth in *Roper* and mental retardation in *Atkins* to current facts about mental illness, there is strong support for the notion that, like juveniles and mentally retarded offenders, severely mentally ill criminals ought also to receive categorical protection from the death penalty.

Experts in the legal, psychological, and psychiatric professions as well as the U.N., foreign countries, and other international groups have presented myriad reasons for why persons with serious mental illness should not be subject to capital punishment....

Despite the overwhelming consensus of the international community, foreign nations, and legal and mental health organizations, it is still unlikely that the Supreme Court will decide to immediately exclude mentally ill criminals from the death penalty. This is mainly due to the fact that state counting was the most objective and therefore most significant indicator in *Atkins* and *Roper* of a national consensus, and according to this Note's analysis, there is only tenuous evidence of state death penalty laws providing categorical exemptions for the mentally ill. Undoubtedly, current practices of juries and courts in sentencing, examples of clemencies for mentally ill death row inmates, opinions of state justices, moratoriums, and public opinion about executing the severely mentally ill are all relevant in assessing whether standards of decency are evolving in the United States about the appropriateness of imposing capital punishment on the mentally ill. As Justice Lundberg Stratton pointed out, however, without the requisite evidence of state legislation outlawing the practice, it is difficult for judges to impose bans on executing mentally ill defendants based on other persuasive reasons offered by foreign countries, relevant expert organizations, and the American public.

Given the strong opinions of the world community, mental health experts, and legal organizations, and the public's changing views about permitting mentally ill offenders to be sentenced to death, legislatures and courts in death penalty states ought to evaluate existing statutes using the framework of *Atkins* and *Roper*. As a starting point, they can examine whether such a punishment achieves the proper penological purposes of deterrence and retribution for mentally ill offenders. Enactment of appropriate legislation protecting the narrow class of severely mentally ill offenders from execution should be considered if there are sufficient reasons to believe that the characteristics of mentally ill offenders render them less culpable and less susceptible to deterrence than the average capital criminal. In addition, with respect to retribution, which requires that the severity of a punishment be commensurate with the offender's culpability, state legislatures can use the analyses of *Roper* and *Atkins* to investigate and determine whether mentally ill offenders have diminished culpability. Given the inability of many severely mentally ill people to control their behavior or thoughts, this Note argues that the penological goals of the death penalty are not met by permitting such people to be executed. States that perform the proportionality analysis outlined will likely conclude that the death penalty is a disproportionately harsh punishment for mentally ill offenders, which does not advance the states' goals of proper retribution and deterrence. If states determine that neither retributive nor deterrent goals are satisfied by permitting the mentally ill to be executed, the states' justifications become significantly weaker for allowing the imposition of the most extreme criminal sanction on offenders with diminished culpability. Therefore, they will be compelled to reform their laws accordingly.

At the present time, evidence is lacking of a national consensus in state legislation that would suffice for the Supreme Court to grant a categorical exclusion for severely mentally ill criminals from the death penalty. Although the current legislative landscape may render the Supreme Court, and courts in general, unable to provide severely mentally ill defendants with categorical protection, state legislatures do have the ability to examine factors such as those discussed above. In other words, notwithstanding the state legislation obstacle which courts would encounter, state legislative bodies have wide discretion to pass and amend laws concerning the matter. Legislatures, therefore, ought to fashion more protective laws for the courts to apply based on proportionality analyses and social, professional, and international opinions condemning the death penalty as a form of punishment for the mentally ill.

*"[Children's rights advocates] contend
the March 1 ruling raises the possibility
that the Eighth Amendment prohibition on cruel and unusual punishment
could also be applied to cases in which
juvenile offenders are sentenced to life
in prison without possibility of parole."*

Roper v. Simmons May Lead to Arguments That Life in Prison Without Parole Is Cruel and Unusual Punishment

Mark Hansen

*Mark Hansen is a senior writer for the American Bar
Association's* ABA Journal. *He has written for the* ABA Journal
since 1991.

Written in the wake of the U.S. Supreme Court's Roper v. Simmons *ruling prohibiting the execution of juvenile offenders,
Mark Hansen asks how this ruling might change the way the juvenile justice system in the United States responds to juvenile offenders. Noting that the majority based its finding on "evolving
standards of decency," children's rights advocates wonder whether*

life in prison without the possibility of parole might come to be considered "cruel and unusual punishment" for juveniles and whether the courts will place a greater emphasis on rehabilitation.

The U.S. Supreme Court's recent [March 1, 2005] ruling prohibiting the execution of juvenile offenders will likely affect how lawyers and judges view juvenile criminal behavior.

Children's rights advocates say the decision, *Roper v. Simmons*, raises the broader question of whether juveniles are less culpable than adults and less deserving of adult-style treatment.

[Children's rights advocates] contend the March 1 ruling raises the possibility that the Eighth Amendment prohibition on cruel and unusual punishment could also be applied to cases in which juvenile offenders are sentenced to life in prison without the possibility of parole.

And they say the Court's consideration of international law opens the door to the possibility that courts might consider foreign authorities when examining other aspects of the juvenile justice system.

"This decision could help shift the thinking about the sentencing of juvenile offenders in courts throughout the country," says Angela Vigil, a children's law specialist and director of pro bono and public service at Chicago-based Baker & McKenzie.

Nova Southeastern University law professor Michael Dale, who teaches and practices juvenile law, says he does not know if a lawyer could walk into court with the *Simmons* opinion and say to a judge that a disposition or a sentencing is unconstitutional.

"But I do think that some of what the court talks about in *Simmons* suggests that more attention should be paid to the issues of culpability and deterrence as they relate to juveniles," he says.

A more immediate question, says Vigil, a member of the ABA [American Bar Association] Litigation Section's Children's Rights Litigation Committee, is what happens to the seventy-two juvenile offenders on death row in twelve states. It's not clear, she says, whether those sentences automatically revert to mandatory alternative sentences or whether those inmates are entitled to new sentencing hearings. "Every state's sentencing scheme is different," she says.

Evolving Standards of Decency

The unanswered questions stem from the Court's landmark five-four decision that the execution of juvenile offenders violates the Eighth Amendment ban on cruel and unusual punishment.

"The age of eighteen is the point where society draws the line for many purposes between childhood and adulthood," Justice Anthony M. Kennedy wrote for the majority. "It is, we conclude, the age at which the line for death eligibility ought to rest."

The decision marked an about-face by the high court, which in 1989 [in *Stanford v. Kentucky*] found no reason to outlaw the execution of 16- and 17-year-olds who commit capital crimes.

The majority based its decision on the "evolving standards of decency" analysis that has shaped the Court's view as to what constitutes cruel and unusual punishment under the Eighth Amendment for nearly fifty years.

In his opinion, Kennedy said the evidence of a new national consensus against the death penalty for juveniles is similar, and in some respects parallel, to the evidence the court held sufficient in 2002 [in *Atkins v. Virginia*] to demonstrate a national consensus against the execution of the mentally retarded.

Besides relying on that trend, the majority cited scientific and sociological studies on the differences between juveniles and adults. The research indicates juveniles have an underdeveloped sense of responsibility, have a greater susceptibility to negative influences and lack a fully formed character. The Court also found that the two social purposes the death penalty serves with respect to adults—retribution and deterrence-have little or no effect on juveniles.

In finding a new consensus against the execution of juveniles, the majority also acknowledged what it called "the stark reality that the United States is the only country in the world that continues to give official sanction to the juvenue death penalty." Since 1990, only seven other countries have executed juvenile offenders, the court said, and all seven have either abolished or publicly disavowed the practice.

A Need for Wholesale Reevaluation

For the past fifteen to twenty years, state policy makers have been passing laws premised on the idea that teenagers are as responsible as adults are for their criminal behavior and should be punished accordingly. But *Simmons* suggests teenagers are less culpable than adults and less deserving of the most extreme punishment society has to offer, children's law experts say.

"The court's recognition that teenagers are not fully formed and that their criminal behavior is likely limited to their teenage years should lead to a wholesale re-evaluation of the laws in every state that have made it easier to prosecute children as adults and bring rehabilitation back to the forefront of our sentencing policy concerning youthful offenders," says Northwestern University law professor Steven Drizin, an authority on juvenile justice policy.

Mark Soler, president of the Youth Law Center, a public interest law firm based in Washington, D.C., that works on juvenile justice issues, says the Court had previously issued conflicting opinions as to whether immaturity was a critical factor in assessing the culpability of juvenile offenders. But *Simmons*, he says, has made it clear that the majority believes it is.

"If you believe that juveniles are less mature and less responsible than adults, as the majority said in *Simmons*, that's a strong argument for keeping them out of adult court," he says.

Before *Simmons*, it also wasn't clear how influential international laws and norms would be in how the courts look at the issues of immaturity and culpability, Soler says. But *Simmons* makes it possible for juveniles' defense attorneys to use such evidence to try to influence what happens in juvenile court.

One example, Soler says, is a provision of the United Nations Convention on the Rights of the Child, which says juveniles should not be incarcerated alongside adults.

Drizin notes that a broad coalition of medical, religious, child welfare, human rights and juvenile justice organizations had come together to call for an end to the death penalty for juvenile offenders. If the same type of coalition can be put together around other juvenile justice issues, such as life imprisonment without the possibility of parole, he says, it could lead to the first real reform in juvenile justice policy in this country in fifteen to twenty years.

"That means reaffirming the idea that children are different than adults, which makes them less culpable, and requiring that we invest our resources in rehabilitation rather than just locking up kids and throwing away the key," he says.

Organizations to Contact

The editors have compiled the following list of organizations concerned with the issues debated in this book. The descriptions are derived from materials provided by the organizations. All have publications or information available for interested readers. The list was compiled on the date of publication of the present volume; the information provided here may change. Be aware that many organizations take several weeks or longer to respond to inquiries, so allow as much time as possible.

Center for Children's Law and Policy (CCLP)
1701 K Street NW, Washington, DC   20006
(202) 637-0377 • fax: (202) 379-1600
e-mail: info@cclp.org
Web site: www.cclp.org

The Center for Children's Law and Policy (CCLP) is a public interest law and policy organization focused on reform of juvenile justice and other systems that affect troubled and at-risk children and protection of the rights of children in those systems. The Center's work covers a range of activities including research, writing, public education, media advocacy, training, technical assistance, administrative and legislative advocacy, and litigation.

Center for Juvenile Justice Reform
Georgetown University, Washington, DC   20057-1485
(202) 687-7657 • fax: (202) 687-3110
Web site: http://cjjr.georgetown.edu

The Center for Juvenile Justice Reform at Georgetown University advances a balanced, multisystem approach to fighting juvenile crime that holds youth accountable and promotes positive child and youth development. It supports this reform agenda through a variety of activities, primarily a program of intensive study designed for public agency leaders responsible for policy development and implementation in their jurisdictions. This program of intensive study has been formally established through two Certificate Program sessions conducted annually, one designed for individuals and one for multisystem jurisdictional teams. The Center also provides guidance and instruction on how to reform the juvenile justice system through the adoption of sound policy and practice. In this regard, the Center supports the development of stronger leaders in juvenile justice and related systems of care and helps them to achieve better outcomes for the young people in their care.

Children's Defense Fund (CDF)

25 E Street NW, Washington, DC   20001
(800) 233-1200
e-mail: cdfinfo@childrensdefense.org
Web site: www.childrensdefense.org

The Children's Defense Fund (CDF) is a national organization that provides a strong, effective voice for the children of America who cannot vote, lobby, or speak for themselves. It pays particular attention to the needs of poor and minority children and those with disabilities. CDF encourages preventive investment before children get sick, get into trouble, drop out of school, or suffer family breakdown. Publications include *Protect Children, Not Guns* and *America's Cradle to Prison Pipeline*.

The Coalition for Juvenile Justice (CJJ)

1710 Rhode Island Avenue NW, 10th Floor
Washington, DC   20036
(202) 467-0864 • fax: (202) 887-0738
e-mail: info@juvjustice.org
Web site: www.juvjustice.org

For nearly twenty-five years, the Coalition for Juvenile Justice (CJJ) has served as the national association of governor-appointed state advisory groups and has included members from many walks of life and professional disciplines who—with allied individuals and organizations—seek to improve the circumstances of vulnerable and troubled children, youth, and families involved with the courts and to build safe communities. CJJ informs policy makers, advocates, and the public about the interplay of prevention, rehabilitation, and accountability in reducing juvenile crime and delinquency. CJJ also issues reports and statements on topics such as mental health, conditions of confinement, racial inequality, and disturbing trends and best practices in juvenile justice.

Juvenile Law Center (JLC)
1315 Walnut Street, Philadelphia, PA   19107
(215) 625-0551 • fax: (215) 625-2808
Web site: www.jlc.org

The Juvenile Law Center (JLC) is a nonprofit public interest law firm for children in the United States. JLC promotes juvenile justice and child welfare reform through litigation, policy initiatives, and public education forums. JLC uses the law to protect and promote children's rights and interests in the child welfare and juvenile justice systems, with a particular emphasis on ensuring that public systems do not harm children and youth in their care. JLC works to ensure that the juvenile justice and child welfare systems, which were created to help vulnerable children and youth, provide them with access to education, housing, physical and behavioral health care, employment opportunities, and other services that will enable them to become productive adults.

Models for Change: Systems Reform in Juvenile Justice
Center for Children and Youth Justice, Seattle, WA   98104
(206) 272-0195
e-mail: mlcurtis@ccyj.org
Web site: www.modelsforchange.net

Models for Change: Systems Reform in Juvenile Justice is a national initiative funded by the MacArthur Foundation that partners with selected states to advance reforms that effectively hold young people accountable for their actions, provide for their rehabilitation, protect them from harm, increase their life chances, and manage the risk they pose to themselves and to public safety. The initiative's goal is to accelerate progress toward more rational, fair, effective, and developmentally sound juvenile justice systems in selected states—in the process developing models of successful systemwide reform that can be emulated. With its partners and grantees, Models for Change produces a variety of reports, research summaries, issue briefs, working documents, and other materials related to system change efforts.

National Center for Juvenile Justice
700 S. Water Street, Pittsburgh, PA   15203
(412) 227-6950 • fax: (412) 227-6955
Web site: http://ncjj.servehttp.com/NCJJWebsite/main.htm

The National Center for Juvenile Justice is a resource for independent and original research on topics related directly and indirectly to the field of juvenile justice. The Center is the research division of the National Council of Juvenile and Family Court Judges, and it consists of systems research, applied research, and legal research. Publications include *Juvenile and Family Law Digest.*

National Center for Mental Health and Juvenile Justice
345 Delaware Avenue, Delmar, NY   12054
(866) 962-6455 • fax: (518) 439-7612
e-mail: ncmhjj@prainc.com
Web site: www.ncmhjj.com

The National Center for Mental Health and Juvenile Justice was established to improve policies and programs for youth with mental health disorders who are involved with the juvenile justice system, based on the best available research and practice. The Center aims at providing a centralized national focal point that pulls together and links the various activities and research that are currently underway, using the best available knowledge to guide practice and policy. Publications include *Adolescent Girls with Co-Occurring Disorders in the Juvenile Justice System*; *Blueprint for Change: Funding Mental*

Health Services for Youth in Contact with the Juvenile Justice System; *Mental Health Screening Within Juvenile Justice: The Next Frontier*; and *Youth with Mental Health Disorders: Issues and Emerging Responses*, among others.

National Juvenile Defender Center (NJDC)
1350 Connecticut Avenue NW, Suite 304
Washington, DC   20036
(202) 452-0010 • fax: (202) 452-1205
e-mail: inquiries@njdc.info
Web site: www.njdc.info

The National Juvenile Defender Center (NJDC) was created in 1999 to respond to the critical need to build the capacity of the juvenile defense bar and to improve access to counsel and quality of representation for children in the justice system. NJDC provides support to public defenders, appointed counsel, law school clinical programs, and nonprofit law centers to ensure quality representation in urban, suburban, rural, and tribal areas. It offers a wide range of integrated services to juvenile defenders, including training, technical assistance, advocacy, networking, collaboration, capacity building, and coordination. Publications include *Juvenile Defender Resource Guide*, *Principles in Practice*, and *Juvenile Indigent Defense Archives*, among others.

National Juvenile Justice Network (NJJN)
1710 Rhode Island Avenue NW, 10th Floor
Washington, DC   20036
(202) 467-0864 ext. 105 • fax: (202) 887-0738
e-mail: info@njjn.org
Web site: www.njjn.org

The National Juvenile Justice Network (NJJN) is an initiative of the Coalition for Juvenile Justice, a national nonprofit comprising governor-appointed advisory groups on juvenile justice from the United States, its territories, and the District of Columbia. The National Juvenile Justice Network supports state-based, juvenile justice coalitions in their efforts to advocate for fair, equitable, and developmentally appropriate adjudication and treatment for all children, youth, and families involved in the juvenile justice system.

For Further Research

Books

The Advancement Project and the Civil Rights Project, *Opportunities Suspended: The Devastating Consequences of Zero Tolerance and School Discipline Policies.* Cambridge, MA: Harvard University, 2000.

Stuart Banner, *The Death Penalty: An American History.* Cambridge, MA: Harvard University Press, 2002.

Hugo Bedau and Paul Cassell, eds., *Debating the Death Penalty: Should America Have Capital Punishment?* New York: Oxford University Press, 2004.

Fred Bemak and Susan Key, *Violent and Aggressive Youth: Intervention and Prevention Strategies for Changing Times.* Thousand Oaks, CA: Corwin, 2000.

John Bessler, *Kiss of Death: America's Love Affair with the Death Penalty.* Boston, MA: Northeastern University Press, 2003.

Joan N. Burstyn et al., eds., *Preventing Violence in Schools: A Challenge to American Democracy.* Mahwah, NJ: Lawrence Erlbaum Associates, 2001.

Steven M. Cox et al., *Juvenile Justice: A Guide to Theory, Policy, and Practice.* Los Angeles, CA: Sage Publications, 2008.

Laura L. Finley, *Juvenile Justice.* Westport, CT: Greenwood Press, 2007.

Clayton A. Hartjen, *Youth, Crime, and Justice: A Global Inquiry.* New Brunswick, NJ: Rutgers University Press, 2008.

Charles Haynes et al., *The First Amendment in Schools*. Alexandria, VA: Association for Supervision and Curriculum Development, 2003.

David L. Hudson Jr., *The Silencing of Student Voices: Preserving Free Speech in American Schools*. Nashville, TN: First Amendment Center, 2004.

H. Roy Kaplan, *Failing Grades: How Schools Breed Frustration, Anger, and Violence, and How to Prevent It*. Lanham, MD: Rowman & Littlefield, 2004.

Ricardo M. Marte, *Adolescent Problem Behaviors: Delinquency, Aggression, and Drug Use*. New York: LFB Scholarly Publishing, 2008

Mark H. Moore et al., eds., *Deadly Lesson: Understanding Lethal School Violence*. Washington, DC: National Academies Press, 2002.

Office of National Drug Control Policy, *What You Need to Know About Drug Testing in Schools*. Washington, DC: Office of National Drug Control Policy, 2002.

Justin W. Patchin, *The Family Context of Childhood Delinquency*. New York: LFB Scholarly Publishing, 2006.

Helen Prejean, *The Death of Innocents: An Eyewitness Account of Wrongful Executions*. New York: Random House, 2005.

Jamin B. Raskin, *We the Students: Supreme Court Decisions for and About Students*. Washington, DC: CQ Press, 2003.

Susan F. Sharp, *Hidden Victims: The Effects of the Death Penalty on Families of the Accused*. New Brunswick, NJ: Rutgers University Press, 2005.

Randall G. Shelden and Daniel Macallair, eds., *Juvenile Justice in America: Problems and Prospects*. Long Grove, IL: Waveland Press Inc., 2008.

Denise Smith, ed., *Bulletproof Vests vs. the Ethic of Care: Which Strategy Is Your School Using?* Lanham, MD: Scarecrow, 2003.

Traci Truly, *Teen Rights: A Legal Guide for Teens and Adults in Their Lives.* Naperville, IL: Sphinx, 2002.

Julie A. Weber, *Failure to Hold: The Politics of School Violence.* Lanham, MD: Rowman & Littlefield, 2003.

Periodicals

Julie Adams, "Seasonal Trends in School Violence," *Psychology Today*, March/April 2002.

Marc D. Allan, "Behind Bars," *Indianapolis Monthly*, November 2007.

Robert H. Bork, "Travesty Time, Again: In Its Death-Penalty Decision, the Supreme Court Hits a New Low," *National Review*, March 28, 2005.

Bruce Bower, "Teen Brains on Trial: The Science of Neural Development Tangles with the Juvenile Death Penalty," *Science News*, May 8, 2004.

———— "Adult System Fails Young Offenders," *Science News*, April 21 2007.

Judith A. Brown, Daniel J. Losen, and Johanna Wald, "Zero Tolerance: Unfair, with Little Recourse," *New Directions for Youth Development*, Winter 2001.

Katherine T. Bucher and Lee M. Manning, "Challenges and Suggestions for Safe Schools," *Clearing House*, January/February 2003.

Julie Bykowicz, "Juveniles Trade Jail for Promise of Jobs: 11 Graduates Look to Work in Construction," *Baltimore Sun*, July 25, 2008.

Nicole Carr, "Gender Effects Along the Juvenile Justice System," *Feminist Criminology*, Winter 2008.

Justin Chen, "Under Scrutiny: Privacy on Campus," *Yale Herald*, September 6, 2002.

K. Daly, "Girls, Peer Violence, and Restorative Justice," *Australian and New Zealand Journal of Criminology*, April 2008.

Kathy Davis et. al., "Surveillance in Schools: Safety vs. Personal Privacy," University of Illinois at Urbana-Champaign. http://students.ed.uiuc.edu.

Lance Davis, "Parks Programs Reduce Juvenile Crime," *Nation's Cities Weekly*, November 17, 2003.

Dana Difilippo, "Life Without Parole Unfair to Juveniles?" *Philadelphia Daily News*, July 25, 2008.

R.F. Eme, "Attention-Deficit/Hyperactivity Disorder and the Juvenile Justice System," *Journal of Forensic Psychology Practice*, 2008.

D.K. Frasier, "Juvenile Crime," *Choice*, February 2004.

Robert K. Goidel, Craig M. Freeman, and Steven T. Procopio, "The Impact of Television Viewing on Perceptions of Juvenile Crime," *Journal of Broadcasting & Electronic Media*, March 2006.

W. Hinton, "Juvenile Justice," *Criminal Justice Policy Review*, Fall 2007.

E.Q. Hoang, "Addressing School Violence," *FBI Law Enforcement Bulletin*, August 2001.

I.A. Hyman and P.A. Snook, "Dangerous Schools and What You Can Do About Them," *Phi Delta Kappan*, March 2000.

Kenneth Jost, "Death Penalty Controversies," *CQ Researcher*, September 23, 2005.

Richard Lawrence, "Special Theme Issue: School Crime and Juvenile Justice," *Criminal Justice Review*, December 2007.

Mike McKee, "Court Weighing Juvenile Strikes," *The Recorder*, July 22, 2008.

Steven Messner, "Law Enforcement DNA Database: Jeopardizing the Juvenile Justice System Under California's Criminal DNA Collection Law," *Journal of Juvenile Law*, 2007.

John Minkes, "Change, Continuity, and Public Opinion in Youth Justice," *International Criminal Justice Review*, December 2007.

John Muncie, "The 'Punitive Turn' in Juvenile Justice: Cultures of Control and Rights Compliance in Western Europe and the USA," *Youth Justice*, 2008.

Christian Nolan, "Budget Squeeze May Affect Juvenile Reforms," *Connecticut Law Tribune*, July 21, 2008.

Brianne Ogilvie, "Is Life Unfair? What's Next for Juveniles After *Roper v. Simmons*," *Baylor Law Review*, Winter 2008.

H. Ted Rubin, "Prosecutors in Juvenile Court: Compatibility and Conflict," *Juvenile Justice Update*, February/March 2008.

Robert E. Shepherd Jr., "Who Are the Victims of Violent Juvenile Crime?" *Juvenile Justice Update*, October/November 2004.

R.A. Wahl, "Spirituality, Adolescent Suicide, and the Juvenile Justice System," *Southern Medical Journal*, July 2008.

Brandon Welsh, "Costs of Juvenile Crime in Urban Areas," *Youth Violence and Juvenile Justice*, Spring 2008.

K.P. Winokur, "Juvenile Recidivism and Length of Stay," *Journal of Criminal Justice*, May/June 2008.

Index

A

Adequate notice, minors, 58–59
Administrative discretion, 165–166
Adult court
  criminal, 72–73, 79–80, 197–205
  developmental/psychological considerations, 199–200
  vs. juvenile court, 71–73, 189–191
  juvenile culpability, 200–202
African Americans, 11–12, 166
Age. *See* Chronological age of juveniles
A.J.M v. State, 142
Alder, C., 44
American Academy of Child and Adolescent Psychiatry (AACAP), 201
American Bar Association (ABA), 216–217, 224
American Civil Liberties Union (ACLU), 155–156
Amicus curiae, 127
Amnesty International, 219
Arizona Juvenile Court, 55–56
Arizona State Dept. of Public Welfare v. Barlow, 60
Atkins v. Virginia. See Death penalty
Attorneys/lawyers
  challenges, 101–102
  competency issues, 103
  defense, 99, 101–105, 226
  juveniles denied, 16, 55
  as legal advisors, 93
  vs. non-lawyer support, 100

proactive *vs.* reactive, 102–104
representation improvement, 98–100, 105
transfer decisions, 75
underrepresentation by, 95–105
waiver of rights to, 176
Automatic transfer statutes, 75, 81

B

Beger, Randall R., 132–144
Bishop, Donna, 82
Blackmun, Harry, 207
Brandeis, Louis, 125
Brutal murders, 176–177
Burdeau v. McDowell, 111
Buss, Emily, 84–94

C

California v. Brown, 193
Camara v. Municipal Court, 112, 113, 116
Capital punishment. *See* Death penalty
Caseload sizes, 99–100
The Changing Borders of Juvenile Justice (Fagan, Zimring), 82
Chao, Raymond E., 47–53
Chen, Yihsuan, 159–170
Child Rescue Movement, 15, 22
Children
  government protection, 24–28
  improved representation, 98–100, 104–105
  participation, 93–94

test for, 147–148

warrantless, 126–129, 146–147

weapons searches, 139

See also Fourth Amendment

V

Vernonia School District v. Acton, 148–149, 162, 169

Vigue, Marcia, 138

Violence issues

for girls, 41, 44

legislation, 78, 133

in schools, 127, 133–135, 143–144, 157, 159–170

sexual abuse/assault, 41, 43

See also Crime/criminalization; Murder/murderers

W

Waiver proceedings, 61, 68, 79–80, 102–103

Warrantless searches, 126–129, 146–147

Weapons in school, 137, 139

Welsh v. Wisconsin, 128

Westborough Reform School, 33

White, Byron R., 109–121

World opinion of death penalty, 185–187

Y

Yell, Michell L., 145–153

Youthful offender rights, 66–67, 90–92

Z

Zimring, Franklin, 77, 82